PLAYING FOR *keeps*

BETH BOLDEN

Prologue

Preseason Camp

Sebastian had lost a step.

Not even a whole step. Two thirds of a step. Three quarters, maybe.

He huffed out his breath as he desperately tried to catch it again. Two-a-days were always brutal, especially in the heat of summer, especially in the heat of a *Florida* summer—the memory had faded in the eight years since he'd played at the University of Miami, considering he'd spent them practicing in Arizona in a temperature-controlled stadium—and they were even worse when he wasn't as fast as he used to be. As fast as he'd always counted on being.

"Howard! Where are you at?" a voice called out across the field. "You can't just let Nicholson speed right past you."

Sebastian did not roll his eyes. Not because he wasn't tempted. But because with his breath still coming in heavy pants, his muscles burning with exertion, he was just too caught up in recovering from the last play he hadn't kept up with Tristan on.

"Fucking rookie wideouts," he muttered.

Tristan Nicholson was fast as hell, but hadn't been particularly good at route running, and the first week of camp, Sebastian had outsmarted him more than he'd outrun him.

That's because you can't outrun him, not anymore. The voice not only taunted him with the bald truth, but in the last few months it had come to sound just like his shitty high school coach.

The one who'd told him repeatedly that he'd never make it. Not in college and not in the NFL. Well, joke was on him. Sort of.

"Howard!"

He raised his head.

A younger version of the Piranhas' head coach was marching across the field.

Great. This asshole again.

"Howard," the guy repeated, shading his eyes from the brutal sun. He was wearing glasses with thick black frames and a Piranhas hat, decked out in their signature yellow and turquoise, but he'd turned the spotless cap backwards, which, as far as Sebastian was concerned, was stupid as hell.

It was not the first stupid thing he'd seen the coach's son do, and it probably wouldn't be the last.

"What," he spat out.

"You gotta stay . . ."

Sebastian was generally a laid-back, good-natured guy. A beast on the field, of course, but in practice and in the locker room, and with his friends and his family, people gravitated towards him because of his low-key demeanor.

He rarely got pissed off.

He was pissed off now.

"I know," he interrupted, "I gotta stay with Nicholson. He's like . . . a fucking energizer bunny out here." *And I'm not, not anymore. You know it, and you're still giving me shit about it.*

The guy stared at him. What was his name, again? They'd been introduced, of course, but all Sebastian had registered were two thoughts: 1) he was a chip off the old Dawson block, nearly a photocopy of Asa Dawson, the new coach of the Piranhas, with his dark hair and chiseled jaw and intense stare, just about twenty-five years younger, and 2) he had never, not once, thought that Asa Dawson was hot, but the son? Hot as lava, walk-across-the-sun-and-still-beg-for-more hot, hot like Sebastian would have crossed ten clubs to talk to him, definitely hot enough that every time they met, he felt fourteen and awkward again. Like he-had-to-fight-every-urge-to-drop-to-his-knees-and-grovel hot.

Sebastian ground his teeth together.

"If it's too much," the guy said thoughtfully, casually, like he wasn't demolishing Sebastian's career one word at a time, "I can always put Rose on him."

"Don't you fucking dare," Sebastian said.

The guy tilted his head, considering. "Then keep up with him, Howard."

He wanted to say he was trying.

He wanted to say it was still early, only a few weeks into camp.

He wanted to say that he was going to find that lost step, because not finding it again was akin to failure, and Sebastian Howard never fucking failed.

Not in high school. Not in college. Not in the NFL.

But he didn't. It was humiliating enough that he found this guy hot. It was an extra dollop of humiliating that the coach's son knew better than apparently anyone else how slow he was now.

"Or," the guy added, "we could try something else."

Sebastian was afraid he already knew the answer, but he asked anyway. Gave himself another precious second to catch his breath. "Try what?"

"What we discussed before you were signed. Playing safety. You've got the brain for it, you've always been able to see the whole field, and it's a position that's better suited to your speed."

"No," Sebastian said.

"No, it's not?" The guy shaded his eyes again. "Actually . . ."

"No," Sebastian repeated with a grimace. "No, I'm not going to play safety. I'm a *cornerback*. The best damn corner in the NFL."

The guy winced. "You *were*. But you're thirty-two now, Howard. Things change. You have to change with them."

The only changing he was going to be doing was changing *back* to what he'd once been. He could do it. He just had to work harder. That was all. Longer hours in the gym. More time on the field. Additional effort in practice.

Yeah, that annoying voice wondered, *where you gonna find all that?*

He would, because he *had* to.

He loved playing football. But it wasn't just that. When he walked into a locker room, everyone was on an even playing field. And he'd never be if he was just walking down the street.

Just yesterday, at his brand-new condo, one of the residents of his building had given him an uneasy sideways glance as he'd walked into the atrium. Sebastian had known exactly what he'd been thinking.

This guy doesn't belong here. He might be here to do . . . something. Something scary.

It was the tattoos. Sebastian knew that. But it was also the color of his skin.

He couldn't give up that level playing field he'd won, one agonizing practice, one shutdown play, one triumphant game at a time. Not without working as hard as he possibly could, first.

"Try the play again," Sebastian said instead. "You'll see."

The guy, as hot as he was, did not look convinced.

But that was okay, because Sebastian believed enough for both of them.

"Fine," the guy said, raising his voice and clapping his hands sharply, "let's run this again."

They lined back up again, Sebastian on one side, covering Tristan, who was the fastest guy on the team by a mile, and Rose on the other. His assignment was Carter Johnson, who had a good ten years in the league and who was a decent slot receiver, but who had lost at least two or three steps since he'd been drafted.

It was good practice for Rose, who *was* fast—"faster than you," that annoying voice pointed out—but who needed more experience covering good receivers, who could find a sliver of an opening and then pry it open with a metaphorical crowbar before you could even blink.

Sebastian bent over at the line, muscles screaming with that all-too-familiar mixture of tension and exhaustion.

How you gonna find that extra step again when you're so fucking tired already?

The quarterback, Paxton Kelly, crouched behind the center, and the second the ball moved, Sebastian exploded off the line, eyes tracking Nicholson as he sprinted down the field.

This time he took a more aggressive line, moving his legs faster and then faster still. Nicholson was five feet away, then four, then three, as they ran down the sideline together. An elbow jabbed him, just inside what was allowed, and Sebastian took it right into the pads, absorbing the impact but not letting it slow him down. He glanced back, watched as Kelly pulled his arm back, about to throw the ball.

No way he wasn't going to throw it in Nicholson's direction, even though Seb would have told him he was wasting his time, because Nicholson was *covered.*

But then Nicholson veered sideways and, somehow, hit a different gear, a gear that Sebastian hadn't possessed in at least a few years, and then he was gone, sprinting down towards the end zone, the ball falling easily into his hands.

Sebastian slowed to a stop, panting.

It was hard to be angry at Tristan's enthusiastic celebration. He was a rookie, and had a lot of talent, and on one hand, Sebastian was happy for him.

On the other, he wished that Tristan was maybe a little slower.

Once he'd caught his breath, he jogged back to the sideline.

Coach Dawson was standing there, tablet in his hands, eyes glued to whatever was on the screen.

Maybe I can just slink by and hit the oxygen by the bench, Sebastian thought, but then Coach glanced up and saw him.

"Howard," he said, "did Beau talk to you?"

That was his name. Beau. Sebastian remembered now, and also remembered why he'd felt it was so appropriate.

Do not think that it suits him. Do not even go there.

"Did Beau talk to me?" Sebastian questioned back.

Coach's gaze narrowed, and he lowered the tablet. "Cut the crap," he said, tone still surprisingly pleasant, "I know he talked to you."

"Yeah, he talked to me." Sebastian lifted his hand to swipe his hair back, and then realized, a second too late, that he'd shaved his locs off before camp started, in some misguided idea that losing some hair might make him faster.

Spoiler alert: it hadn't.

"And?"

Coach Dawson had been arguably the most successful, most popular coach in modern-day NCAA football. He'd built a generation of winners at Tennessee, with half a dozen national titles and more Heisman winners than any other collegiate program.

As far as Sebastian was concerned, he should have stayed in Tennessee.

There was nothing to be gained but failure in this NFL experiment for Dawson—he'd already crafted his legacy, and all he was going to do was potentially tarnish it.

As someone currently grappling with a legacy that felt like it was rapidly turning to shit, he didn't understand why Dawson had taken the risk.

"And I'm not a safety, I'm a cornerback."

Coach rocked back on his heels and hummed under his breath. "You're still a damn good corner, Howard, nobody's saying that. I don't think many teams are gonna have a player who can keep up with Nicholson. Not if his routes keep improving."

"No shit," Sebastian said. His breathing still wasn't steady, and Tristan was further down the sideline, laughing at something with Wade Lewis, the rookie tight end.

"Next series," Coach said, "I'm going to put Rose on him—"

Sebastian opened his mouth to argue. Not something he usually did, but this was his *life*—and his legacy and his future—they were discussing, as casually as you ordered a burger at a fast-food drive-thru.

But Coach shot him a look. Sebastian was reminded how he'd been notorious for laying down the law at Tennessee.

"Rose needs the practice, too, and so does Nicholson," Coach said. He still sounded all friendly, like they were just having a nice chat, but Sebastian would have to be a lot denser not to hear the steel underneath it. "And I'd like to see you at safety."

"But—"

Coach turned to him. "This can't be a surprise, Howard. We discussed this when we offered you a contract."

"As an experiment . . ." Sebastian stumbled.

"I get it." Coach gazed out onto the field. "You thought you could work hard all spring, summer, come here, and put in some hard camp time, prove to us that you were just as good as you'd always been. And we still needed a corner—we have Rose, of course, but he's a rookie, and you're Sebastian Howard. And you're *still* Sebastian Howard."

It was so accurate, Sebastian nearly cringed.

But he hadn't been wrong.

He could still do it.

Coach was right; he *was* still Sebastian Howard. He'd won two Defensive Player of the Year awards, and would have won more if Spencer Evans could stop sacking the quarterback every other goddamn play.

"Fine. Let Rose kill himself keeping up with Nicholson," Sebastian said.

"See?" Coach patted him on the back. "I know you've studied the plays. I know you can do it."

"Safety is a poor man's corner," Sebastian argued.

But to Sebastian's surprise, Coach didn't flinch. In fact, Coach didn't look perturbed in the least. "You're not ever going to be cheap, Howard, we both know that. You're too goddamn smart, and far too driven. Why don't you prove to me you can be the most expensive safety in the league?"

"For a series, sure."

The thing was, if they wanted him to play safety, he would play safety. They'd just tell him that his position had changed. But

Rose, his supposed replacement, was still young, still unformed, and still a rookie. Still played like a rookie.

Then there was the way that both father and son were pushing Sebastian to *want* to change.

Well, they could keep waiting for that.

"I like you, Howard," Coach said, grinning. "I don't want to, but I do. But I don't think Beau was wrong about this. And you'll see it too."

Coach turned back to his tablet then, dismissing Sebastian, and as he marched over to the bench, he realized that his biggest problem, the singular pain in the ass that wasn't going to let up for one fucking minute, wasn't going to be Coach Dawson.

It was going to be Beau.

"Ready to see your experiment in action?"

Coach turned towards him, a mischievous glint in his dark eyes.

Was he ready to see Sebastian Howard play safety?

Beau wasn't going to lie to himself; he'd watch Sebastian Howard do just about anything. He'd watch him sit completely, utterly still.

But watching Sebastian Howard play football—no matter what position—was captivating. Enthralling. Fascinating.

Beau told himself it was because Howard was a great player, a once-in-a-generation talent, even if he wasn't quite as fast as he'd been in the first few years of his career, and nobody could read the field or anticipate a receiver's routes the way he could.

But he knew that wasn't all of it.

Sebastian Howard was a gorgeous man.

He was tall, easily over six feet, and two hundred pounds of lean brown muscle. For the last few years, he'd been growing out his hair, and the locs he'd worn it in had been gorgeous. But then he'd shown up at camp, and to Beau's surprise, he'd shaved his head, and all that had done was put his stunning face into even sharper relief.

The first time they'd met, Beau had felt himself babbling painfully, and the second, the third, and the fourth times hadn't been improvements. He'd told himself that the zing of attraction he felt was one-sided. He'd never even heard if Sebastian was queer.

But no matter what Beau felt about the man personally, he'd long felt, with extensive study of Sebastian's film, that he would be an exceptional safety, and that was how he had pitched his joining the Piranhas to his dad.

Now he'd finally get to see if he was right.

"Yeah, if he actually plays," Beau said with trepidation.

"He'll play," Coach said. "That's how he's built."

Beau hoped so, even though he knew just how much Sebastian hated this possibility.

He's just not looking at it the right way; you can convince him. If you do one thing this season, let it be saving Sebastian Howard's career.

The play unfolded as they watched.

It was a pass over the middle, developing late, with the ball either going Wade's direction or a long pass to Nicholson. Except that Rose was giving him hell, making the most of his opportunity, and Beau rocked forward, eyes glued to the field, watching as Sebastian had a good, long moment to look over the field before he decided to commit to a particular direction.

He decided correctly, crossing over, and tackling Wade just after he'd caught the ball, four yards short of a first down.

"You were right," Coach mused, as he glanced over at Beau. "But then you usually are."

"He's always seen the field, and it was a waste to put him at that position. But he had the speed and the hands, so they made him a corner, not a safety. But I bet you if you move him, he picks off more balls than he ever did at corner."

"I told you," Coach said, "I'm not gonna do it if he's not on board. Sebastian Howard is like a priceless racehorse. You can't force him to do anything. He's gotta decide on his own."

Beau rolled his eyes. "You're the head coach. You make the rules."

"Luckily for us I don't have to make any rules right now. We've got a pair of decent corners, and then Rose, and a safety in Vaughn West. We're fine."

"You want to trade Vaughn West," Beau murmured under his breath.

"Sure I do," his father said. "He's never gonna be as valuable as he is this year, but I'm not gonna do it, not if Sebastian decides he's gonna go down in flames."

"He won't," Beau said, watching as another play unfolded, and Sebastian helped contain the running back.

"No?" Coach looked his direction, surprisingly away from the action on the field. "You don't think so?"

"No, 'cause I'm gonna make sure he doesn't," Beau said.

Beau walked through the locker room.

Saw Tristan's hand lying casually on Wade's shoulder as he excitedly described how he'd scored the touchdown. The last thing he'd expected was for their rookie wide receiver and their rookie tight end to fall in love—he knew *they* certainly hadn't expected it either—but they had.

Beau wasn't jealous. Not exactly.

He worked hard, and not just because he had to, but because he wanted to, and he *had* found time over the years to date casually, but the casual dates never seemed to turn into love.

Twenty-six and the only relationship you've ever had has been to your job.

Beau had witnessed firsthand how that turned out. When he'd been twelve, his mom had divorced his dad, and he couldn't even be *mad* about it, because they'd both been so much happier afterwards.

She'd moved to New York City, found a circle of artists who understood her, and his father had gone on much as he had before, coaching throughout the day, and spending nights in his office, long after the rest of the building had emptied. Beau had started going into work with him at first just to make sure he came home. Then he'd found out that he loved the work, too, and it surprisingly suited his analytical mind.

"I see he caught you too," Lynn, his mother, had said mournfully, when he'd told her he was staying in Tennessee for college, and not trading in Knoxville for New York. "You were accepted to Columbia *and* NYU, Beau, you could do *anything*."

"And I want to do this," Beau had told her.

She'd sighed, resigned, but she'd accepted his choice.

Over the years, Beau had always expected that he'd end up meeting a player, because he spent so much time with them, and they'd fall in love; at first his dad would be annoyed, but eventually he'd get over it. And he wouldn't just have his job, and a dad who sometimes felt more like a boss than a close relative—but it had never happened.

He continued walking through the locker room, not stopping in his dad's *other* office, because his father was a masochist who never knew when to quit working, and decided he'd head to the main building. The weight room would be empty right after the second of two grueling practices today, and he could get some reps in. Maybe work off some of this frustration.

This sexual frustration, he internally corrected, because that was what it was, wasn't it? It was easy to forget about his pathetic excuse for a life normally, but when Wade and Tristan were *right there*, it was a whole lot tougher.

"Beau!"

The voice was low, rough, and determined.

Only one man sounded like that.

Beau turned, and Sebastian was standing there, eyes narrowed, only wearing a pair of gray slacks, slung low and partially unzipped, barely hanging on to his hips.

"I need to talk to you," he said.

Let's do more than talk, Beau nearly said, because the sight of him was like a punch to the solar plexus. No—it was more than that, it was like staring into the brightest fireworks display—so dazzling he couldn't tear his eyes away.

You don't even know if Sebastian Howard is queer, and you're better off not knowing.

"So, talk," Beau said, more brusquely than Sebastian probably deserved.

It was not his fault he was so gorgeous Beau's mouth went dry every time he saw him.

"Not here," Sebastian said and grabbed his arm, leading him to, of all freaking places, his father's surprisingly empty office, shutting the door behind them, but not turning the light on.

Beau wished that the location made it impossible to fantasize about what all that smooth skin felt like, but it would take more than the smell of his father's cologne lingering in this office to stop him.

"What's . . ."

But before Beau could get the rest of the sentence out, Sebastian prowled closer, a lion on the hunt, and he stopped abruptly, every thought in his not-inconsiderable brain going blank.

"Coach said this was *your* idea," Sebastian said. It was not quite dark in here, but dim instead, light filtering in through the partially open blinds on the window that looked out into the hallway. But it was just bright enough that Beau couldn't miss the frustration and the anger in his gaze.

He swallowed hard. Didn't ask what was his idea, because he knew exactly why Sebastian was pissed off. "Yes."

"You think you can waltz in here, no consequences because your daddy is some big hotshot coach, and change players' jobs—their *lives*—without permission?" Sebastian's stare pinned him in place.

Sebastian wouldn't have been stupid enough to talk to his father this way, but Beau knew his last name would only protect him so far. Howard wouldn't be the first player to get into his face, and after the first time, when his dad had told him to suck it up, to prove he belonged, that his decisions were solid, he'd dealt with it on his own. He wasn't going to get a rep for running to his father, all the time.

Yeah, you're going to really love dealing with Sebastian one-on-one, a sly voice told him.

"You knew coming in that we wanted you to switch to safety," Beau said.

"I knew it was a *possibility.*"

Sebastian began to pace in front of where Beau was pressed up against the front of his father's desk.

"You thought you could show up in camp and prove yourself," Beau guessed.

Sebastian shot him a glare from underneath eyelashes a model would've killed for. "You and your daddy really are the same, aren't you?"

"What?" Beau couldn't follow. "We're not . . . *no,* we're not alike at all, really."

"That's what he said." Sebastian breathed out, and for a moment, he was silent. "That I planned to come to camp and prove you wrong, that I should stay a corner."

Sebastian unsettled him so much, he could barely think. "It was a reasonable conclusion," Beau said. "It's not like a big injury slowed you down—a bunch of little ones, more like, and *age.* You've been playing ball since you were what, twelve? Thirteen? It's a lot of wear and tear, it's going to happen . . ."

"So you thought you could push me, teach me a lesson, huh?"

"No. *No.* I want . . ." Sebastian took a step closer, and Beau's breath clogged in his throat. He gripped the edge of the desk and told himself firmly, even though he'd never, *not once,* been tempted to touch a player who hadn't clearly wanted to be touched, that he would not reach out and press a palm to Sebastian's bare chest.

"What I want," Beau started over again, "is for this to be mutually beneficial for both of us. You want to keep playing. *We* want you to keep playing."

Sebastian's lip curled. "Oh, you're two regular do-gooders."

"No. We want to win football games. And you're gonna help us."

For a long moment, Sebastian just stared at him. Like he was assessing him. Beau found himself standing a little straighter, and hoping that after pulling off his cap, his hair wasn't too much of a mess.

Like *any* of that mattered.

"I think," Beau continued, uneasily, "that this could be a real good change for you. Honestly. What I *want* is for everyone to succeed."

"What if what I want is to play corner?"

Beau shrugged. "You can teach Rose everything you know. He's got potential. He won't be *you* in your golden years, sure. But he could still be really, really good."

"Sure," Sebastian retorted.

"Listen"—Beau found his voice growing sharper—"you want to know what I really think?"

Sebastian gestured like, *sure, might as well*, and Beau kept going. "I think that you're miserable trying to be your old self. You're working yourself so hard, you're going to end up with another injury, and it's going to end up being a vicious cycle. You played safety this afternoon, and I saw a dynamic, aggressive player who got to be *himself* again because he wasn't worried about outrunning a guy he couldn't outrun anymore. You saw the field, analyzed it, and attacked the play."

Sebastian stared at him.

Long enough that Beau told himself not to squirm under the intensity of that gaze, but he couldn't help it.

Finally, he spoke. But only after taking another step closer, and then another to be even closer still. Beau swallowed hard. All he'd have to do was lean in and their chests would touch. He was wearing a cotton polo, but he bet that he'd feel the warmth of Sebastian's skin, even through the fabric.

"You think you know me?" Sebastian's voice was low and quiet and so dangerous.

Dangerous to Beau's peace of mind.

"I . . . I . . ." Beau stuttered.

Players always tried to intimidate him—usually because he was his father's son, but had never been a player himself, so they always thought they could push him around. That was until they discovered that where it counted, Beau was Asa Dawson's son, and could outdo that ornery sonofabitch with his own stubborn streak.

But this felt nothing like any intimidation tactic that Beau had ever experienced.

Instead it felt hushed and quiet and intimate . . . like any second, Sebastian was going to stop warring with himself and lean down and . . . kiss him.

He's not, he's really not, Beau reminded himself, before he could get his hopes up and his heartbeat could accelerate any further.

But then Sebastian's eyes dropped, unmistakably, to his lips, and Beau realized that maybe he wasn't imagining things after all. Could Sebastian be . . . attracted to him?

It seemed like a wild assumption, but then Sebastian's eyes flicked back up, and Beau swore that it wasn't only his breath that was coming faster.

"You," Sebastian said softly, his voice like velvet, "are gonna be a pain in my ass, aren't you?"

"Not on purpose."

But maybe he would, if Sebastian kept staring at him like that, like he wanted to dig into his chest, and see how he ticked, like he wanted to turn his mind inside out, like he wanted to lean in and close the last bit of space between them.

It felt like an eternity—the best and worst eternity that Beau could possibly imagine—but finally Sebastian pulled away. Turned to head out the door, but before he could open it, he glanced back.

"I'm a cornerback in the NFL," he said, his jaw jutting out in a stubborn angle that should have made him unattractive, but instead made him impossibly more handsome. "I'm the best damn corner in the NFL. I'll show you."

Not the team. *You.*

When the door shut behind Sebastian, Beau realized his knees were wobbling.

And he was no longer quite as convinced that the man was straight as the day was long.

Chapter One

Regular Season, Week One

"We need to talk about Sebastian."

Beau glanced up from his laptop, and hated how his fingers trembled just at the mention of the man's name. He took a minute, taking his glasses off and cleaning them meticulously to cover for his own hesitation.

It had been weeks since their confrontation in the dark office—if confrontation was even the right word for it; Beau could be a veritable thesaurus and he still hadn't figured out what to call it—and Sebastian had avoided him since then, except for a handful of tense, terse conversations about football.

Your confrontation was all about football, too, Beau reminded himself.

Except that it hadn't felt like it was about football. It had definitely started that way, but then it had veered sideways, unexpectedly, and Beau was still trying to find his equilibrium.

He had a feeling that Sebastian was too, because of how he avoided meeting Beau's gaze directly, and how he avoided ever being alone with him again.

They'd put him in at safety half a dozen times in the preseason games, hoping he'd get a feel for the spot, and see what was so

"

obvious to them. But Sebastian had maintained, whenever he was asked, that he still wanted to play corner. He'd worked hard there, too, but Beau knew he was right, and all he'd bring himself was misery if he kept pushing for such an unattainable goal.

"What about Sebastian?"

Asa sighed, and stood, pacing behind his desk, finally resting his hip against the back corner. "You know what happened to Jonah?"

Beau nodded. It was a brutal blow, losing Jonah to a torn Achilles tendon. He'd been one of the few rock-solid pieces they'd inherited when taking over the Piranhas organization, a reliable kicker who knew the culture, and could be depended on in a jam. His had been a non-contact injury, going down while he'd been jogging around the stadium, warming up for the last preseason game, only a few days ago.

"There's some decent kickers around," Beau said. "We can bring some in for a tryout if you wanted."

His dad shook his head. "The Raiders are carrying two; their kicker from last year, a solid guy who can reliably nail a fifty yarder. And a young rookie phenom."

"You think they're going to drop the experienced guy for the rookie."

"It's the Raiders," Asa said with a shrug. "They like to take chances. It's baked into that organization. But they're not going to just release the veteran. They want something for him, because he's valuable."

"You want to trade for him."

Asa sighed. "They want a safety. It's their big missing piece. And they're willing to throw in a few more draft picks, too."

"They want Vaughn West," Beau guessed, naming their starting safety. He could see where this was going.

"I said I didn't want to push Sebastian into a position he doesn't want, but my hands are tied here. The deal's good. He's worked hard at corner, but he's a natural fit for safety. You were right."

Normally, Beau would feel damn good about a compliment like that from his dad, but right now, all he was thinking was how Sebastian was going to react to being permanently moved to safety to fill their gap.

"Rose can play corner, decently enough," Asa continued, "and there's a guy I want to pick up who can take the other side. And let's face it, we'll need *less* corner help, if Sebastian is covering the middle of the field."

"What's the problem, then?" Beau asked, even though he already knew what it was.

Asa sighed.

"Strong-arming him into where we want him isn't going to produce the best results," his dad admitted. "And I told him he'd get to choose."

Beau thought back to the last two preseason games, games where Sebastian had split time between the two positions. He'd not argued once, and while he was still giving his all, trying to win the corner job, Beau realized that *he* hadn't decided yet.

Before he could think better of it, he said, "Let me talk to him."

Asa's head snapped up. "What?"

Beau was ninety-nine point nine percent sure that his father, while knowing *everything* that happened in the Piranhas organization, did not know what had occurred between him and Sebastian. He definitely hadn't confessed, and not just because he didn't want either his father or his boss to know, but because he still wasn't exactly sure what *had* happened. And there was no way Sebastian would tell the coach that he'd tried to physically intimidate his son, and it had all gone sideways.

No—there was no way Asa knew the truth.

But he looked surprised anyway.

"Is there a problem with me talking to him?" Beau kept his voice and his gaze steady.

"No, not at all, I just got the impression you've been avoiding him." Asa hesitated. "Avoiding each other. I thought you were trying not to push him. And he didn't *want* to be pushed."

"I made my feelings on the situation clear, same as you," Beau said. "I think he's just been keeping his head down. And I've been busy."

It wasn't a lie. Not technically. All of that was true.

But Beau knew they *had* been avoiding each other.

Maybe it was time to clear the air.

"He's gonna be pissed."

"I . . ." Beau paused. He'd have said the same as his father, but now that he was considering it, maybe Sebastian wouldn't be as angry as they'd both thought.

He'd certainly been taking the snaps at safety without a hint of protest.

Beau remembered what he'd said. *I think that you're miserable trying to be your old self.*

Sebastian was hardly stupid; he'd been in the NFL for eight years now. He knew what that felt like, and he wasn't the kind of guy to live in denial, either, though he'd been doing a fairly decent job of trying, before.

Maybe what the last few weeks had been were Sebastian considering his options.

"I think I can talk him around," Beau finally said.

The only way to deal with this was to just bite the bullet and talk to the guy. Keep it professional. Keep it light.

You can do this, Beau told himself. *You have to do this.*

"If you want to try, be my guest," Asa said, waving him off. "I'm gonna finalize this deal."

"Tonight?" Beau was surprised. He hadn't realized that things were so far along.

Asa nodded. "They want to get it done."

"That means I need to tell him tonight."

But Beau knew Sebastian had already left the building. Which meant there was no way around it. He was going to have to go to Sebastian's home. Where he *lived*.

"Yep," his father said, "let me grab you the address. I think he mentioned he bought a penthouse condo, right here in downtown Miami."

So much for totally professional and non-intimate.

Shit.

It had been a long day.

If Sebastian was being totally honest with himself, this pre-season had been longer and harder than any he'd ever had as a professional athlete.

It's 'cause you're fighting too hard.

Beau's words from their argument weeks ago echoed in his head.

I think that you're miserable trying to be your old self.

Sebastian stared out at the lights of Miami laid out beneath him like a shiny, flashy blanket, swirling the rum in his glass. He'd bought this condo for the view, thinking not just that real estate was always a solid investment but that he might want to permanently move back to where he'd gone to school.

Arizona had been fine, but he'd missed Florida. And half of his family lived in Florida. At least the half he gave a shit about.

But ever since coming back, he'd been preoccupied by too many questions and not enough answers.

The one haunting him most recently was all Beau Dawson's fault.

Was he miserable trying to be his old self again?

Of course it would be easier to just let the fight go, to settle for this new position they had gift-wrapped for him. But would giving up on his goal make him happier? Maybe he'd feel like he was settling, and he'd be even more miserable than he was now. Sebastian didn't know the right answer.

Lifting his glass to his lips, he took another sip of rum.

Next to him on the glass-topped-table set on the open patio, his phone buzzed. He almost ignored it. Sebastian was sure it was some of his old college buddies, back in town, their own NFL careers much shorter and much more uneventful than his, probably hoping for a night out. But when he glanced at the screen, he saw it was the doorman calling from downstairs.

He picked up, hoping that it wasn't his friends—anticipating that it would be easier to convince Sebastian to go out if they came to him in person instead of calling.

"Hey, Luis," Sebastian said. "What can I do for you?"

"Mr. Howard, there's a gentleman here, says he works with you, for the Piranhas."

Sebastian's insides coalesced into ice. His first thought was horrible. He'd been traded. But if he had, his agent would have been the one to call him. They wouldn't have sent a rep from the Piranhas.

"Says his name is Beau," Luis continued, and it was funny how Sebastian both unclenched and also tensed up, all over again.

God, he didn't want to talk to Beau.

He didn't know what had happened between them in the office, but he'd avoided him since, because that had seemed easier.

Simpler.

Now he was here, at his condo, after nine on a Thursday night.

Not many people knew Sebastian was queer. Maybe Beau had figured it out, and was here to collect on the promise of the charged atmosphere from their argument in the office.

Would Beau do that?

Sebastian didn't know, but if he was here for that, then Sebastian would politely decline, and then show him the door.

He *would*.

"I'll talk to him," Sebastian told Luis.

"Sure thing, Mr. Howard. And thanks so much for the tickets. Manuel is so excited for the game."

"Can't promise a win, but it'll be a party," Sebastian said wryly.

"Still, it's a big deal. Thank you."

"You're welcome," Sebastian said, hanging up the phone and setting it back on the glass table.

Luis was a nice guy; why wouldn't he give him a pair of tickets to the Piranhas' home opener? But even though Luis worked at the most expensive high-rise in Miami, *and* the one that happened to be closest to the stadium and that he knew housed a bunch of players, it seemed nobody had ever bothered to give him tickets.

Sebastian knew what it had meant to go to his first football game. He'd gotten to see a whole new way to exist. He was happy to give Manuel that same opportunity.

He straightened, standing and stretching out his sore muscles. He was halfway to the front door of the spacious penthouse when he heard a knock. He considered turning on a few more lights; but he couldn't decide, so finally just went to the door.

When he opened it, and Beau was standing there, dark hair ruffled from the breeze, dark blue eyes shadowed by his glasses, and just as enticing in the half-dark as he was in the bright light of a midday football practice, he realized that it wouldn't have mattered how many lamps he turned on.

He was going to be attracted to him, no matter what.

"Hey," Beau said, "I'm sorry to bother you, but I wanted to talk to you about something."

Sebastian raised an eyebrow, playing it cool. Not wanting to betray his anxiousness about this late-night visit. "And it couldn't have waited til tomorrow?"

"No." Beau's voice was firm, and there was a resoluteness in his gaze that Sebastian normally would have found refreshing.

"Well, come on in, then," Sebastian said, opening the door further.

The condo had been staged for sale with a bunch of cool beige furniture—low-slung couches, all shiny glass and hard white lines. He'd bought it all, and then hung up some of his favorite art pieces on the wall. Art from Africa and from the South. Art that illustrated his history and his background. He thought it had a juxtaposition that most people found unexpected. Kind of like himself. Sebastian stood back and watched as Beau took in the decor.

He turned back after a long look around the room. "It's a great place," Beau said. "I especially like this one," he added, walking a few steps closer to Sebastian's favorite piece, with the multicolored scraps of indigenous fabrics, woven together to create an abstract yet concrete pattern.

"It's got a great texture," Sebastian agreed. "Can I get you something to drink?"

He watched as Beau considered the question.

Lots of people had told him, both before and after he'd signed with the Piranhas, that Coach Dawson's son was brilliant. "A genius," more than one of them had named him.

Sebastian didn't know him well enough to tell if that was true, but what he had noticed about Beau was that he never answered anything quickly. Every word out of his mouth took consideration.

"We might both want one," Beau finally said with a hint of a smile that was gone as quickly as it had appeared.

"Bad news?" Sebastian couldn't help the apprehension in his voice as he led them to the patio, grabbing another glass from the liquor cabinet.

"No, not exactly," Beau admitted as he took in the view. "Wow, this is incredible."

Sebastian poured another few fingers of rum into his glass, and then some into the one he'd brought for Beau.

"Should be," Sebastian admitted, handing the glass to Beau, "for what I paid for it."

"What is it?" Beau asked, swirling the dark liquid.

"Sipping rum. You'll like it. Everyone likes it," Sebastian said, grinning before he could stop himself. "This one is from the Bahamas. Spice, bananas, and caramel; it's really nice and full-bodied without being overpowering."

Beau sniffed at it, and then took a sip. "Yeah, it's really good," he said. "Who knew rum was good for anything else other than tropical cocktails topped with frilly umbrellas?"

Sebastian nodded and set his glass down. "What's going on?" he asked. "What's so important that it couldn't wait?"

"You heard about Jonah and his Achilles?"

"Yeah, he tore it. Rough stuff. But I don't get what a kicker has to do with me."

Beau stared out at the lights sprinkled below them. It was safer, no doubt, when they weren't looking at each other. Sebastian knew he was attracted, even though he knew he'd never act on it; and it seemed, at least from the fraught tension between them, that it wasn't one-sided. So it was better and easier if Beau *didn't* look at him.

But Sebastian was feeling the warmth of the rum spreading through his stomach. He wanted Beau's eyes on him. So he walked up next to him.

"There's a kicker that the Raiders have, they want to trade him. Coach wants him."

Sebastian still wasn't sure he understood. "But if you were trading me to the Raiders, my agent would be here, not you."

He watched as Beau took another drink. "The Raiders want Vaughn West." The current starting safety.

It all clicked.

"You want me to play safety full-time." Sebastian would have expected to be a lot angrier in this moment; he didn't think it was the rum keeping him calm. Or the man telling him. Though neither of those hurt. "Your dad told me that it was going to be my choice."

"He *wanted* it to be your choice." Beau finally looked up at him, and Sebastian felt a jolt as he saw the frustration *he'd* expected to feel reflected in Beau's eyes. Beau was frustrated *for* him? That didn't make much sense. It shouldn't matter to this guy what position he was playing, and yet, it seemed like it did.

"But circumstances, blah blah blah," Sebastian retorted without heat. He'd been sure he'd be furious at this moment. Angry, resentful, and resigned.

But only felt a vague echo of any of those emotions.

"Exactly. And I thought I should be the one to tell you . . ." Beau took another drink. A gulp, really. Despite his self-possession, he was clearly nervous. Sebastian knew why. He could feel the same edginess vibrating through him.

He shoved his hands into his pockets. Better than using them. Especially on Beau Dawson.

What he *should* do was apologize to Beau and promise that he'd never make him uncomfortable again.

But when he opened his mouth to say the words, something else came out instead. "Because you wanted to clear the air?"

Beau's lips clamped together. "Why would we need to do that? It was . . ." Sebastian could see him struggling with the right thing to say; he should put him out of his misery. Dismiss it as unimportant, but the way they seemed to vibrate on the same frequency wasn't unimportant at all.

It wasn't something he was ever going to act on.

But that didn't mean it wasn't meaningful.

Finding a genuine connection to another human being was hard as fuck. *Naturally,* Sebastian thought wryly, *you found one with the worst possible person. If Coach Dawson found out, he'd feed me my own balls, and then bury me so deep that no other NFL team would touch me with a ten-foot pole.*

It wouldn't even matter if it was because he was a player or because his skin wasn't the same color as Beau's.

"This matters a lot to me," Sebastian said.

"Playing corner? I know, I know, and I'm . . ." Beau hesitated again, but this time he plowed ahead before Sebastian could interrupt. "I'm sorry. But I meant what I said then, no matter what it . . . what it was like, when I said it. I think this could be a whole new chapter for you, an extraordinary chapter actually. It's not the end, it's the beginning and I want you to . . ." Beau wet his lips. "I want you to see it, too."

"I don't know why," Sebastian said frankly.

"We want to win football games, of course, and we'll win more with you than without you," Beau said hurriedly. It was the first time he'd answered quickly, without considering every word out of his mouth.

That made it pretty easy to identify as the first lie Beau had told him.

He could let it go.

But the problem was that Sebastian didn't want to.

"No," he said.

"No?" Beau's gaze locked with his. Suddenly, just like a few weeks ago, in Coach's office, the space between them grew fraught. Sebastian felt like he could barely breathe in and out, like there just wasn't enough air.

And there was air all around them.

"Yeah, of course Coach wants to win games. This is his rep on the line, after all. His legacy. And frankly, nobody expects us to win very many of them. But that's not why you give a shit."

But Beau didn't answer. Instead, he finished the rest of his rum and held out the glass. "I'd better be going. I just wanted to come by and tell you, because I guess the deal's getting finalized tonight, and by tomorrow . . ."

"By tomorrow I'll be your new starting safety," Sebastian said dryly.

"Yes. Exactly."

"Rose isn't ready." Sebastian didn't say it because he wanted to keep his position, though he did, he still *did*, even as he knew he was beginning to acknowledge that it was a pointless exercise to keep trying. He said it because it was the truth.

"No, but he's going to get there," Beau said as they walked through the dark living room towards the door. "I'm going to help him, my dad's gonna help him, Brett's gonna help him, and I hope . . ." He hesitated. "I hope you'll help him, too."

Sebastian raised an eyebrow as Beau turned, back to the door.

It would be so damn easy to press him to the door, like he'd nearly pressed him to the desk, and kiss him and take what they both wanted.

He knew he wanted it.

And there was no way Beau didn't want it. Every line of his body screamed how much he did, and he didn't know what to do about it.

Probably because Sebastian hadn't told him that he was queer too, and to make a move on a player, on one of his *dad's* players, without knowing for sure it would be reciprocated, would be a disaster.

It would be a disaster, even if it was reciprocated, and it most definitely is, Sebastian reminded himself firmly.

"You want me to teach my replacement all my tricks?" Sebastian questioned. *Keep him—and you—focused on football, and not on this . . . whatever this is.*

"No. Yes. I . . . yes," Beau stuttered.

Sebastian leaned in a bit closer, put a hand on the door, next to Beau's head. Watched as Beau's eyes dilated.

Not being publicly out like a few of his fellow players, Sebastian was used to practicing restraint, but it had never felt so difficult.

"And what about me?" Sebastian asked quietly.

"What about you?" Beau's eyes were glazed. Dazzled. Having him look at him that way was addictive.

Don't let it become a habit.

"Who's gonna help me?"

Beau swallowed hard.

If he kissed him, he'd taste like rum. Rum and secrets.

Because nobody could know what they'd done—or *almost* done—in his condo, late on a Thursday night.

"Me," Beau murmured, tilting his head.

"You've never played safety. You've never even played football." Sebastian could hear the dark amusement threading through his voice.

"I know, but . . . I can still help. I'm . . . I'm good at this."

"So I've been told," Sebastian said. "People keep telling me you're a genius."

"I'm not. No. But I'm good at this." Beau met his gaze dead-on. Confident now. The desire was still there, but he was trying to overcome it. Probably thought he *had* to.

He does, he absolutely fucking does. And so do you.

"I guess we'll find out if you are," Sebastian said, and it took all his strength to push away. To reach for the door handle and pull it open.

Beau licked his lips and looked at Sebastian. One last, long, nearly irresistible look.

"Yeah," he said. "I guess we will."

Chapter Two

It wasn't until the bright light of the next morning—brutal in only the way that the Florida sun could be—that Sebastian realized that he'd been played.

Yeah, Jonah had torn his Achilles tendon. But as he'd said last night, when Beau had just arrived, it didn't have anything to do with him.

Could the Raiders genuinely want West? Of course, West was a reliable safety. Reliable but nothing spectacular.

As Howard sat up straight in bed, frustration coursing through him, he saw exactly how he'd been played.

By Beau Dawson, of all people.

Beau Dawson had played *him*.

No doubt he'd been the one to plant the seed in his father's head, suggesting the Raiders would trade for West, thus eliminating the one player standing in the way of Beau's grand plan. The plan he'd designed to prove himself.

Because as of now, Beau was just another coach's relative, hoping to establish himself.

Convincing him, *Sebastian Howard,* to not be a corner, but to be a safety, would be considered a coup in a lot of corners of the football world, and if it was a *successful* experiment, it would be even more impressive.

But this was Sebastian's *life*. His job. The only thing he'd lived for, for more years than he cared to count. The one thing he could always reliably count on.

He was not going to get bullied into playing a position by someone who thought he could manipulate him.

Beau had orchestrated this whole situation, and then had come here last night, and used Sebastian's attraction against him to convince him to go along with it.

He'd been so dazzled, which was completely unlike him, that he'd just let it happen. But he didn't *have* to let anything happen.

"My choice, my ass," Sebastian growled as he pushed the sheets back and swung his legs over the floor. The marble floor was cold, but he didn't flinch.

He grabbed his phone from the bedside table, dialing his agent.

Alec answered on the third ring. "Mitchell."

"What do you know about Beau Dawson?"

Alec was silent a minute. "Is this going to be a problem?"

Sebastian, on the way to the kitchen for his morning protein smoothie, stopped short. "You didn't answer the question."

"No, I asked another one." Alec sounded amused. "*Is* this going to be a problem?"

Sebastian yanked open the fridge. "He's a problem, yeah."

"A football problem or *I want to fuck him* problem?"

His fingers froze on the bag of fresh spinach he liked to blend with the frozen berries and the protein powder. "Jesus, Alec," he said. "It's a football problem."

Sebastian could see his agent throwing up his hands. "Listen, for a time, Beau Dawson was, maybe still *is*, one of the more famous queer people associated with the game. He's young. He's not unattractive. It's not a wild assumption to think this isn't strictly a football problem."

It isn't, Sebastian thought sulkily.

"Listen, whatever Beau is up to or not up to, this is about how he keeps trying to fucking manipulate me."

"I heard about the trade, and I thought I'd call you, but you've informed me I'm not allowed to call before eight."

"You'd really be up at five?" Alec lived on the West Coast, in Los Angeles. Sebastian tried not to take it personally that he was currently shacked up with the man who'd been his Defensive Player of the Year nemesis, Spencer Evans. "How does Spence feel about that?"

"Spencer knows all about my job," Alec retorted crisply. "And why do you keep trying to change the subject? Beau isn't manipulating you. You knew what was going to happen. They *told* you they wanted you to play safety, Sebastian. When they offered you a lot more money than other teams this season, I told you that was why. And then they *told* you that was why. You had other teams you could go to, but you wanted to go back to Florida, and you wanted the money they were handing out." Alec sounded annoyingly pragmatic. "Besides, what's the difference between playing corner and safety?"

"You know what the difference is," Sebastian scoffed. "Not everyone can play corner."

"And what," Alec interrupted sharply. "Just *anyone* can play safety? That's a lie, and you know it. You're feeling stung because you've got the wrong impression that changing positions means that you weren't good enough. You were a great corner, Sebastian, and you're going to be a great safety. If you can get over your own goddamned pride."

Sebastian wasn't proud, but he heard how sulky he sounded. "I thought they'd figure out that it was a stupid idea, and keep me at corner. Besides, they had West at safety."

"Well, they no longer have West."

Sebastian reminded himself that he'd always liked that Alec was the most straight-shooting agent he'd ever met.

"Yeah, exactly. They did that. *Beau* did that. Beau came over here, all cute and shit, and all flirty bedroom eyes, and convinced me not to fight it. Convinced me that it was the best thing for me to do, to just give in."

Alec didn't say anything for a long, drawn-out moment. "So, this *is* an *I want to fuck him* problem."

"No, it's not. It's really not." It really wasn't, not now. Sebastian wasn't going to fuck some guy who thought he was smarter. Especially one who thought he was so goddamned smart that he could run circles around him.

Beau Dawson was going to be in for a rude awakening.

"Then it was. And now you're angry because he convinced you to give in? I hate to break it to you . . ."

Sebastian knew what his agent was going to say, and interrupted before he could. *I told you so* always stung, no matter how pleasantly it was delivered.

And Alec Mitchell was the king of the pleasant *fuck you* speech.

"But they don't need my permission?" Sebastian leaned against the counter, smoothie forgotten. "I know that. They can say, *hey, Howard, good morning, fuck you, you're gonna play safety,* and I'll play safety."

"I'm sure Dawson didn't want to do that because he's not stupid," Alec said mildly. "He knows players. He'd get more out of you if you were on board."

"Exactly. So he sent Beau in to soften me up . . ."

It was Alec's turn to interrupt.

"Listen, I know Beau, and I don't think he did. At least . . . at least not on purpose."

"What," Sebastian demanded flatly. "You *know* him?"

"Sebastian," Alec said coolly, "I've been around a long time. Of course I know Beau. I know his father. And I know they want the best for the Piranhas and for you."

Great, now he'd pissed off his agent. "I didn't mean . . ." Sebastian took a deep breath. "I know this is to their advantage, to get me to play safety, and to get me to agree to it on my own terms."

"You think Beau persuaded his father to trade Vaughn West away, and then persuaded you to accept the change in position?"

"Yes."

Alec laughed. "You must really not know Beau Dawson very well. I hate to break it to you, but he makes suggestions. Asa is Asa and he does whatever's best for the team. Not for his son or his reputation. And as for persuading you . . ."

Alec was quiet for so long that Sebastian almost barked at him to get it over with, because he was *obviously* not going to like it.

"Well," Alec finally continued, huffing a laugh under his breath, "maybe you *wanted* to be persuaded, Sebastian."

It would have been less annoying if it had been less true.

But like hell he'd admit it to Alec.

Or to himself.

"Fuck no."

"You called because you wanted my advice," Alec said, "and here it is. Try it out."

"Even if they manipulated me into this spot?" Sebastian demanded.

"Even if they did, which for the record, is probably not what happened."

"*Probably*," Sebastian retorted, latching on to the one word he liked in that sentence.

Alec sighed. "It's the National Football League, Sebastian, and you know how it works. They want you to play safety, you're going to play safety."

"They can *try*," Sebastian said.

He'd begun to really respect Coach Dawson, at how he didn't want to push Sebastian into doing something he didn't want to do. How he'd wanted Sebastian to have a choice. Like he'd known just how few choices Sebastian had had in his life. But then this bullshit had happened.

"I don't even want to know what that means, do I?" Alec said with resignation. "Just think about it, okay? And I'll reach out, see if I can shine any additional light onto this situation."

"Good." But Sebastian already knew that he wasn't going to let Alec handle this entirely on his own. Beau Dawson thought he could manipulate him? Oh, that road worked both ways. Especially because while Beau didn't know Sebastian was attracted, Sebastian definitely knew Beau was.

Beau looked up as his father trudged down the sideline of the practice field like a man on a mission.

"What?" he asked. Coach rarely walked down this far. He liked to stay focused on the players on the field, not on the coaches and players milling on the sidelines.

"Just before practice," Coach said, "I got an interesting phone call from Alec Mitchell."

"About?"

But Beau already had a feeling he knew what it was about. Had Sebastian pretended that everything was okay last night only to turn around and decide that it wasn't? Was he trying to use his agent to intervene? Not that Sebastian was the only player on the team who had Alec as an agent, but him calling this morning? It seemed extremely likely that this was about Sebastian.

Coach sighed. "You texted me and said that Howard was on board. And now he's pissed? Asking his agent to get involved? What on earth did you say to him?"

Beau told himself that his father's tone, strident and annoyed, was not his fault. He hadn't done anything—or, rather, he'd done exactly what his father had asked and what he'd promised.

He'd told Sebastian the trade situation. Sebastian hadn't even seemed particularly angry about it. Resigned, more like. And then there'd been . . . well, things had gone sideways again.

Even though Beau had very specifically told himself that they wouldn't. That they *couldn't.*

But there'd been that moment at Sebastian's front door. When he'd leaned in close, so close, *far too close . . .*

Oh shit.

Had Sebastian complained to his agent about Beau flirting with him? Even though it had definitely been Sebastian who had flirted first?

Beau had always been so fucking careful—but sometimes, there was a guy, a guy who was too caught up in all the toxic masculinity of football, who wanted more, but couldn't even admit it to himself.

That didn't seem like the Sebastian that Beau knew.

But you don't know him. You barely know him at all.

"I said exactly what I was supposed to say. I told him that we were trading Vaughn West to the Raiders in exchange for one of their kickers and some draft picks. I told him that he was the new starting safety. I asked him to help Rose out, if he could. I told him . . ." Beau swallowed hard, remembering that charged moment at the front door, when Sebastian had wondered who would help *him*. Like he'd done everything his whole career all by himself, and he couldn't even imagine someone wanting to give him a hand. "I told him I'd help him, if he needed to study film or plays, or whatever. That's it." Beau had to stop himself from making any more excuses or apologizing.

He hadn't done anything wrong. But sometimes, when he looked at his dad, he wasn't his dad at all, he was Coach Asa Dawson, with a whole room full of trophies and hardware and the adulation of every collegiate football fan on the planet.

And Coach Dawson always made Beau want to apologize for letting him down.

"He seemed resigned to it, you said?" Coach's gaze narrowed.

"He said he'd do it. I . . . I even told him that it was better for him. You know this is better for him."

"I do, but it seems he doesn't," Coach said flatly. "Considering he's got his agent calling me to bitch."

"About me?"

Coach looked at him more closely. Then glanced away. "I don't know," he said with a hesitant drawl, "Alec didn't say anything about you *particularly*, but he made it clear that Howard's not happy."

Football was a game of inches, and also a game of patience. He'd learned, the hard way, just how difficult that could be. His dad had never ruled at Tennessee through fear, even though everyone had been afraid of him, and Beau had learned at his side to keep his temper, to sit back and wait, and to never let anger get in the way of success.

But Beau couldn't help himself. He was fucking pissed.

"He doesn't need to be happy," Beau said between clenched teeth.

He knew what his father wasn't saying.

They'd only had one—and that had been plenty—conversation about Beau working with him. Asa had told him, "I don't care what you do in your off time, or who you do it with, as long as it doesn't spill into the locker room, or onto the field."

Beau had made sure. Frankly it had never been an issue until Sebastian.

And now he'd just made it an issue.

Coach sighed. "I wanted it to be his choice, because I didn't want any of this bullshit distractin' us."

"It won't."

Except that it already had. Asa was down here, talking to Beau, instead of focused on what was happening on the field.

"Take care of it, Beau," Coach said. "And not like . . ."

"Not like before?" It was impossible not to feel bitter. Not to *sound* bitter. Sebastian Howard had a lot to answer for.

But then Asa reared back, and Beau was surprised to see shock in his father's eyes. Suddenly, then, he wasn't just Coach, he was *Dad*.

"I wasn't meaning . . . I didn't mean . . ."

Beau rarely saw his father at a loss for words.

"It's okay."

"No, it's not." His father frowned. "Did he . . . did he make a pass at you? Is that the problem?"

Beau stared at his father. "Is that what you think happened?"

"I don't know what happened, which is why I'm here talkin' to you. Alec didn't have an issue with you, Beau. Didn't say Howard did either. You didn't even come up."

Beau let out the breath he hadn't known he was holding.

So Sebastian hadn't complained about him after all.

His father patted him on the shoulder. "You've got a good head on those shoulders, son, I trust you'll do the right thing."

The right thing.

Beau eyed where Sebastian was standing on the other side of the field. He'd found an uneasy spot half between the safeties and Rose, the rookie corner.

Like even after all this time, he wasn't sure where he belonged.

And maybe Sebastian's life had been really different from Beau's. But that didn't mean that Beau didn't know how lonely it could be, to not feel like you belonged anywhere.

It shouldn't have made him any less pissed. But it did, anyway.

Beau wasn't stupid. He knew it was a mistake to talk to Sebastian right away.

Instead, he waited and watched.

It was Sebastian's first full practice as a safety, and while it was hardly perfect, being a brand-new position to him, Beau saw the same potential in every play that he'd dreamed of when he'd first come up with the idea.

But there was also a hesitancy in Sebastian's movements. An uncertainty.

He *wasn't* committed.

And every once in a while, Beau would see him glance over at where Rose was trying to cover Tristan. Anyone else would miss it, but for better or worse, Beau had made a study of Sebastian's face, and a split-second, blink-and-you'll-miss-it moment of dissatisfaction and frustration would cross it.

Every time it happened, Beau felt an echo of it. By the time practice ended, he wasn't necessarily any less pissed, but what was painfully obvious was that this conversation was going to be even more difficult than he'd originally anticipated.

He waited longer, until the last shower had turned off, lurking in the darkened doorway of his father's office, right outside the locker room. Coach had already returned to his upstairs office, no doubt so he could question Foreman, the passing coordinator, and Davis, the quarterbacks coach, on why the offense kept stalling out.

Which, thankfully, would distract Coach from the defense for just long enough.

Long enough for Beau to convince Sebastian that this was the best possible outcome for both of them.

You thought you already did that, and you didn't, not even close. What makes you think this'll be any different?

The answer was easy enough: *because it has to be.*

Sebastian was one of the last guys out of the locker room, eyes glued to his phone screen as he walked out.

"Hey," Beau said as he passed him.

Sebastian stopped in his tracks and stared.

"I need to talk to you," Beau said, but didn't reach out and tug Sebastian into the office with him. Instead he joined him at his side, and gestured towards the elevator that would take them to the top floor and its attached parking structure. "Can I walk with you?"

The look on Sebastian's face was deeply suspicious but he nodded anyway. "Sure, I guess."

Beau shoved his hands into the pockets of his athletic shorts and tried to keep his face casual. "Coach said that your agent called this morning."

Sebastian hit the elevator button. "Alec said he was going to."

"I thought this was all settled last night," Beau said.

He was surprised when Sebastian leveled a glare at him. "Yeah, I just bet you did."

"Is there a problem?" He kept his voice calm, even though it was a struggle. "Because I don't usually expect players to go around me, and have their agents call Coach."

The elevator dinged and they got in. Too late Beau realized that he should have made small talk til they'd gotten to the parking lot, because now they were closed in together in a space that normally didn't feel too small, but now felt inescapably tiny.

Sebastian shook his head in disgust. "Why do you bother calling him Coach?"

"Because he's the coach of this team."

"He's your *father*," Sebastian growled.

Beau had been trying to tamp down his temper, but it flared. "You think I ever forget that?"

"I think," Sebastian said, eyes narrowing, "that you *count* on that."

He should be used to the insinuations by now, but this wasn't exactly an insinuation, was it? It was a blatant accusation.

"This doesn't have anything to do with that," Beau said angrily. "This is the best move for the team, and the best move for you, if you would get your head out of your ass long enough to see it."

"So, you didn't manipulate your father to trade Vaughn West, so you could see your master plan in action? You didn't come over, to my *house*, interrupting my night, hoping to manipulate *me*?"

Beau stared at the man for a long second. He felt dizzy with the smell of Sebastian and his sandalwood and lavender cologne, and the anger surging through him. The elevator dinged again, but neither of them moved.

"Is that what you think I did? This is *football*, that's it. I'm in charge of putting the right pieces in the right spots. That's what you are. A right piece that I'm trying to position into the right spot. Coach gave me that job because I'm really fucking good at it, not because I happen to be his son."

Sebastian reached over and hit the button to close the elevator doors harder than was entirely necessary. "If you're so goddamned smart, then why are you working for him?"

Beau had asked himself that question dozens of times. His mother had wondered, too, because after all those successful years in Tennessee, he'd had plenty of job offers.

But he'd followed his father to the NFL instead.

"Because I want to," Beau said bluntly. "Not that it's any of your fucking business."

"You've made it my business now," Sebastian retorted.

"Your business," Beau said, poking him hard in the chest. His *hard* chest. Which he wouldn't think about. Nope. No way. Never. Not in a thousand years. "Your business is to play fucking football. To play *safety*, whether you like it or not."

Sebastian stared at him for a long second, and Beau realized he was breathing hard. That hard chest was rising and falling at the same speed as his own.

Then he realized that he'd done exactly the thing he'd told himself he couldn't do: he'd lost his fucking temper. Epically.

"Hey, I fucking did it, didn't I? I stepped out onto that field to-day, and did exactly what you wanted." Sebastian sounded bitter. The expression in his eyes was enough to curdle milk. "If I want to bitch to my agent, and my agent decides to bitch to you about it, that's my right."

"Yes," Beau said smoothly. "It is. Just like it's my right to put the pieces where I want them."

Sebastian shook his head. "You're a cold sonofabitch," he said. The elevator dinged open again, and this time he strode out of it, leaving Beau scrambling to keep up. "But," he added, turning his head just enough that those hot golden-brown eyes met Beau's, "since I'm not worried about the state of my balls, that's not my business, either."

Beau pulled up short, not sure *what* he should say to that. Sebastian stomped off, finally disappearing from sight, leaving Beau behind, confused and weirdly, oddly turned on.

Had Sebastian just insinuated that his balls . . . that he'd like . . . that he'd *want* . . .

No. No way. And even if he did, which was surprising because Beau hadn't ever heard a peep about the man being queer, that door had just slammed shut.

Sebastian Howard thought he was a spoiled, manipulative asshole who'd only gotten this job because the coach was his father.

Beau squeezed his fingers into a fist, ignoring how they were still trembling.

If Sebastian wanted to throw his career away with both hands, that was his business. As long as Beau got what he needed—not what he wanted—out of the man, first.

Chapter Three

Even though Sebastian had been in the NFL for almost ten years, he'd only played for the same team—and the same coach. Both his coaches at Arizona had never been too into pre-game speeches. They'd let the coordinators talk to each side of the ball, had usually said a few words at halftime, and maybe at the end of the game. But that was it. He wasn't used to a big pre-game pep talk, and that was fine, because he didn't need one.

But then, right when he was getting into the zone by himself, focusing on his job—on his *new* job—Coach Dawson walked into the middle of the room, and to his surprise, climbed onto the seat of a chair that to his eye, didn't look particularly sturdy.

But Coach didn't look even the slightest bit concerned.

"Listen up," he said, raising his voice until the noise of fifty or so players getting ready for a game died down. "I don't always do this . . ."

"Yeah, you actually do."

Sebastian didn't have to glance behind him to see that the man who'd interrupted was Beau. The prickling on the back of his neck would have made it apparent even if he hadn't recognized the voice.

He'd spent the last few days actively avoiding the man.

And now, of course, he was here.

He's supposed to be here, he's a coach on this team, and it's the first game of the season. But Sebastian wasn't interested in reasoned arguments.

Just the thought of Beau Dawson set his blood on fire.

In all kinds of ways.

Even ways he didn't want, at all.

Especially now that he'd discovered that Beau would do anything to get what he wanted.

"Well, maybe I do," Coach drawled, "but I like doing it, because I like to set the tone for our games. So you're gonna have to bear with me, each week, getting up on this rickety-ass chair and giving y'all a piece of my mind. Here's the piece you get today: we're playing seventeen games this season, and it's not news to you, but despite winning a few games in the preseason, nobody thinks we can win more than a couple of regular season games." Coach paused. "I don't know about you," he said, "but that makes me angry enough to spit. I didn't come here to lose. I came here to change the way this city and our fans and the NFL see our franchise. I want to bring it back to the days when the Piranhas were part of the conversation, not an afterthought. Do you know how that starts?"

Sebastian thought he had some idea. But then the team he'd played for the last nine seasons had never had a losing one while he was there.

He'd known coming here was going to be a brutal uphill battle, but the money had been so good—so much better than he'd thought he could expect, enough to set him and his momma up for life—that he'd decided that winning games meant less than getting paid to play the game he loved.

Of course, Sebastian thought, staring moodily at his cleats, he'd thought he'd still be playing the *position* he loved too, but maybe

Rose would be terrible enough out of the gate that Coach would rethink Beau's plan, whether he was his son or not.

"It starts," Coach continued, "by running onto that field believing that we can win one game. Just one. *This* one." His eyes suddenly gleamed, and Sebastian felt the jolt of Coach's commitment hit him square in the chest. Suddenly, his devoted following at Tennessee made more sense.

Coach was magnetic enough to motivate a dead man, and none of them were dead. Not yet, anyway.

His voice rose. "This is the game that matters. Not next one. *This* one. If we win this one, then we get another chance. And then another and then another. Defeat the odds, exceed expectations, and then we get another season. I'm not here to tell ya that we can win a Super Bowl. But next year? Or the year after?" Coach smiled, like a cat that had just won the cream. "Then we can get serious. But it starts right here, right now, with this one game."

The room erupted into enthusiastic yells. And Sebastian, despite his jaded bitterness over this whole fucking experiment, found himself whooping right along with everyone else.

Sebastian had played at safety during a handful of plays during the preseason, but this was his first game playing *only* safety.

It was weird, and even though he'd spent the last few days studying the defensive playbook, he found himself in the wrong spot twice in the first drive.

The first time it happened, he realized it right before the snap, the play gelling in his head with a sudden clarity, as he watched the offense line up on the other side, setting up for what Sebastian was pretty sure was going to be a run play.

But then the ball snapped, Rodgers falling back into the pocket, and he realized a half second too late that it had been a run-pass option, and with Sebastian and some of the other defense clustered in the middle, he'd decided to go with the pass option, holding on to the ball.

Sebastian watched him for a half second, wishing he'd had more time to prepare. He'd rarely had the need to study the different ways quarterbacks telegraphed their intentions. When he'd played corner, he'd covered his man, no matter if he was going to get the ball or not.

But as a safety, he needed to learn to read better. Beau had said he had the instincts, but as he hesitated, muscles tensed and poised for his next move, he realized that he hadn't had any time to develop them yet.

He was so fucking raw. Clueless and confused.

And just like all his worst nightmares come to pass, Rodgers threw the ball, right over the side where he couldn't possibly get to, to a slot receiver who'd wormed his way past the first line of defense.

First down, and an extra fifteen yards.

It was hard not to feel demoralized, as they lined up for the next play.

Hard not to feel like he'd personally fucked up.

It's okay, he told himself, as Rodgers passed the ball to the running back. He was in a better position that time, though only by accident, and he helped bring the ball carrier down, tackling him to the ground. *You're gonna be fine.*

Except when he jogged back to the bench after the defense gave up a touchdown, right down the middle to the receiver that Rose was trying to cover, he wasn't sure that was true.

They were a bunch of rookies and has-beens, who were trying to hold back one of the best offenses in the NFL. It was hard not to take it personally, even though, like Coach had said, nobody expected them to win this game.

Nobody expected them to win *any* games.

Beau was there, on the sideline, head buried in his tablet, a frown on his face.

Sebastian walked by him in search of a towel and some Gatorade, and for a split second, he thought Beau was just going to let him pass. He *hoped* Beau would just let him pass. Yeah, he'd fucked it up, but he was trying, damnit.

Unfortunately trying did not amount to much in the NFL.

Especially when the offense was counting on the defense to give up less points, because they were still trying to find their own groove.

It was not a recipe for success.

But instead, Beau reached out and grabbed his arm as he walked by.

"Hey," Beau said, pulling down his headset. "You wanna go over that series?"

Did he *want* to go over that series? No. He absolutely fucking did not. He wanted to bury his head in a towel, down some water and forget that it had happened. But then, it was inevitably going to happen again, and then again, and then about a dozen times more, for good measure.

Sebastian slowed and nodded, and looked down at Beau's tablet, which he angled towards him.

"Here," Beau said, pushing his glasses up and then touching the screen, pointing at where the figures were moving at a fraction of their regular speed, the play unfolding slow enough that Sebastian could recognize it. "That's a tell," he added, repeating the play over and then over again. "RPO."

Run-pass option.

That was one of his primary responsibilities as safety—to cover the new developing kind of play where the quarterback could make the decision at the line. And he'd done a shit job of it during the last series.

"Yeah," Sebastian said shortly. "It's funny how fucking fast the game moves, when I'm not just trying to cover one guy."

"It's a change, a big change," Beau said, nodding solemnly. No judgment. When as far as Sebastian was concerned, he should be judging the hell out of him. Had the Packers scored solely because of him? No, but he hadn't helped stop them either.

If you do this, then he's justified in all the shit he did to get you here, Sebastian reminded himself. *He's not helping out of the goodness of his heart.*

Except that yes, Coach was right. Nobody expected them to win many games. And if they did, and if Sebastian helped them do it, he'd get another season. And then maybe another. Then things could get serious. He didn't have a ring, and he'd always wanted one. But he'd never let himself wish for it, because it had felt like he was always choosing between the money and the championships.

"Show me again," Sebastian said, reaching out and snagging a towel from an assistant carrying a load of them to the bench. "Slower this time, and then I want to see the last play, the one they scored on."

Beau shot him a look. "Shouldn't I be showing that to Rose?"

Sebastian gave a shrug. "Yeah, you should, but I want to see it too, because I think if I'd seen it coming, I could have disrupted it better. Covered that guy better. He was out in the flat first, before he came into Rose's zone."

"Hmmm," Beau said thoughtfully as Sebastian took in the first play again, the arrangement of the players on the screen finally beginning to gel in his head. "Yeah, I can see that."

"The best defenses have corners and safeties that work together," Sebastian pointed out. "And you said you wanted me to help him."

"I do," Beau said. "*We* do. Why else do you think we got him in the first round?"

"Because he's fast as hell and can sort of cover, if he gets his head out of his ass," Sebastian said. All things he was going to point out to Rose.

He might not have wanted to be his mentor, but the first series had thrown into stark relief that he *should* be.

"Because," Beau said, "if you two can get on the same page, you're going to wreak holy hell on any offense."

"What," Sebastian retorted, "my days of wreaking holy hell aren't over?"

Beau grinned. "Not by a long shot."

"Long and short of it is," Coach drawled, hip perched on the side of his enormous desk, "we need to score more points, and give up less points."

It was an obvious statement, so obvious that Beau heard a few chuckles and saw a handful of tight smiles around the room. But after a loss, nobody was in a particularly joking mood, especially his father.

But then, nobody, least of all him, had really expected to pull out a win.

His father rarely screamed at a loss—even once when they'd lost a National Championship they should have won, he hadn't yelled. But he'd agonized over it for months.

The first and last person his father blamed for a loss was always himself.

"Tomorrow," he continued, "we'll come back here and figure out how to do that. But for tonight? Give yourselves a break."

Even though Beau knew he wouldn't be giving himself a break.

Slowly the rest of the coaching staff filed out of the office, leaving just Beau and his father, who was sorting through some paperwork on his desk.

"Hey," Beau said, nudging his side with an elbow. "That means you, too."

His dad glanced up. "What means me too?"

"What you said, about giving ourselves a break. You're included. Which means you can't stay here all night, agonizing about what you could have done to change the scoreboard."

"Unless we managed to find thirty extra points, I don't think I *could* change it," Asa said wryly.

"Yeah, exactly. We knew this game was going to be tough. First time out, tough opponent, still getting our balance."

His father's gaze was steady. Honest. Beau found it ironic that Sebastian was so convinced that he'd manipulated his father into doing what he wanted, when he'd always been the most straightforward person that Beau knew. The least likely person to get suckered into something because he always saw the board and the pieces better than anybody else.

Even Beau.

"Doesn't excuse losing by thirty points," his father said, then sighed. He looked concerned, which was worrisome, because he rarely let people see the baggage he carried around with him. Even Beau. "Maybe I shouldn't have dragged you here. Shouldn't have dragged myself here."

"I wasn't dragged, and neither were you," Beau said firmly. "This was a once-in-a-lifetime opportunity, and we took advantage of the money and the prestige of it."

"I doubt anyone's gonna be talking about prestige when we lose every game."

"Then we won't," Beau said simply, even though, deep down, back in the recesses of his mind, he worried about the same thing. So much of their game plan was built on *ifs* and *maybes*. Maybe Sebastian Howard would develop into a legendary safety. If Paxton Kelly could become a franchise quarterback for the Piranhas like Colin O'Connor had. Maybe Micah Rose would be even better than predicted. If Tristan Nicholson could learn to run an NFL-caliber route.

They all bounced around in his mind, like too-ephemeral dreams and hopes and wishes.

But it was his father's job and *his* job, too, to make them solid fucking reality.

"Go home," his father said. "Go have a drink. I will, too."

Beau raised an eyebrow. "Will you? Or will I come back tomorrow morning and see that you slept on the couch again?"

A tiny smile cracked through the worry on Asa's face. "I won't sleep on the couch. That much I'll promise you. If only because my back can't handle it anymore."

"Good." Beau put a hand on his dad's shoulder. They didn't do this, not much. Not ever, really. But . . . he already knew this would be a loss his dad would think about for a long time.

At least before every kickoff of every game to come this season.

And, Beau realized as he walked out of the office and down the hallway to the elevator, he wouldn't be alone.

He and his father had both gotten condos in another one of Miami's high-rise buildings. They weren't the penthouse, but then he wasn't making Sebastian Howard kind of money, either.

But still, when Beau exited the facility, the air still muggy and warm even though it was almost midnight, he didn't turn towards it. Instead, he went the other way.

He'd seen a bar in the ground floor of Sebastian's building, and his father's words were ringing in his ears as he walked the few blocks that direction.

It had looked nice, even low-key, with low lights in the corners, and palm trees on the patio, and it was late enough, and the loss had been brutal enough that Beau didn't think any fans would be hanging around, celebrating the opening game of the season.

He was right.

When he walked in, the bar was nearly empty.

Only one seat at the bar was taken, and when the man sitting at it glanced up, Beau realized that it wasn't the bar's attractive laid-back quality that had brought him here, but the hope that something like this might happen.

Sebastian didn't wave him over, but Beau didn't care, he walked over anyway.

"Tough loss," he said, as he slid into the barstool next to him.

Sebastian didn't say a word. Just stared, unblinking, at the drink in front of him.

It looked strong.

It *smelled* strong.

"What is that?" Beau asked.

Sebastian finally glanced over at him. "A caipirinha," he said.

Beau didn't know what that was, but then he wasn't a big drinker. Alcohol dimmed focus, and Beau never liked giving up the mental upper hand. But tonight had been rough enough, his father's anxious expression still burned into his brain, that he decided that maybe losing a bit of focus wouldn't be a terrible thing after all.

"Same," he said, when the bartender came over to get his order.

Sebastian slid his gaze over again. "Are you sure you know what you're doing with that?"

Beau had no fucking idea. "No," he said honestly.

A corner of Sebastian's mouth quirked up. "Telling the truth is hot," he said.

It reminded Beau of what else Sebastian had said—that time out of anger and frustration—that he'd deliberately *not* asked about.

But since I'm not worried about the state of my balls, that's not my business, either.

He'd wanted to ask, of course.

The words had gone through his mind a hundred times in the last few days, even though he'd tried hard to push them away.

It really wasn't his business what Sebastian had meant.

But he wanted to know anyway.

His dad had always said that his capacity for curiosity was lethal, but Beau was always surprised where it led him.

"What else is hot?" Beau wanted to know.

"Winning." Sebastian's retort was immediate, and delivered in a hard-edged voice.

The bartender appeared with the caipirinha, setting it on a napkin in front of Beau.

He leaned forward, swirling it with the straw, then taking an experimental sip.

It was strong, *really* strong, with an enticing sweet and sour flavor that he really liked.

"This is good," Beau said, with surprise.

"And lethal," Sebastian said with a humorless chuckle, holding up a finger to order another round.

Beau took a closer look, and realized that Sebastian had had more than one already. His eyes were slightly dilated, and his face was flushed, barely evident in the dark room.

He took another sip of his own drink, and couldn't disagree.

"I don't usually do this, you know," Sebastian said, turning towards Beau, surprising him.

"Get drunk after a bad loss? Why not?"

"Do you?" Sebastian countered.

Beau shook his head.

"This one . . . made me think too much. Too much noise."

"About?"

Sebastian laughed humorlessly. "Anyone ever tell you that you're too curious for your own good?"

Beau hesitated, not wanting to piss Sebastian off by bringing up a sore subject, but also wanting to tell the truth. "My father, all the time," he finally said. He took another long drink, feeling the booze burn all the way down. Lighting a fire in his stomach.

Sebastian's thoughtful gaze resting on his face pushed it into a conflagration.

"I can see that," Sebastian said with a thoughtful hum. "Today made me think how much I really want this job, want this chance.

And if things go this way the whole season . . ." He made a sudden, brutal slice with his hand. "That's what'll happen to it."

Beau couldn't help it; he latched on to the one thing they actually had in common. "I want mine, too. And I want . . . I want people to take me seriously. More than just as Asa Dawson's son." He hesitated. "More than just as Asa Dawson's *gay* son."

Sebastian didn't even look surprised, so Beau continued, aware somewhere that was still sober that he shouldn't have drunk that so quickly, especially when he was unused to such strong liquor. "I want people to not look so goddamned surprised when I have a good idea. I want them to not sound shocked that I like working in football. That I want to do it as a career. That I'd have wanted to do it even if my father wasn't who he is. And that I still want to fuck men, afterwards."

Sebastian still didn't blink.

And then he blew Beau's world apart.

"Yeah," he said, lifting his glass and knocking it gently against Beau's, "I want that, too."

Maybe Beau wouldn't have taken the most direct route if he hadn't had most of a caipirinha, but he had, and there was no stopping the question now. "Are you saying what I think you keep saying?"

Sebastian's smile was wry. "How much more obvious do I need to be? I've almost kissed you twice. I didn't think it was much of a secret after that."

Beau was sure he looked shocked. More than shocked. Fucking astonished. He'd *guessed*, or hoped, or dreamed, or something like that, but he'd never expected that all those fantasies would turn out to be right.

"If you look this surprised, it's been too long since someone almost kissed you," Sebastian said, sounding amused.

"I'm just . . . it's not . . ."

But before Beau could get his thoughts together—not helped in the least by the alcohol now swirling through his system—Sebastian interrupted. "Ah, I get it," he said. "You just didn't think *I* was queer, huh? Big tough guy? Yeah . . ." Sebastian grimaced. "I get that."

Beau's first inclination was to nod his head and agree that *yes*, he'd had no idea because most guys, even guys who were still in the closet, were more relaxed these days about people finding out the truth. But he'd never heard even a single whisper about Sebastian.

But luckily he *didn't* say the first thing that popped into his head, because if Sebastian chose to make sure nobody knew, that was his choice, and it wasn't Beau's place to question it.

God knew he'd questioned his own decision to come out at seventeen more than once. Usually he ended up being glad, but occasionally . . . he wished he hadn't been so sunny-eyed and optimistic, thinking that nobody would give a shit.

Because people definitely had given a shit. And even though they should know better, they *still* gave a shit.

Would they have given a shit about Sebastian? Probably.

"I'd have expected you to know better." Sebastian didn't even let him answer and his tone was reproachful.

"I might be a little surprised, yeah, but also . . ." Beau covered for his pause by finishing the rest of his drink, and prayed that he wasn't saying the wrong thing *again,* but then, Sebastian had said *I've almost kissed you twice.* "Also grateful. Really fucking grateful."

Sebastian's face broke into a big, happy grin. "Yeah?"

Beau ducked his head, his own smile nearing Sebastian's in wattage. "Yeah."

The bartender set a new round of drinks in front of them.

"I shouldn't," Beau said.

"Why not?"

Because if I have another drink, I'm going to think it's a really, really good idea to have sex with you, and it's not.

Sebastian broke into laughter then, and Beau realized, humiliation flushing his cheeks, that he'd said that *out loud*.

"Maybe you *shouldn't* have another one," Sebastian said, still chuckling as he swirled the straw in his own drink. But then he shot him a speculative glance, and Beau realized he wasn't the only one thinking about it.

Sebastian had been checking him out all night.

Sebastian had almost kissed him *twice*, even when he was pissed as hell at him.

"Is that why you thought I manipulated you?" Beau asked before he could stop himself.

You're the worst. The absolute fucking worst. You're supposed to be flirting with the super-hot guy you haven't been able to stop thinking about since he showed at camp, and instead, you're bringing up that he hates you. A+ work, Beau. Really brilliant. You must *be a genius.*

At least, Beau thought as Sebastian continued to stare and swirl his drink, he hadn't said any of that out loud.

Thank God for small miracles.

"Naw," Sebastian finally said, another glimmer of a smile emerging on his handsome face. "You tried your level best *not* to flirt with me. It's not your fault you trying to be all brilliant and professional about it made me hot."

"No?" Beau squeaked.

Sebastian leaned in, and Beau could smell him again. Lavender and something darker and richer, and he wanted to lick up the neck that the open collar of his white button-down shirt had exposed and taste it, too. Wanted to trace the tattoo peeking out of his collar with his tongue.

Maybe he really shouldn't have another drink.

Except . . . he *could* sleep with Sebastian. That wasn't off-limits. But if they made it a habit, it would inevitably spill into the locker room, and then onto the field, and that was the one hard and fast rule his father had given him.

And he was going to want it to be a habit. They hadn't even kissed, and Beau already knew it, as easy as breathing.

No, he should really keep his hands in his lap, and his drink un-drunk, but then Sebastian's eyes practically sparkled with the dare of it and he leaned in another fraction of an inch.

"Don't you want to know how hot it made me?" Sebastian crooned in that dirty, sexy voice of his, all low and enticing, and Beau lost the fight with himself.

He reached out and laid his hand on Sebastian's thigh. His hard, muscular thigh, hot beneath the light wool of his slacks. He'd already removed his jacket, and rolled up the sleeves of his shirt, exposing those rippling forearms that had taken up residence in too many of Beau's fantasies already.

He swallowed hard. But didn't move his hand either.

"I think you do," Sebastian said lowly.

Beau reminded himself that he was no slouch in the suggestive flirting department. He could do this too. He was a fucking genius. He could do this *even better* if he wanted to—if only he could get a little more blood in his brain and a whole lot less in his cock.

"Maybe I want you to show me," Beau said.

Sebastian looked visibly shaken by his confident statement, fingers trembling on his glass, like Beau was stripping away his self-control one word at a time. Like he hadn't expected Beau to call him on his bluff.

Nerves and anticipation jangled in his stomach, along with the liquor, and he took a chance, and squeezed Sebastian's thigh.

It twitched under his touch, and Sebastian's fingers drummed arrhythmically on the bar top.

"You're playing with fire," Sebastian said. "We're not . . . we shouldn't . . ."

Beau batted his eyelashes shamelessly. He'd made up his mind now, and he wasn't going to let Sebastian take this away from him. From *them*.

If he had to go back to his condo alone, he'd end up with the worst blue balls of the century.

It wouldn't matter how many times he touched himself. His hands weren't going to magically morph into Sebastian Howard's hands, and that was what Beau really wanted.

"It's not off-limits," Beau said firmly, squeezing again. God, he wanted to know what Sebastian felt like, under this fabric. Spread out across his bed.

Sebastian's gaze narrowed. "I find that hard to believe," he said.

Beau grabbed his last chance, and shoved them into the fire.

He trailed his fingertips up Sebastian's thigh, feeling it tense under his exploration. And then he found what he was looking for—the hard ridge of Sebastian's erection. He barely had to graze it, with only the barest touch of his palm, before it twitched, undeniably, incredibly interested in whatever Beau might do next.

"Come on," Beau said. "You can agonize over this in the morning. I think you live upstairs . . .?"

Sebastian downed the rest of his drink, and Beau only had a split second to move his hand before he was sliding off the barstool, peeling a few twenties off the stack in his wallet, then swirling his jacket over his arm. Conveniently, Beau realized, hiding his erection. He tilted his head arrogantly towards Beau. Like he knew just how hot he looked. "Are you coming, then?"

I sure hope so. More than once.

Beau had no illusions about how unsexy he was as he scrambled off his stool, but Sebastian didn't even blink. Just settled a hand proprietorially in the small of his back, and guided them out the door, into the lobby of the building, and towards the elevator.

Sebastian hit the up button and they stood, waiting for the elevator, and Beau shuddered, with anticipation and with a sudden terror that this was a huge fucking mistake.

It's a huge fucking mistake, all right, his brain thought evilly, *emphasis on the fucking.*

But because nerves always made him chatty, he started talking. "I don't see Luis," he said, craning his head around Sebastian's body, noticing he didn't recognize the concierge at the front desk.

"Luis went to the game with his son," Sebastian said, voice low. "I got him and his son, Manuel, tickets."

And this right here was why following Sebastian into his elevator and then up to his penthouse, where they would inevitably—and hopefully—get naked, was an egregious mistake.

Because that was so fucking sweet.

Sebastian was such a good guy. A *great* guy. And Beau already knew he didn't want just a one-night stand with him. To get naked together and then go their separate ways the next morning.

But then the elevator dinged, and Sebastian pressed him forward, that hand large and warm even through Beau's polo shirt.

This was happening, good idea or not.

Chapter Four

The ride up to the penthouse was interminable, Beau watching with nerves blooming along every inch of his skin as each floor ticked by.

The only other time Beau had made this ride, it had felt the same. He'd been nervous that night, too, worried that he wouldn't be able to keep things professional between them.

But tonight there was no way things were going to stay professional. The moment Sebastian's door closed, they were both going to cross a line.

With enthusiasm and hopefully at least twice, Beau thought.

Finally the elevator reached its destination, and a few seconds later, they were walking towards Sebastian's door. And then they were through it, and to Beau's surprise, Sebastian wasn't immediately on him.

Instead, he hung back, at least a foot too far away, as the door shut behind Beau. He tossed his coat onto a nearby low sofa, but didn't come any closer.

Beau shifted weight from one foot to the other, and then pulled his glasses off, shoving them in his pocket. He'd barely had a sip or two of his second drink, and he was sobering up every minute they stood there, staring at each other.

He didn't want to be sober. Sobering up meant logic and coherency, and anyone who was thinking clearly would not be doing this.

He tossed the dice again, and leaned back against the door.

"I'm assuming," he said, gesturing to himself, "that this was time number two."

Sebastian straightened, like Beau had just caught him out. "Time number two?"

"You said, *I almost kissed you twice*, and I can only assume the first was the argument we had in my father's office, and this was the second."

Sebastian gazed at him. "Yes," he said. His tongue darted out, licking his bottom lip. His full, generous bottom lip. The same one that Beau had imagined licking himself.

Why was he not doing it? Oh, that's right. Because Sebastian looked like he still didn't know if this was a smart move.

"Well," Beau said, recklessly, because it really *wasn't* a smart move, but he was going to do it anyway, fuck the consequences, "there shouldn't be a third."

He closed the distance between them and reached up, cradling Sebastian's cheek, smooth as butter, in his hand, and reaching up onto his tiptoes, kissed him.

Sebastian tasted like sugar and mint, with something so much deeper and spicier underneath, and Beau tensed. Trying not to fall headlong into the kiss, because Sebastian hadn't exactly kissed him back.

He pulled back, and Sebastian's hands, just grazing his sides, trembled. Sebastian stared at him for a moment longer, and then it was like a dam broke, all of a sudden, and with force. With *feeling*.

One moment, Beau was about to apologize and excuse himself with an astonishing amount of embarrassment, and the next,

Sebastian pulled him into his arms, so tightly against him that Beau could barely breathe, Sebastian's cock a hard, hot line against his thigh. *He's still interested, he still wants this*, was all Beau had time to think, and then he was kissing him fiercely. Catching and captivating him so completely that Beau ceased to simply think at all.

He only felt.

Sebastian's hands on his ass, gripping it in rhythm with his tongue delving into his mouth. One moment, he'd been his own, and the next he was this man's, for whatever he wanted.

Yes, please, Beau's cock screamed. *Let him take us. Make us his.*

Sebastian tilted his head and, somehow, impossibly devoured him even further, until all Beau could do was hang on to his shoulders, turned on beyond anything he'd ever experienced before.

Then the kiss was over, almost as suddenly as it had begun, and *oh God*, Beau thought unsteadily, as he watched Sebastian drop to his knees, mouthing at the fabric of his khaki slacks, right over where he was the hardest, the most sensitive. He couldn't help it; he gasped.

"Did you know," he said, in a low rough voice, "I thought about this the first time I saw you. You walked into the room, and I could only think about one thing. Getting your pants off, and your cock in my mouth."

"Oh," Beau gasped as Sebastian tugged his pants down, and then his briefs, and then his cock was being engulfed in the hottest, sweetest mouth he'd ever felt.

Sebastian pulled back for a second, tongue dragging along the underside, making Beau see stars. "Is this okay?" he asked.

"Is it . . . is it okay?" Beau stuttered.

A hand gripped his thigh, pushed him against the door. "It's a question. Needs an answer," Sebastian said. His mouth, already red and wet, hovered right over his cock.

"Yes," Beau said in a rush. "Yes, absolutely fucking yes."

"Good." Sebastian sounded delighted. "You can come now, and then you're going to fuck me after."

Sebastian's mouth and *then* his ass . . . Beau groaned a little, his head hitting the back of the door, as Sebastian began to work him over.

It was sloppy and wet, and not as quick as Beau had expected, with the way the evening had changed course so abruptly. Sebastian made it slow and deliberate, long slow slurps and an almost unbearable suction as Beau hung on and tried not to embarrass himself by coming too fast.

There wasn't much on Sebastian's head to hold on to—Beau found himself missing the long, luxurious locs, that he'd imagined tugging on hard while Sebastian blew him—but he reached down and caressed Sebastian's head anyway. Marveling at the beautiful way he was put together, and how he was Beau's to enjoy, at least for tonight.

Sebastian's hand cupped his balls, tugging on them just enough that Beau found himself rushing, far too quickly, into what promised to be a mind-blowing orgasm.

His fingers dug into Sebastian's scalp, and then he took him even deeper, his throat vibrating around his cock, already so sensitive, and that was all it took. He tilted his head back and embarrassingly yelled as he came.

It was a long moment before he opened his eyes, and he twitched, slowly softening in Sebastian's mouth, as he took in the gorgeous sight beneath him.

"That was . . ." Beau was supposed to be a genius, why couldn't he come up with a single word that could properly describe the most incredible experience of his life?

But Sebastian didn't look insulted; instead he looked happy. Thrilled, in fact. He stood, pulling himself to his feet slowly, as Beau realized belatedly that he probably looked like an idiot, with his cock hanging out, and his pants around his ankles.

He was still wearing his shoes, for God's sake.

"Good?" Sebastian's eyes twinkled at him as he held out his hand.

"Unfuckingbelievable," Beau confirmed. He reached down and decided he would shed his clothes right where they stood, before he took Sebastian's hand.

Sebastian nodded thoughtfully. "Not a bad idea," he said, tilting his head at where Beau's clothes piled in front of the door. But instead of stripping himself, he pulled him along, deeper into the penthouse, in a different direction than Beau had been before.

The master suite was huge, with an enormous bed at the center of it, big enough for at least six. Beau considered making a joke about how many people would be joining them, but then Sebastian pushed him gently to the bed, and began to unbutton his shirt.

He'd seen Sebastian Howard in various states of undress in the locker room, and in the weight room, and once memorably in the showers, though he'd *tried* very hard not to look, because if anyone caught him looking, it was going to be a problem.

But they were all dwarfed by this moment, because now not only could Beau look without a frisson of unease running through him, but Sebastian wanted him to look. Was taking his clothes off just for him.

He thumbed each button carefully, deliberately, and then tugged the shirt out of his slacks, dropping it to the floor.

Sebastian looked like he'd been carved by a master. Every ridge of muscle was glorious, so perfectly formed that Beau ached with the beauty of it. Tattoos swirled over his light brown skin, adding to and never detracting from the flawless way he was constructed. He was so fucking gorgeous, he could have anyone on earth he wanted.

And with the way his eyes were burning as he stared at Beau, his fingers fumbling with the button and zipper of his slacks, who he wanted was Beau.

It was humbling, and it was exhilarating.

He stripped his shoes off, and his socks, and then his pants followed, and *God*, Beau realized unsteadily, he wasn't wearing anything under them. This had already been the sexiest, hottest encounter of his entire life and now nothing else would ever touch it again.

Now, whenever he saw Sebastian dressed up, or dressed down, or dressed any which way, he was going to imagine that he was naked underneath. That alone was going to make keeping this out of the locker room and off the field almost impossible. But before Beau could hesitate, Sebastian dipped his head, kissing Beau again, slow and deliberate, his movements surprising considering how hard his cock was.

Beau broke the kiss, leaning away. "You said . . ." He hesitated. "You said you wanted . . ."

Sebastian's eyes glowed gold. "Yeah," he said unsteadily. "You good with that?"

Beau had let him take charge from the bar up til now. But if he was going to do this, he was going to do it right.

He put his palm against Sebastian's gorgeous chest and pushed him back onto the bed. God, his pecs, his abs, his arms, Beau was going to be jacking off just to the image of him from now until the end of time.

"Drawer," Sebastian rasped out, "you'll find what you need."

He did, pulling out lube and a condom.

His cock was already starting to get hard again, because this was the hottest thing that had ever happened to him. But first, he needed to get Sebastian as desperate as he felt.

He leaned over and gave Sebastian's cock, long and hard and thick, an experimental lick. Yes, he tasted just as good as Beau had imagined. And Sebastian's reaction to just that one touch was unbelievable. He threw his head back and groaned, fingers knotting in the sheets.

Beau could feel the blood throbbing in his head. And his dick.

But instead, he leaned in and this time took Sebastian's cock into his mouth, letting it slip further into his mouth, enjoying the stretch of it, the weight of it on his tongue.

He made it plenty wet, nearly as sloppy as Sebastian's blowjob had been, and with a finger he swiped through the mess of his saliva and Sebastian's precome, and slid it slower, circling his hole with his thumb.

"Oh fuck," Sebastian moaned the moment he touched him there.

So apparently Sebastian might be deep in the closet, but he had no qualms about enjoying this. Beau hummed with approval, sliding in his thumb further, loving the sounds spilling from Sebastian's lips as he sucked his cock and fingered him.

When he took a break to grab the lube, he chanced a look at the man beneath him and found him panting, his chest rising and falling fast, his face flushed, and his pupils totally dilated.

"God," Sebastian groaned, sounding totally wrecked, "just get on with it. I can take it. I can . . ."

Beau took him at his word, sliding two slicked-up fingers into him, giving a few experimental, gentle thrusts before Sebastian thrust his own body, trying to get Beau to go faster.

Beau stopped instantly, and shot Sebastian a look. "You gonna behave?" he asked.

Sebastian froze. His mouth went slack. And somehow, impossibly, his cock grew even harder.

"Good," Beau said. His answer had been clear enough even if he hadn't said a word.

He took his time fingering Sebastian, gliding his fingers in and out, then reaching up higher, curling them, trying to find the spot that would set Sebastian on fire.

Sebastian didn't try to push him again, just took what he was given, clearly loving every moment of it.

Beau realized as he reached for the condom that he was hard as a rock, too, now and straining to come again.

He'd have to . . . well, he'd have to do whatever it took to make sure Sebastian got what he needed.

"Please," Sebastian begged.

He clearly did not beg very often, because the word looked wrenched from his mouth.

Beau decided they'd both waited long enough. He lifted one of Sebastian's thick, muscled legs in his hands, and positioned himself, slowly beginning to sink in.

Sebastian was slick and hot and tight, so fucking tight that Beau felt the stirrings of his orgasm begin before he'd even slid all the way home.

When he did, Sebastian moaned, all those glorious muscles tensing up with how good it felt.

You can't, you've got to give him what he needs. You want to give him what he needs, Beau reminded himself. But the fire was already starting in his blood, racing through his veins, and he could barely hold back as he began to fuck him.

Then Sebastian reached down and gripped his own cock, twisting it in time with Beau's thrusts.

Just when he'd thought this had been as hot as it could possibly be, Sebastian somehow effortlessly made it sexier. Beau screwed his eyes shut, hoping to hold on just long enough to feel him come around him.

He tilted Sebastian's hips a little, searching desperately for that spot, and he knew when he hit it, because Sebastian yelled and then he was squeezing him, over and over and over again, come splattering over both of their chests.

Sebastian in the throes of an orgasm was an incredible sight, his back bowed, the tendons in his neck thrown into sharp relief, and Beau gave one last unsteady thrust, and followed him into bliss, pulsing endlessly into the condom.

When it finally ended, he pulled out, collapsing next to Sebastian, his breath wildly unsteady as he tried to catch it.

Sebastian didn't say anything. Just stared at the ceiling, unblinking.

Beau knew he had to get up. Deal with the condom. But he didn't even know where the bathroom was.

Finally, just as he was about to awkwardly ask—*and destroy the best sex of your entire fucking life*, he thought—Sebastian pointed to a dark shadowed doorway at the other end of the room. "Bathroom's through there," he said, voice low and gritty.

Beau both wanted to get up and escape and also stay here, forever.

They weren't quite touching, but the presence of Sebastian next to him was enough. More than enough, because then Sebastian glanced over at him, and there was affection and sweetness and satisfaction in those golden-brown eyes.

"You good?" Beau asked. Kicking himself for how silly he sounded. But there were no words left in his brain. Sebastian had blown them all away.

"Yeah," Sebastian said. Voice still gravelly.

Beau got up then, and headed to the bathroom, feeling Sebastian's eyes on him the whole way.

The bathroom was just as palatial as the bedroom.

Beau disposed of the condom, and after cleaning himself up, considered bringing a damp washcloth into the bedroom to help Sebastian, but before he could make up his mind, Sebastian walked into the bathroom behind him, headed straight for the shower.

He flipped it on, and stared, unblinking again, at Beau.

He still didn't say anything.

Maybe I should just go, Beau thought. *Things are getting awkward.*

More than awkward.

But then Sebastian spoke. "You need help getting home?"

It wasn't like Beau had expected Sebastian to invite him to stay, but it stung anyway.

"No," Beau said, turning towards him, making sure he sounded confident.

"Good." Sebastian paused. "'Cause I'm . . . well, I'm not entirely sober yet. Not even close."

Had Sebastian been that drunk? Beau hadn't thought so. But then he didn't know the guy all that well.

How much had he had to drink before Beau showed up? Beau considered asking but decided against it because then it sounded like he'd taken advantage, and truthfully, they'd taken advantage of each other.

"I'll just grab an Uber," Beau said. Remembering at the last moment that he was still naked and that his phone was in the other room.

Sebastian nodded. He turned to get into the shower, and Beau thought with disappointment that the message was clear enough—when he was done, Beau had better have cleared out. This was just sex, it had been great, but now it was over.

But then, before Beau could slink out of the room to make his walk of shame, Sebastian pulled him in and kissed him. *Hard.*

The kiss was ravenous, like they hadn't gotten nearly enough of each other. *You haven't, not by a long shot*, Beau's uncooperative brain proclaimed.

Sebastian's fingertips dug into his waist, and for a single wild second, Beau thought he might actually be able to get hard again—but no, there was no way that was happening. He wasn't sixteen anymore.

He was the one who pulled away.

"That was fucking amazing, from beginning to end," Beau said.

Sebastian nodded. "I knew it would be," he added.

"The two almost kisses?" Beau questioned, and Sebastian laughed.

"Among other things."

Beau almost asked what the other things were, but he'd wanted a way to exit gracefully, and this was it.

He couldn't stop remembering his father's edict: *not in the locker room, and not on the field.* If they kept kissing, and Beau stayed, then there was no way that was going to happen.

It was going to be tough enough as it was, now that Beau knew how Sebastian kissed and fucked and looked and *was.*

"I'll see you on Tuesday, then," Beau said.

"Monday," Sebastian called out as Beau left the bathroom. "We lost, ain't nobody taking a day off around here."

Sebastian woke with an ugly throbbing in his head, and a warmer, much more pleasant throbbing in his ass.

Had he . . .

Oh, he had.

He'd gotten drunk and then he'd gotten fucked.

By Beau Dawson.

Sebastian groaned, and rolled over in bed. He'd fallen into bed still tipsy and still blissed out from the great sex, and he'd forgotten to lower the blinds that kept the bright Miami sunshine from flooding the entire condo.

He hadn't been drunk, not exactly. He'd had a few shots before Beau had ever showed up, because it had seemed like a good idea when he'd been feeling so goddamned sorry for himself.

Of course he'd lost plenty of games before.

But never with the expectation looming that he'd lose a lot more.

That had been the painful knowledge he'd been trying to face, staring down at the bottom of a glass, along with the inescapable fact that even switching to safety might not be enough to save his NFL career.

Then Beau had walked in—that awe in his gaze that stoked Sebastian's own ego mixed with his own brand of cocky confidence.

He'd taken advantage of both, because he hadn't been able to help himself.

Or, Sebastian thought ruefully as he stared up at his vaulted ceiling, maybe they had used each other. At the very least, he hoped they'd both gotten this inconvenient sexual attraction out of their systems.

He should get up, make his morning smoothie, stretch out his sore muscles from the game, and head over to the complex to get his workout in. But something stopped him. The inevitability of seeing Beau?

You're not going to want him, still, no matter how good it was, how much you enjoyed it.

But it didn't matter how firmly he told himself that inescapable fact.

It still didn't quite feel like the truth.

And if it didn't feel like the truth, here and now, alone in his bed, how was it going to feel when it was the two of them alone in an otherwise empty office, late at night, with all the memories crowding them?

This right here was why Sebastian had *never*, not once, gotten involved with another player, or another person associated with an NFL team. Because it was never simple or straightforward and the cut was never clean.

This one, he was afraid, was going to be messy as hell.

There was a gym somewhere in this building, and Sebastian was just considering how cowardly it would be to stay here today, instead of going to the Piranhas' facility—especially since he'd *have* to return on Tuesday, no matter what—when a knock on his front door echoed through the room.

Sebastian, working his way to upright, froze.

It couldn't be Beau, back again, but there were only a few people on Sebastian's automatic permissions list with the concierge, and it was entirely possible that Luis had added Beau the last time he'd been here.

The person at the front door knocked again, and Sebastian grumbled, sliding out of bed, grabbing his pants, still crumpled on the floor from where he'd dropped them the night before.

He'd barely gotten them fastened when he made it to the front door, pulling it open, both hoping and dreading that it was Beau.

Hoping because the sex had been incredible, and he would be stupid not to want to do it again.

Dreading because they couldn't. No matter how good it had been.

But it wasn't Beau.

It was Alec, holding two takeout cups with the logo of his favorite Cuban bakery emblazoned on the side.

Alec raised a dark, flawlessly groomed eyebrow at Sebastian's lack of clothing. "Rough night?" he asked.

"You could say that," Sebastian said, pulling the door open further and then shutting it behind his agent.

They walked together into the kitchen. It turned out that Alec was also holding a *bag* from his favorite Cuban bakery, and he could smell his absolute favorite pastelitos filled with cream cheese and guava as Alec set the bag on the counter and began to unpack it.

Sebastian turned away to find plates and two mugs for their coffee.

"So, not that I'm not always happy to see you on the East Coast, but I wasn't expecting you," Sebastian pointed out.

"I thought the surprise would be a good one," Alec said dryly. "I was already in Tampa for the Riptide game, and it was easy enough to grab a flight to Miami."

"You gonna tell me why?" Sebastian asked, pouring his coffee into a mug. It was already doctored with the sugar mixture that made the incredibly dark, rich coffee drinkable. He grabbed a pastry and watched as Alec did the same, settling onto one of the barstools opposite him.

"It was a bad loss," Alec said simply.

"If it was just the one, I'd be fine," Sebastian said.

"But it won't be. More of a chance the rest will be just like this one," Alec agreed with a nod. He sipped his coffee and made a face. "God, I don't know how you drink this when it's so fucking strong."

"Puts some hair on your chest," Sebastian teased.

Alec shuddered and eyed Sebastian's bare chest—which was devoid of hair. "And yet," he said dryly.

"So you flew here to console me?" Sebastian asked. *Beau did it better. Beau was the best goddamn consolation prize I've ever been lucky enough to win.*

He took a bite of his pastry and it was totally worth the workout he'd have to put in later to make up for the calories.

"I flew here because you're a mess, Howard."

"I'm . . . I'm getting there," Sebastian said, guardedly. "Less of a mess than I was, anyway."

"Freaking out that Beau Dawson was manipulating you, of all fucking things, and what about yesterday? You looked only sort of committed out there, like you were only playing safety because you *had* to, not because you wanted to."

"I thought you were watching the Riptide play Tampa Bay yesterday," Sebastian said sulkily. Annoyed because if it had been evident enough to his agent, then it was inevitable that Beau *and* his dad were going to be able to spot it too. And they wouldn't just give him a hard time about it, like Alec would.

No, they would exact their retribution in sweat and blood.

So there was that to look forward to.

"I was, but you're a client, and even more, you're a *friend*, and you're kinda all over right now. Not like the usual dialed-in Sebastian Howard."

"The dialed-in Sebastian Howard plays corner." Yes, he was absolutely still pouting about it. Was it attractive? Sebastian didn't think so, but then it must not be *unattractive* either because Beau certainly hadn't hesitated at the chance to climb into Sebastian's bed.

"He *used* to play corner. He *could* play safety, if he could get his head out of his own ass," Alec said bluntly. "Beau is good at this, you should let him help you."

"Why does everyone think he's so fucking brilliant anyway?" Sebastian grumbled, even though he was already beginning to see it.

He was halfway to hungover, and both regretting last night and wanting to repeat it at the soonest possible opportunity, and the impossibility of that was making him cranky.

"Because he is," Alec said simply. "The fact that he came up with this idea in the first place proves it. Because you're a perfect candidate to make this switch."

"If I get my head out of my ass?" Sebastian grumbled.

Alec nodded.

"I'll talk to him," Sebastian said. "I know I wasn't . . . I wasn't my normal self out there yesterday." *And all you're gonna do is talk. That's absolutely it.*

"Good." Alec looked satisfied by this. "And the other thing . . . that's not going to be a problem?"

Sebastian knew exactly what Alec was talking about. The *I want to fuck him* problem.

If only Alec knew what had happened here last night—but he wasn't going to be stupid enough to tell him, because he'd never hear the end of it. Besides, it had been one time, and it was going to *stay* the only time.

"Nope," Sebastian said. Because *technically*, Beau had ended up fucking him.

Though if Beau wanted to, he'd have been just as eager to return the favor.

"You're doing that shifty-eye thing," Alec said. "He's cute, he really is, I get it. And y'all work too much. No time for . . . well, for anything resembling a social life."

"What would Spence say if he could hear you?" Sebastian teased, trying to change the subject.

Alec rolled his eyes. "The best thing about Spencer is that he's aware I'm human, and also madly, completely in love with him. He doesn't have anything to worry about, and he knows it."

"Must be nice."

Alec had the nerve to look smug. "Oh, it is."

And the truth was, Sebastian thought Alec was not only a freaking fantastic agent, but a great guy, and he deserved love and happiness.

"Also, you're one to talk about not having anything resembling a social life," Sebastian pointed out.

"It turns out," Alec said, and he was smiling now, like he only did when he talked about Spencer, "that there's more to life than work. A lesson you should be learning. You're not getting any younger."

"So everyone keeps telling me," Sebastian retorted bitterly.

Alec stood, having finished both his pastry and his coffee. He patted Sebastian on the shoulder sympathetically, but his voice was brisk when he said, "Stop feeling sorry for yourself and embrace this new path you've got. Not everyone gets a second chance, you know."

"Time for the tough-love portion of the pep talk?" Sebastian asked, raising an eyebrow.

Alec shot him a look. "You should be glad I didn't *start* with the tough-love part."

Sebastian couldn't help it, he laughed at that. "That would be your regular MO, for sure."

Alec grinned. "It's why you love me, and also as a bonus, employ me."

"Hey," Sebastian said, as they walked towards the door. He pulled Alec into a tight hug. "I'm really glad you came, actually."

"You looked like you needed it," Alec said, his gaze turning serious.

"I . . ." Sebastian wanted to say that he *had*, but then he'd run into Beau—or Beau had run into him—and somehow, he'd made it both better and also worse.

But it had been good to see Alec, anyway. He didn't get to, not nearly enough anymore, now that he'd moved back to Florida.

"I know," Alec said. "But chin up, you *can* do this, Sebastian."

He chuckled. "That's exactly what I'm afraid of."

Not only was he going to have to ask for Beau's help, he was going to have to ask for it *and* figure out how to keep his hands off him in the process.

"You can do anything you set your mind to," Alec said confidently. "You're Sebastian Howard, and you're gonna be the best damn safety the NFL has ever seen."

CHAPTER FIVE

After Alec left, Sebastian made his smoothie, got dressed in his workout clothes, and decided going to the gym in his building was not only fucking cowardly, it set the wrong tone.

He and Beau had had sex.

Really, really good sex.

It would be easier to confront it head-on, instead of trying to pretend that it hadn't happened.

That might even help them get past it quicker.

A few years back, the Piranhas, during the massive overhaul of their stadium and its offices, had bought up a few blocks of property and converted it to a smaller practice facility right next door to the main field.

It was within easy walking distance of his condo, so even though most of the guys still drove in, showing off their flashiest rides, Sebastian preferred to walk.

It was muggy this morning, but Sebastian still hustled, warming up and loosening his muscles for his workout to come.

Since it was a Monday after a game, they technically had the day off, but when Sebastian walked into the weight room, to his surprise there was already another player in there.

Logan Banks, the center newly signed from Minnesota, was sweating as he benched an absolutely ridiculous amount of weight.

Niko, the assistant strength coach, was spotting him.

"Hey," Sebastian said, approaching after Logan had finished his set. "I thought I'd be the only one crazy enough to be here today."

Logan grinned. "Not just us. Pax just finished his workout, and he's already cloistered away with Abernathy, breaking down yesterday's plays. Coaches are all here, too."

"It was a tough loss," Sebastian said.

After a few last warmup stretches, Sebastian sat down on a weight bench. He'd spent so long trying to be both strong *and* fast that he'd made compromises. But he could already tell, after one full game at the position, that he needed to be stronger. Better arm strength and much better core strength, to improve his tackling.

"Still glad I came here, though," Logan said.

Sebastian frowned as he picked his weights, and started his reps. "Even if we lose every game?"

He hadn't wanted to say the words out loud, but it was a possibility, lurking in the back of everyone's mind. It had happened before, and it would happen again. And they were positioned for that kind of disastrous season with a brand-new coaching staff inexperienced in the NFL and a whole bunch of rookies and veterans who, just like Sebastian, had lost a step.

But Logan just nodded. "Better to lose here than win in Minnesota," he said. Dropped his voice, and then winked. "You know what I mean, Howard."

Beau had told him last night that he'd never heard a rumor that he was queer, but clearly Logan Banks had, and so had Tristan Nicholson, earlier in the summer.

Alec was probably right; Beau was working way too hard to have anything resembling a social life. Was it any wonder they hadn't been able to deny their mutual attraction? Clearly it had been way too long for him.

And for you too, an annoying voice in Sebastian's uncooperative brain pointed out.

"Yeah," Sebastian said. He couldn't deny that the money hadn't been the *only* reason he'd agreed to come to Miami.

Their reputation as one of the more queer-friendly NFL teams had definitely helped. It wasn't like the Cardinals were particularly bad—there technically hadn't been any "out" players on the team when Sebastian had played for them, but there'd been more than one who hadn't really bothered with the closet. They'd just lived their life, not worrying about questions or speculation or gossip.

Sebastian had always considered making that transition, but at first he'd been so tired of fighting about his race, that he hadn't wanted to fight, too, about who he loved. And then he'd hated even the thought of anyone speculating about his private life—so he'd kept it entirely private.

But maybe this move to Miami, with its more queer-positive atmosphere, would reduce the amount of questions.

Maybe he could be more open—at least maybe he could be *less* private.

"Now," Logan said, as he moved towards one of the mats, "I certainly don't intend to lose every game. We're gonna get on track."

"I like your optimism," Sebastian said, meaning it.

Logan grinned. "All you gotta do is just believe. And work your ass off, too."

He thought about what Alec had said this morning. "Gotta get my head out of it first."

"I wasn't always a center, you know," Logan said as Niko tossed him a medicine ball and he began doing a complicated set of crunches. Sebastian was going to need to do those, too, as painful as they looked. "I started as a right tackle in college."

"What happened?" Sebastian knew that offensive linemen often switched positions. At Arizona, they'd had some backups who could theoretically play any spot on the line.

"Center got injured, and then the backup went down mid-game," Logan said. "Didn't have a choice. Took a few practice snaps on the sideline, and got sent out on the next possession."

"How was it?"

Logan laughed, and Sebastian, who'd already liked what he'd seen of the guy, liked him even more. "Oh, it was fucking terrible," he said. "I hated it. I couldn't wait to go back to tackle. I'd spent all this time teaching myself to pull, and centers don't traditionally do that. I thought I was being moved to a position that was easier than what I'd already learned to do. I thought it was beneath me."

Sebastian nodded. That he could understand. Not that safety didn't have its own share of difficulties, but corner was challenging in an entirely different way—a way he'd always connected with.

"The original center came back, but then Coach called me into his office. He wanted me to keep playing center."

"What did you say?" Sebastian asked, panting through his next set of reps.

Logan shrugged. "Do any of us really get a choice?"

At one time, Sebastian had thought he might, because Coach had told him that he wanted him to make the change willingly, but then Jonah had torn his Achilles, and they'd traded West to the Raiders in exchange for their kicker.

He could've protested, insisted on competing with Rose for the open cornerback spot, but he hadn't. Probably because he'd been terrified that he'd lose.

"How did you make your peace with it?" Sebastian asked.

"I decided that if I was going to play center, I was going to be the best. And along the way, I discovered that it was just as hard to play center as it was to play right tackle," Logan said, shooting him a grin. "Maybe harder. At least if you do it right."

Alec had been right; Sebastian had been going through the motions yesterday. He'd been playing safety, but he hadn't been *committed* to playing safety. He wasn't trying to be the best safety on the field.

He'd just been *a* safety on the field.

There was a distinct difference.

To learn how to really commit himself, he was going to have to do what Alec suggested and talk to Beau.

Even though what he wanted to do with Beau had nothing to do with talking.

"That . . . that helps, actually," Sebastian said, panting through the last bit of his reps. He set the weights down and straightened, wiping his face with a towel. "I think I'm gonna need to approach it differently."

"I think," Logan said seriously, "if anyone can do it, it's you. You're Sebastian Howard. You're a fucking legend."

Before, that proclamation would have boosted his ego nicely. Would have made him feel more secure in the fact that he was *right*, that he should never switch positions. But now, considering what else Logan had told him, the words hit him differently.

He could be a legend at corner, and *become* a legend at safety. Rod Woodson had done it, hadn't he?

He had the skills. He just needed to refine them. Learn how to utilize them better. Prepare differently.

And as much as it sucked, it was going to have to be Beau who helped him.

Beau walked into the practice facility an hour later than he'd originally intended. And, if he took an entirely different route than he normally did, he told himself that it did not mean anything.

Except it totally did, and he'd done it because he'd hoped to entirely avoid the part of the facility that housed the weight and locker rooms.

The places Sebastian was most likely to be this morning.

He wasn't proud of it. But he still hadn't figured out how he was going to see him today and resign himself to the fact that what had happened between them wasn't going to happen again.

It would have helped his whole reconciliation thought process if it hadn't been so fucking good.

"You're in late."

Beau looked up and saw their defensive coordinator, Brett Jackson, leaning against the side of the doorframe.

Brett had an even thicker Southern accent than his father, having spent most of his career in New Orleans, coaching the Saints.

But his father, who'd always been a friend, had hired him to be the Piranhas' defensive coordinator because first, he trusted Brett, and second, because Brett would listen to him when he had suggestions for strengthening the defense. Which, because he was Asa Dawson, was inevitable.

His father was full of opinions, but *especially* opinions about the defense.

"Not so late," Beau said, somewhat defensively.

"Asa was in hours ago," Brett drawled.

He liked Brett. He really did. But sometimes he also had to fight the urge to punch Brett in the face.

As it was, Beau decided that comment didn't deserve a response.

He worked just as hard as, if not harder than, anyone else in the building, and he didn't need to justify his behavior to anyone, especially Brett Jackson.

"I wanted to chat with you 'bout Sebastian," Brett said, when his previous comment was met with Beau's pointed silence.

Beau forced himself not to turn bright fucking red.

Brett was one hundred percent *not* here to talk about how he'd fucked Sebastian the night before. Nope, he was definitely, absolutely, with zero questions, here to talk about Sebastian's first game playing safety.

"Could've gone better," Beau allowed.

Brett raised an eyebrow. "Better? He looked lost on the first two drives."

"On some plays, yeah," Beau allowed. "But he got better. He's learning. There's going to be a learning curve, I told you there would be."

"I can't believe your fucking dad traded West away," Brett said. Beau had already suspected that Brett wasn't happy Vaughn West was gone, and so this wasn't exactly a surprise.

No doubt Brett had been bitching to Asa about it for days.

"Doesn't matter," Beau said with a clipped voice. "We're going to make the defense work with Howard at safety, and Rose at corner. He played well."

"Hope you're talkin' 'bout Rose," Brett said.

Beau nodded.

"Yeah, he wasn't *too* bad, considering," Brett agreed. "I gotta get Howard to work with him some before the next game."

"And I've got to work with Howard," Beau said, even though he'd already known it. There just hadn't been enough time. Not enough hours in the day to get Sebastian properly prepped for the first game.

Never mind that Sebastian hadn't seemed to want to.

But now, hopefully, with one game under his belt, and the way he'd floundered, they'd both be on the same page.

"You'd better," Brett said.

Beau shot him a look. He hadn't exactly been against his father's hiring of Brett, but he'd had a few other candidates in mind. Unfortunately his father hadn't gone for any of those, because none of them would have stomached taking so much of Asa's pointed advice.

But Asa had also made a point that he didn't want to just hire white coaches. "We can't only think people of color are valuable on the field, Beau," he'd repeated dozens of times, even though Beau had agreed with him every single time.

"You could *also* help," Beau said slowly.

"Don't you worry, I'll be sure to be giving him lotsa drills tomorrow. So many he's gonna hate me. But still . . ." Brett paused, about to turn away and leave. *Thank God,* Beau thought. "Still, he's got fire, and I can't say that 'bout everyone here."

Possessing "fire" was the greatest compliment that Brett Jackson had, and Beau supposed as the defensive coordinator turned and left, that was at least someplace to start.

Because the last thing Beau needed was for Sebastian to realize just how unhappy his coach was that Vaughn West had left, leaving only Sebastian to cover the center.

Only.

Beau chuckled to himself.

"What's so funny?"

Beau looked up and there he was, *only* Sebastian Howard, standing in his doorway, looking somehow, impossibly, hotter than ever, and also slightly sheepish.

No, they absolutely should not have slept together, whether his dad would go ballistic or not.

Why? Because they were going to want to do it again and again and again.

They'd be stupid not to, considering how goddamn good it had been.

"Hey," Beau said, trying for anything but awkward, but not quite managing it. "Uh, it's . . . uh . . . good to see you . . . again."

"Is that what was so funny?" Sebastian asked, walking into his office and, without an invitation, flopping into the chair opposite Beau's. "How incredibly awkward we were going to be today?"

Beau sighed. "No, but it *is* awkward, isn't it?"

"Only if we make it awkward," Sebastian declared. "I just finished my workout, and now I'm here."

He seemed to think this was a declarative sentence, but Beau was still stuck back in the *it's only awkward if we make it awkward,* which might theoretically be a good plan, but all it made Beau think was last night hadn't been the same for Sebastian as it had been for him.

Maybe it hadn't been.

Maybe he did this kind of thing all the time.

After all, you practically had to seduce him.

"Now you're here," Beau said, struggling to keep up. "For . . .?"

Sebastian shot him a cocky, confident smile that absolutely should not have made Beau hard.

But it did. Anyway.

"So you can teach me?" Sebastian said slowly. "I . . . I'm out of my depth here. I don't like admitting it, but it's the truth."

No, he wouldn't, and as a result, his sexy, cocky edge dimmed a bit at the admission, but that, Beau decided, was better for everyone, if they were going to be keeping it in their pants.

"I didn't get the impression from yesterday's game that you were really interested in being a better safety." He'd only been in the office an hour, but Sebastian's film had been the first thing he'd gone over, as potentially risky as that was, but he'd needed to know if his gut impression had been accurate.

What he'd told Brett had been true; as the game had gone on, Sebastian had gotten better, but even then, it was clear—he *wasn't* committed.

"Maybe I wasn't committed then, but I'm committed now," Sebastian said firmly.

"What changed your mind?" It didn't really matter what was causing this change of heart; only that it was happening. But Beau was curious.

Sebastian leaned back in his chair, all coiled, leashed strength, and he considered Beau for a long moment before answering. "A lot of things," he finally said.

It wasn't an answer, but then Sebastian didn't really owe him one.

"Okay," Beau said. He picked up the remote for the large television mounted on the wall, and clicked a button so the image on his laptop appeared about ten times bigger.

"What's that?" Sebastian asked, leaning closer.

"Footage from last night's game. I've been going over the defensive plays."

"Is that your job?"

"That and a whole lot more," Beau said. He shouldn't be hurt that Sebastian had no idea what he did; most of the players didn't, and that was fine by him. He literally did not have the time to coach each of them one-on-one using his film techniques.

"Right," Sebastian said uncertainly, staring at the screen. "This is the first play of the game."

"You were in the wrong spot."

Sebastian glared at him. "Maybe I thought this was a better spot. I thought safeties could make those kinds of adjustments."

Beau pressed another button and the video moved forward, showing, at a much slower speed, the way the play had unfolded.

The Packers had moved the ball twenty-five yards.

"I didn't guess that Rodgers would hold on to the ball," Sebastian said in a clipped voice.

No player liked analyzing all their mistakes. But in this case, it was unavoidable. Because Sebastian was so raw at the new position and had made so many, going over each and every one was inevitable if he wanted to learn to be better.

And he was in front of Beau, in his office, because he said he did.

Time to figure out if he really meant it.

"It was an RPO," Beau said. "Run-pass option."

"I know what that is," Sebastian retorted, sounding testier.

"The Packers use RPOs a lot, but more and more teams are, as well. You've got to be prepared. And every team is going to have different ways of executing."

"I'm going to have to do a lot more film study before games," Sebastian guessed, correctly.

Beau nodded. "You played on instinct before this. Your instincts were good, so that was fine. Besides acquainting yourself with the receiver you'd be covering and their general tactics and plays, you didn't have to pay much attention to the rest of the offense. But now, you're going to have to. If you don't, this . . ." He pointed to the screen, where the Packers had essentially gone down the field unchecked. "Is going to happen every single game."

"I don't . . ." Beau watched Sebastian carefully as he hesitated. This was a lot for the ego of an NFL player to take. Not every player could have handled it.

He still wasn't sure Sebastian could.

But if he wanted to make the transition *successfully,* he wasn't going to have another choice.

"I don't know how to do this, the film-study part," Sebastian admitted.

"It's okay," Beau said gently. "Because that's my job. To help you do it. To teach you how."

Sebastian smiled wryly. "So that's what you do. This. And you're a genius at this."

"You keep saying that."

"I keep getting told that," Sebastian corrected.

"Well, I guess I've got to prove myself," Beau said. "No pressure."

"You know you're good at it. You sit up a little straighter, speak with more confidence and certainty." Sebastian eyed him coolly. "Just like you fuck."

Beau, in the middle of sipping from a bottle of water, choked on the liquid. "You really can't do that," he said. "You really, really can't do that."

Sebastian grinned. "Do what?"

"Bring up fucking," Beau hissed. "And definitely not here . . ." He gestured around his office. "Where I'm supposed to be *working.*"

"Oh, is that gonna make it hard . . . on you?"

Beau glared. "Seriously, what happened to *it's only awkward if we make it awkward?*"

Sebastian shrugged. "Making jokes about it, that's how I'm trying not to make it awkward."

"Well, stop," Beau said.

"You weren't all this buttoned up last night."

"No, and I wasn't *working* either," Beau said. "Or"—he paused—"*trying* to work."

"Point taken," Sebastian admitted. "No more jokes."

"It happened," Beau said, "and it's not going to happen again. So let's just move past it."

The gleam in Sebastian's eyes seemed to tease that it wouldn't be quite so easy to forget.

But Beau was going to, because he refused to let the tension between them distract him any further.

"So what should I have done on this play?" Sebastian asked, gesturing towards the screen, where Beau had paused the video.

"First, you should have identified that Rodgers was going RPO," Beau said.

Sebastian nodded. "You showed me during the game."

"Where would you have put yourself if you'd known Rodgers could hold on to the ball? That this wasn't going to be just a simple, straightforward running play?"

Sebastian took a minute to think it over, gave his answer, and then Beau refuted it, offered another option, and for a few minutes they had a nice healthy debate about it.

And then they moved on to the next play. And the next play after that.

They'd covered the first two drives of yesterday's game, when a knock on the doorframe broke Beau's concentration.

"You're exactly who I've been searching for," Helen said, reaching out and shaking Sebastian's hand. "I should have expected that you'd be in Beau's office."

"I'm sorry . . ." Sebastian shot the woman one of the most charming smiles in his arsenal. From Beau's experience, it took a lot to fluster Helen, but he'd had one of those smiles turned on him and he knew how captivating they could be. "You are?"

"Helen Gibson. Head of Public Relations for the Piranhas." She returned Sebastian's charming smile with one of her own. "I was hoping to check in with you really quick, as I'd like to get you on the schedule for a few events."

Sebastian raised an eyebrow. "Events?"

"Events," she said firmly. "You're the number-one-selling jersey in the last month, and one of the most recognizable faces of the franchise. We need to get you out there."

"Congrats," Beau inserted dryly.

"Shouldn't Pax be selling the most jerseys?" Sebastian questioned.

Helen shrugged. "He did last year."

"What Helen is too diplomatic to say is that our second-year QB is struggling, and nobody wants to buy the jersey of the guy who can't move the offense down the field."

Helen shot him a half-hearted glare. "That's . . . that's neither here nor there," she said. Beau was amused, because it wasn't exactly a denial. "But I *was* hoping we could set up some time to get our schedules in sync, some events onto your calendar that I know you'll want to attend. Perhaps with your family . . .?"

"I'll attend whatever you want, but not my family. They stay out of it."

"But . . ." Helen wheedled. "You're not married and you're the face of the franchise . . ."

"No," Sebastian said, in a tone that brokered no arguments, even as Helen spluttered and continued to make them.

Finally, after agreeing to meet with him the next afternoon, she gave up and left.

"No family?" Beau asked, raising an eyebrow. Thinking that while Sebastian might not want to share the reasons why he had that rule with Helen, he might be more willing to tell *him*.

"No," Sebastian said, in the exact same tone. "And no, I don't want to talk about it, either. Let's re-focus on this play."

"Alright," Beau said, but his curiosity was piqued. He'd have to do a little research on his own. See if his father knew anything.

It wasn't technically any of his business if Sebastian didn't want to get his family involved with team affairs. They hadn't signed his family, they'd signed *him*, but it was unusual, and Beau was just weak enough that while sleeping together was off the table, he still wanted to know more about the man.

They finished up the half, and agreed to meet the next day to go over the second half. "I've got meetings I've got to get to," Beau said apologetically, closing up his laptop and standing, tucking it under one arm. "Coach is all worked up about the offense."

Sebastian's grin was lopsided and not just sexy, but freaking adorable.

This, Beau thought, *would be so much easier if Sebastian didn't make every fucking nerve ending stand straight up on end.*

But he did, and it wasn't going to stop, either.

He was just going to have to get used to it.

"And that's your job, too?" Sebastian asked, standing up with him and stretching, his t-shirt riding up and exposing a sliver of chiseled abs.

Beau had touched those abs last night. He'd had his tongue all over them.

He bit his lip.

"It's part of it, yeah. Fixing problems, that's a Beau Dawson specialty. Not that . . ." Beau cleared his throat. "Not that you're a *problem*, necessarily."

Sebastian just grinned though. "Hey, how can I be a problem if I'm selling more jerseys than Pax?"

"Don't . . ." Beau lowered his voice. "Don't tell him that, okay? He's already, well, he's feeling the pressure, a lot. Too much, in my opinion."

"Shouldn't Abernathy be helping with that? I thought they were close."

"He is. They *are*. But it's . . . imagine you never have a losing season your entire life. And then you lose fifteen games your first year in the NFL, the year you're supposed to step in for a first ballot Hall of Fame quarterback."

Sebastian nodded. "I get it. He's feelin' the crunch. Feelin' like everyone wants him to be Colin O'Connor."

"He's not Colin O'Connor, but he can be Paxton Kelly," Beau said firmly as they exited his office.

Sebastian paused, jabbing a thumb the other way. "That's my direction," he said, "but . . . I appreciate all your help. I guess you do this for all of us. Me, Nicholson, Pax . . ."

"I do it for anyone who needs help or wants an extra edge," Beau said firmly.

"Well, you're really fucking good at it."

But before Beau could respond, Sebastian was already frustratingly halfway down the hallway.

His words shouldn't have affected him that strongly. After all, they'd had *sex* the night before, and that had been . . . well, *spectacular*.

But Beau wasn't sure if he was thankful or something else entirely, that as the offensive production meeting began, his father greeting each of the coaches and then Pax, it was Sebastian's compliment that really stuck with him, not just the memory of his touch.

Chapter Six

"That," Wade said, swinging his leg over the bench that ran the length of the locker room, "was fucking brutal."

Sebastian didn't exactly disagree—the coaches had worked them hard today, but then it had felt *less* brutal to him, because for the first time, after two intensive days of Beau's coaching, he felt like he knew *more* of what he should be doing.

Cover the middle of the field was simple enough, but in practice, it was incredibly complicated and forced him to not only rely on his existing instincts, but to create new ones, too.

And then there'd been the tackling drills, because Coach Brett had decided that he didn't like the way that Sebastian was tackling. That he wasn't *finishing* the tackle well enough, and so they'd done tackling drills for over half an hour.

If he could lift his arms tomorrow, he'd be shocked.

"No kidding," Tristan echoed. He and Rose had been running routes all practice, and Sebastian knew exactly what that was like.

"It was hard because we were shit last Sunday, and we need to get better." Paxton spoke up. "We *have* to get better."

Sebastian didn't think, individually, that they were all that bad. There were some talented players. But they weren't gelling. They weren't playing as a team, yet.

They might not ever get there, but if they didn't, Beau's pessimistic view that they wouldn't win many games was going to come true.

It was absolutely not his job to bring this team together. It was Paxton's. He was the quarterback, the leader of the team, and ostensibly supposed to be the loudest voice in the locker room.

But Sebastian hadn't forgotten what Beau had said about his struggles, and once his own were lessening, it was easy to raise his head and see similar problems elsewhere.

Paxton was one of them.

He was floundering.

"Hey," Sebastian said, cornering him after they'd both dressed and were getting ready to head out. "You wanna go grab some dinner?"

They'd done it once before, in preseason, and it had been good for all of them—to get out of the pressure cooker for an evening.

"What?"

"Dinner," Sebastian repeated patiently. "We should get some."

On a lot of teams, the defense and the offense didn't mix much. But Sebastian had always thought that was stupid. They were a team, weren't they? Why shouldn't they act like it?

"Tonight?"

"Yes. Tonight." Sebastian told himself the guy was struggling. No need to be judgmental, but he was clearly either distracted or stupid.

And he didn't think Paxton Kelly was stupid.

Nobody could have amassed those records, those awards, and that win percentage in college while being stupid.

"Oh. *Oh*." Pax laughed ruefully. "I would, that's a great offer, actually, but Davis and I . . . we're going over some additional film."

"Wade told me you were here at six this morning going over film," Sebastian said. "It's good to take a break." The guy was going to work himself into a nervous breakdown. Where was Davis in all this? Was he the one suggesting that Pax work this hard?

"I can take a break when we start to win games." Pax's jaw jutted out stubbornly.

"Alright." Sebastian reached out and clapped him on the shoulder. "First win, and dinner's on me."

"Alright," Pax said, and immediately turned, heading back towards where the position rooms were.

"Something," Tristan said coming up behind him, "is happening there."

"What?" Sebastian was confused. "Pax working too hard?"

"No," Tristan said decisively. "Something else."

"You're flying your conspiracy flag again," Wade muttered, joining them. "Nothing is going on."

"They spend a *lot* of time together, that's all I'm saying."

"Pax is the QB and Davis is the QB coach, that's supposed to happen," Wade said.

Tristan waggled his eyebrows. "*All* the time? They're supposed to spend *all* their time together?"

"Flounder, you're stupid in love," Sebastian said, calling Tristan by the nickname he'd come up with at preseason camp, as he shook his head, "and as a result, can't help seeing love everywhere. Trust me, Davis Abernathy and Paxton Kelly aren't in love."

"But are they fucking?" Tristan retorted with a grin. "Because . . "

"Is who fucking?" Sebastian looked over to see Logan walking over, a curious look on his face.

"Nobody," Wade said quickly. "Absolutely nobody."

"Except us, of course," Tristan said with a shit-eating grin.

"Of course." Sebastian rolled his eyes. Absolutely not wondering, no way, not even in the slightest, what they'd all say if they knew he'd slept with Beau. The coach's son.

"What are y'all doing over here?" Logan wanted to know. "Gossiping?"

"Sebastian is taking us to dinner," Tristan announced. Sebastian groaned.

He hadn't really intended to take Tristan—or Wade, for that matter. But it sounded way better than going back to his dark, silent penthouse, imagining how much lighter, how much warmer it would feel, if he wasn't alone. If maybe Beau was with him.

"Yes, I sure am," Sebastian said, and both Tristan and Wade looked surprised. "You wanna come?" he asked Logan.

"Sure," Logan said. "But only if Dylan can come with us."

"Dylan? The kicker?"

Logan shot him a look. "Is there another Dylan on this team?"

"No, of course he can, I just didn't realize you and the kicker were so . . . close?" He sounded just like Tristan now, sure that everyone was fucking.

"You didn't?" Tristan sounded surprised.

"Should I have?" The expression on every guy's face around him told him the truth—*yes*, he should have. Clearly he'd been spending too much time with his head down, focused on his own shit.

Team wasn't just everyone doing their own thing, it was *all* of them, together. Guilt swamped Sebastian. He'd made an effort in the preseason, and the moment shit had hit the fan, with the transition from corner to safety, he'd retreated back into his cold, lonely cave.

"Dylan's living with Logan," Wade explained. "Since he hasn't had time to get a place yet."

"I thought . . . I thought the Piranhas had apartments for those guys." Sebastian couldn't believe he'd missed this. But he had.

"Water main burst in the building," Logan said succinctly. "Poor guy didn't have anywhere to go, so I . . . well, it wasn't hard to do the right thing. I've got plenty of space, and he's a good guy. A great guy. You'll like him."

Sebastian realized that he also hadn't given the kicker anything more than a one-sentence greeting.

You're better than that. You've always been a team player.

Except he hadn't been since the season started. He'd been head down, entirely preoccupied with his own insecurities, his own fears.

The irony was that it was the welcoming nature of the locker room that he'd always gravitated to the most in football. And he hadn't been doing any of it.

"I'm sure I will," Sebastian said.

"I'll just go grab him, and then we can take off," Logan said and jogged off, in search of their kicker.

"I thought you'd be all buddy-buddy with the defense," Tristan asked as they waited for Logan to come back with Dylan. "Aren't you defensive guys supposed to stick together?"

"Those guys are great," Sebastian said, even though he was realizing that he'd barely spent any time with them.

"What about Micah?"

"Oh, well," Sebastian hedged, "that's a little tougher. Hard to spend time with the guy who's supposed to replace you."

"But he isn't, he *wasn't*," Wade said optimistically. "You were meant to switch to safety, and Rose was . . . well, I guess in a technical sense, yeah, he replaced you. But it's not like he stole your job."

"And," Tristan said loyally, "he doesn't give me nearly the problems in practice that you did."

"Is it a compliment if he wasn't supposed to be my replacement, but I was still better?" Sebastian wondered, a little bitterly. Yes, he'd told Beau that he was committed—and he *was*, because this was the opportunity this season. There wasn't going to be another one. Not if he wanted to keep playing.

But he also wasn't going to make nice with Micah Rose, either.

Even if it wasn't really Micah's fault.

"Not better, just . . . different. He's got some different techniques," Wade said, shooting a reprimanding glare in the direction of his boyfriend. "Good techniques. He's going to be good."

"He could be better. You should help him."

Of course Tristan thought he should.

"You," he said, jabbing Tristan in the shoulder with his finger, "should not be nearly so . . ."

"Naive?" Wade supplied when Sebastian hesitated, not quite sure *what* Tristan was exactly. "Endlessly optimistic? Sunshiney? Sure that everyone should help each other?"

"We're a team, aren't we?"

They were, and Sebastian felt called out, even though he knew Tristan hadn't necessarily meant to, because he hadn't been acting like a teammate. He'd been acting like a desperate lone island. Ready to shoulder all the burden, and take all the blame.

And that was not how a team was meant to work. No wonder they'd lost that first game by so many points.

"We just haven't been playing like one," Sebastian said, firmly. "But that's gotta change."

"See?" Tristan said excitedly, putting his arm around his boyfriend's shoulders. "See, there *is* someone like me. And his name is Sea Bass."

"Sure thing, sweetcheeks." Wade grinned at him, the love evident on his face, shining so brightly in his eyes that it was impossible to miss.

And Sebastian felt a pang in a place he had absolutely no fucking right to feel a pang.

He'd never felt that way about someone. And nobody had ever felt that way about him. He was almost thirty-three, he'd been playing in the NFL for almost nine years, and all he had to show for it was a new, different position because he couldn't play the old one anymore, a ridiculously expensive penthouse he wasn't even sure he liked, and a string of one-night stands that occasionally might stretch to two nights, if the timing was right.

It was pathetic.

He was pathetic.

He'd thought by now that he'd have found what Tristan and Wade had, but he never had.

You have to be open to find love, an annoying voice that *still* resembled his old high school coach barked at him. *You're not open. You're a fucking closed book, Howard.*

He was. He knew it.

Beau had asked about his family and why he didn't talk about them, and though they'd shared a good night and an entirely different kind of good time working through the last game's film, he'd shut down. Refused to talk about it.

And yeah, it was painful. He didn't *like* to talk about it, but Beau had shared things with him that he obviously wouldn't enjoy talking about. The accusation of nepotism that probably hung over his head all the time, for example.

The fact that he wanted to be taken seriously, as more than just Asa Dawson's son. As more than just Asa Dawson's *gay* son.

Beau had set himself a hard row to hoe, and he hadn't hidden that fact.

Not like Sebastian had hidden his own somewhat ugly history.

"Hey," Logan said, breathlessly as he walked back up with Dylan, the new kicker, next to him. "We ready to go?"

Sebastian stared, his brain whirling so fast with so many hard and unpleasant truths that it took him a second to catch up.

"Yeah, I think so," Wade said, speaking up. He turned to Sebastian. "You okay, man? You look like you just saw a ghost."

"Yeah, yeah, I'm good," Sebastian said distractedly. Because he wasn't. Not really.

Because he'd done here, in Miami, what he'd done in every other facet of his life. When he'd attended the U, and then been drafted by the Cardinals, he'd been folded into an existing organization. Players had been welcoming to *him*, but the Piranhas? They were essentially starting from scratch, with almost no players left from the season before.

It had been *his job* as an experienced veteran, to not just focus on himself, but on the team.

But he hadn't done it.

There's always time to start, his high school coach bellowed in his ear. *No time like the present, Howard.*

"Come on," Sebastian said, gesturing to the guys around him. "Let's go get some grub."

They took two cars to Sebastian's favorite sushi restaurant in Miami.

When Tristan got out of Wade's BMW, he shot the place a dubious look.

"Trust me," Sebastian said as they walked across the ugly pitted parking lot.

"Are you sure you know what you're doing?" Logan said skeptically as he and Dylan joined them.

"I think he does," Dylan said surprisingly.

Sebastian, sure that he was going to have to sign a promise with blood that nobody was going to get food poisoning, because the front of the strip mall sushi joint was unassuming in the extreme, turned to look at the Piranhas' new kicker.

"Not 'cause I've been here," Dylan said. "I went to school in Michigan, we wouldn't know good sushi if it bit us in the ass, but Howard here went to Miami. Which, if I'm right, isn't too far from here."

Sebastian nodded. They were maybe only half a mile from campus.

"That means he knows how to get the best eats for the buck," Dylan finished. "So yeah, I trust him."

"You are not what I expected out of a kicker," Sebastian said, more surprised by Dylan's straightforward logic than he wanted to admit to.

"Told ya," Logan said with a knowing grin.

Sebastian pulled the door open. "And you're from . . . Michigan?"

Dylan nodded.

"God, I'm sorry," Wade said with a snicker.

Tristan elbowed him. "It's not like you've got much room to talk," he told his boyfriend, "you're from *Texas*."

"I'm *also* from Texas, so you'd better watch yourself," Logan joked, high-fiving Wade. "We take our heritage seriously."

"Ugh," Tristan said.

Sebastian left the bickering foursome at the door and spotting his friend Akio in the back, by the sushi bar, gave him a wave.

He'd been back here a few times since returning to Miami—and more than a handful since he'd left, too—but Akio always looked thrilled to see him, and came hurrying out from behind the counter, giving Sebastian a quick hug.

"You brought your friends?" Akio said with a bright smile. "Here I didn't think you had any."

"We're gettin' there," Sebastian retorted. "But yeah, these guys all play with me."

"Sit anywhere you like," Akio said. "I will bring sushi."

"*All* the sushi," Sebastian said. "And some of that sake you poured for me last time. Two bottles, for the table."

Akio shot him a quicksilver grin. "Tryin' to be a big spender, huh?"

"Always trying," Sebastian agreed, and returned to where the foursome stood near the door.

"You know the guy who owns this place," Wade observed as Sebastian led them to a big table in the back.

Big because, even though there were only five of them, he knew that these guys could eat.

Tristan might be built like a stick, but he could put food away.

To say nothing of Logan and Wade.

Dylan was still a wild card, but Sebastian not only liked the bright intelligence in his eyes but the way that he'd shut down Tristan's food poisoning speculation right away.

Logan was probably right—because he had a solid head on his own shoulders—and Dylan was a good guy.

"Yeah, I met him in college," Sebastian said as he took a seat across from Tristan and Wade. "Dylan was right about that."

"Knew it," Dylan said, pumping his fist.

"Lucky guess," Tristan argued. "Why did I think you went to Florida State?"

Sebastian shot him a disdainful look, but couldn't help it, breaking into a smile. "God help me, I have no freaking clue."

"Nothing against Florida State," Tristan said quickly.

Wade side-eyed him. "Just like you've got nothing against Texas, sweetcheeks."

"Hell, I've got something against Texas. Doesn't mean I don't still love it," Logan said. His Texas twang had gone less pronounced, probably during all his years in Minnesota, but Sebastian could hear it now, loud and clear.

"And you're from Michigan." Sebastian, gaze shifting to Dylan, making sure to include him in the conversation.

"Guilty as charged," Dylan said. "Thought for awhile I might play in LA, then bounced around a bit—Green Bay, Tampa, New England, before settling for a few years in Vegas."

"And now you're in Miami, which is better than *all* of those," Tristan crowed.

"That," Dylan said, "remains to be seen."

"God, don't we all know it," Logan said, but then added, "Though I told Sea Bass here yesterday that playing for a team that loses every game and doesn't give a shit who I love is better than winning sixteen games in Minnesota and having to hide every second of every day."

"Preach," Tristan said.

Wade grinned at his boy. "Minnesota was never gonna draft you, you didn't have any of that to worry about."

"Not necessarily," Logan said. "The Stars drafted Spencer Evans, and then regretted it every year, even though he was a fucking beast on the field. There's sometimes this crazy disconnect between what a team is willing to accept and what they *want* to accept."

"Was that how Minnesota was?" Sebastian asked, because he was genuinely curious.

"No, I never told them before I was drafted, because I thought . . . I don't know . . . I could keep it a secret. But it was harder than I thought."

Sebastian thought of the last nine years. Of all the one-night stands. Always being worried that someone would tell. That someone would *see*. He understood Logan's struggle more than he wanted to.

Being ashamed of who he was even though there was nothing to feel shame over.

"Wait a minute," Dylan said suddenly, "am I the only . . . well, the only not queer guy here?"

Sebastian nodded, because he was among friends now. Friends he should be able to trust. He was going to have to work on that part, but this was a good start.

"Not queer?" Tristan asked, his eyebrows rising. "You sure about that?"

"Yes," Dylan said, though there was something in his voice that Sebastian recognized. Something he'd felt, way back in junior high, when he *hadn't* been sure. When he'd only wondered and then prayed that he could stop wondering, because he'd known then that black queer kids didn't play football.

"Nobody is entirely straight," Wade said. "That's my theory."

"What do you think, Dylan? You agree with Wade?" Sebastian said.

Dylan just shrugged. "I'm not against it. I guess it would have to be the right situation. The right guy."

"That," Tristan said, slinging an arm around the guy, "is what we all tell ourselves in the beginning."

Dylan went bright red, and between Wade chastising his boyfriend for flirting with the kicker, and Logan laughing, Akio showed up with the bottles of sake, followed by an employee carrying an absolutely enormous wooden tray shaped like a boat, full of sushi.

"Hell yeah!" Wade exclaimed. "Look at the size of that thing!"

Logan turned to Sebastian. "It looks freaking incredible. Guess we shouldn't have doubted you."

Tristan popped a roll into his mouth, not even bothering to grab his chopsticks. "Tastes incredible, too." He batted his ridiculously long eyelashes in Sebastian's direction. He never quite knew what to do with the rookie wide receiver—but despite his uncertainty, he *always* ended up laughing and enjoying his company.

Tristan Nicholson was just so unapologetically himself, in a way that Sebastian both envied and craved.

"Don't ever doubt the veteran," Dylan said. "Maybe you rookies should be making a list of veteran suggestions."

"Well, what would you add, Logan?" Wade asked.

Logan considered this problem as he deftly picked up a shrimp roll and slid it between his lips. He chewed and swallowed. "I guess," he said, "don't forget that the NFL is brutal."

"I think today's practice was enough reminder of that," Tristan said.

"Yeah, not just physically," Logan said. "But mentally. Look at how it's wearing Pax down."

"We should have made him come tonight," Tristan said, sipping his sake.

"Unfortunately, you can't make someone listen who doesn't want to," Dylan pointed out.

"You'd think Davis would have something to say about it," Wade said. "It's not like he hasn't been through the wringer."

"No ring, and a team that rejected him because he was injured and then traded him so they could bring in some shady-ass quarterback? Yeah, no joke."

"He's done good for himself since then," Logan said. "He's a good coach. Puts in lots of time with Pax."

"Yeah," Tristan said slyly, "I just bet he does."

Sebastian laughed. "Do you think *everyone* is fucking? Trust me there is way less fucking on NFL teams than you think."

"Is there?" Tristan raised an eyebrow. "What about a couple years ago when everyone found out that Heath Harris and Sam Crawford were doing it on the regular?"

"That is *not* the norm," Sebastian said, laughing. "At least not in my experience."

"I don't know," Logan said, "maybe not on the teams you've been on but . . . no one's gonna say anything at all 'bout a little extracurricular in the shower, if you get my drift."

"Oh, we do," Tristan said, leaning forward, his blue eyes gleaming with interest. "See, Sea Bass," he said, gesturing towards Sebastian, "you're just missing out."

"What?" Sebastian said, picking through the sushi offerings on the tray, and picking out his favorite spicy tuna. "Like I'm some old, boring man? Is that what you're saying, Flounder?"

He hadn't been old and boring on Sunday night.

But he definitely was not going to repeat it, and he absolutely wasn't going to talk about it.

Tristan eyed him. "If the shoe fits . . ."

"All I know," Logan added, "is that I've been impressed at how few rumors I hear. You keep your shit locked down. Not that easy to do."

It was easy, when you didn't really *do* anything. Maybe one or two hookups a year. At most.

He could've had far, far more, if he'd wanted. If he'd been interested. But the risks had always seemed to outweigh the rewards. Also, it turned out, being so scrupulously careful kind of killed the inherent sexiness of a potential hookup.

But he wasn't going to let them think he was living like a monk either. He'd just had sex! Three nights ago!

"I do keep it locked down," Sebastian agreed. "But that doesn't mean I spend all my time alone."

"Oooooh, you *hooked up*," Wade said. "Who was it?"

"Probably some random guy he picked up," Tristan teased.

"Y'all think he can pick up random guys *and* keep his shit locked down?" Logan scoffed. "No way. No way. It's someone he knows." He paused. "Fuck, it's probably someone *we* know."

"It would have to be someone who has as much to lose by everyone finding out as he does," Dylan said, chiming in with his own two cents.

Sebastian would have much rather he'd kept them to himself. Because Dylan had already proven to be way too smart for his own good.

He almost categorically denied Dylan's theory, but then he worried, at the last second before he opened his mouth, that he might give more away by speaking up.

He'd clearly already said too much.

Your fucking ego, his high school coach yelled at him, *always getting you into trouble.*

"Well, who's on the team that's single?" Wade asked.

Tristan shot a look at Logan. "It wasn't you, was it?"

Logan laughed. "No, no way. Nothing against you, Howard, but you're not my type."

Dylan looked intrigued. "Who *is* your type?"

"It could be Paxton. He was really into inviting him into dinner," Wade said thoughtfully.

"Wait, Paxton Kelly is gay?" Dylan sounded surprised. But Sebastian was just as surprised.

"I don't know what he is, but he's dated guys before," Tristan said. "I knew one of them." He slid a glance towards Sebastian. "Not the same one *you* dated, however."

"*Dated* is probably too generous of a term," Sebastian said bluntly.

Tristan nodded. "So it's not Pax. It's not Logan. It could be . . ."

"What about Beau?"

Sebastian froze and then forced himself to relax.

"Beau?" Tristan sounded surprised.

"Yeah, Beau," Dylan said. "He's queer, right? And single."

"Famously," Tristan said wryly. "Everyone thought Coach was going to kick him out of the house or something, when he came out. He was only seventeen when it happened."

"People didn't really think that," Wade said staunchly. "Why would they think Coach would be so shitty to his own son?"

"Because Coach is from the deep South and was coaching at Tennessee," Tristan retorted. "I guess they all thought he was allergic to the gays, or something."

Sebastian tried to look normal. He wasn't sure he entirely succeeded.

"Well, he wasn't," Logan said. "What he said was awesome."

Everyone at the table nodded, Sebastian included, because it *had* been awesome, and part of the reason, so many years later, why he'd signed with the Piranhas, and also because he'd look even guiltier of sleeping with Beau if he kept acting weird.

"Clearly Beau knew what was up, because he never looked worried," Logan said.

"I think he just wants to do what he's good at," Sebastian said carefully. "Which is his job."

He thought he'd done a good job at keeping his expression and tone perfectly neutral, but apparently not because Tristan's eyes widened.

"You absolutely fucked Beau Dawson," he said.

Sebastian told himself firmly not to freak out, because Tristan also thought Pax and Davis Abernathy were fucking, and that was a legitimately insane theory with zero basis in reality.

Everyone at the table stared at him, and Sebastian debated whether he should lie. He *should* lie, of course. It was the right thing to do, even though it was almost never the right thing to categorically deny something that had happened only three nights ago.

Tristan leaned over and murmured into Wade's ear—not very quietly. "I think Sea Bass is freezing."

He *was*. What he should do—what he *needed* to do was open his mouth and make the phrase, *no, I never fucked Beau Dawson and he certainly never fucked me* come out.

But he couldn't. His tongue felt stuck.

He felt fucking frozen. Damn Tristan.

Logan nodded. "It seems like he is."

"Listen, we don't judge," Wade said.

"Why would we? In fact, next time it happens, take a few pics. I wouldn't mind having a front-row seat to all that," Tristan teased.

Dylan laughed.

"Well, kudos to Beau," Logan said, clapping a hand on Sebastian's shoulder. "Getting a piece of the famous Sea Bass."

"Listen," Sebastian said when he could finally untangle his tongue, "you really can't . . . and I mean *cannot* . . . say anything to anyone about this. It happened, and it's not going to happen again. It was just . . ." What *had* it been? Sebastian still didn't know, not exactly. "A weak moment," he finished, even though that wasn't quite right.

It had felt the opposite of weak.

It had felt like him standing up to the fear that had governed him for far too long. It had felt like him grabbing what he wanted and *taking* it, damn the consequences.

Wade raised an eyebrow. "Are you *afraid*, Sea Bass?"

"You don't think his daddy would kick my ass for messing with his kid?"

"Well, no, because Beau isn't a kid," Logan said way too reasonably. "And they've worked together for awhile now. I don't think Beau would still be working for him if he thought he'd kick the ass of anyone he slept with."

"Yeah, that's not Coach Dawson's style," Dylan agreed.

"I totally thought he was going to kill us for getting involved," Tristan said, glancing over at Wade. "But he was actually pretty understanding."

"*Pretty* understanding," Sebastian retorted. "I don't think I remember that being the phrase you used afterwards."

Tristan shrugged. "It turned out fine."

"Do *not* say it would turn out fine with Beau," Sebastian said between clenched teeth. "I told you it was just . . . a one-night thing. Don't make a bigger deal out of it than it is. Besides, we're too different. Completely different. Nothing in common."

Except that as he looked around the table, nobody looked particularly convinced.

Maybe because he didn't sound particularly convincing.

"How do you know it was just a one-night thing?" Tristan asked.

"Because it was," Sebastian said shortly. "Seriously, it's not . . . don't make it into more than it is."

"You're saying you wouldn't date him if you could?" Wade asked.

"Was the sex not very good?" Tristan didn't even let Sebastian answer Wade's question before he asked one of his own.

"I'm only surprised that you didn't ask that right away," Sebastian said, rolling his eyes. "Like first thing."

Tristan didn't look even the tiniest bit embarrassed.

"Hey, we all wanted to know, I was just the only one with big enough balls to ask," he said.

"It wasn't bad at all." *It was some of the best sex of my whole life.* "It's just . . . we're trying to do a lot of impossible things this season. It could be a distraction."

"Or," Logan said quietly, "the chance to have something awesome and amazing off the field." *For once.*

Logan didn't say them, but the words echoed in Sebastian's head, anyway.

"Appreciate the advice, but I just really don't want this getting out, okay? Beau isn't going to tell anyone, so if I hear about it . . ."

"Yeah, we get it," Wade said. "Secret's safe with us, man. Don't worry about it."

"We wouldn't," Dylan said solemnly.

Logan shot his roommate a teasing look. "You wouldn't because you don't *know* anyone to tell, yet."

Dylan chuckled. "True story. But the point's still valid. What happens at the strip mall sushi joint, stays at the strip mall sushi joint."

"Yep," Wade agreed. "Now where's the rest of this sushi? I'm still hungry."

Tristan laughed and elbowed his boyfriend in the ribs. "You're a freaking bottomless pit."

"Hey, you were at that practice today," Wade said defensively. "I burned a lot of calories."

Sebastian waved Akio down, ordered more, and another bottle of sake, and settled in to actually enjoy having friends again.

Even friends who were nosy as hell.

Chapter Seven

"And this," Beau said, pointing to a play on the screen, "is what you need to watch the quarterback for. When he goes mobile."

Sebastian raised an eyebrow. "*Can* he still go mobile?"

"He might be nearing retirement, but he's still dangerous as hell with the ball in his hands," Beau said, taking his glasses off and rubbing his eyes. He looked tired. Hot, always, but definitely tired. "You can't sleep on him."

"So as long as he's got the ball, eyes on him." Sebastian leaned back in his chair. "Got it."

It had been two days since Sebastian had had dinner with the other guys and accidentally spilled about his secret hookup with Beau. He'd dreaded the first time he ran into him again, sure that one of the other guys would've gossiped, but Beau had greeted him exactly as he'd have expected. No weirdness, no awkwardness. Except that annoying frisson of awareness that always lit him up from the inside out, like quicksilver.

Did he want to date Beau Dawson?

He'd never answered the question, and he'd found himself thinking about it, far too often, and at times when he was definitely supposed to be focused on other things, but he still wasn't sure what the answer was.

You don't want to know the answer, his high school coach bellowed at him. *You're not fucking brave enough to know the answer.*

He wished that wasn't true, but it kinda was.

Because even if he did know the answer and it was yes, what would he do about it?

A whole lotta nothing, the coach screamed.

"You seem distracted," Beau said, zero accusation in his voice. "We can call it a few minutes short today. I know Brett's been working you guys hard in practice."

"Yeah," Sebastian said, happy to be able to use the excuse. "Apparently my tackling skills were not up to par. Rather they weren't up to *his* par."

"And now?" Beau asked, raising an eyebrow.

"Well, my arms feel like jelly, but we'll see tomorrow," Sebastian said dryly.

If Beau's gaze lingered for a second longer than it should have on his arms, exposed by the tank he was wearing, Sebastian ignored it. He didn't need this. He didn't want it.

Yes, you do. Badly.

"Guess we will," Beau said.

For a single, agonizing moment they stared at each other.

Long enough for Sebastian to know they never should have touched each other, because now it was there, the echo of that touch, in every conversation. In between every single fucking breath.

It was exhausting, trying to fight it. But Sebastian wasn't a quitter.

"Ah, uh," Sebastian inserted awkwardly into the silence. "Wanted to apologize about something."

Beau looked surprised. God, was he that much of an asshole?

"My family," Sebastian said. "I can be really . . . private, I guess, about them. And I realized me shutting you down when you asked, well, that wasn't really fair to you. Not when you've shared . . ."

God, all the things Beau had shared.

His body. His mouth. His fingers. His *cock*.

Not what he needed to be thinking about when he was talking about his family.

"Not when you've shared stuff about you. And your father." Sebastian finished his sentence so clumsily, he had to fight not to flush.

"You aren't obligated to share anything, Sebastian," Beau said. Kindly. Too kindly.

Why did the guy have to be so hot and so goddamn *nice*?

It made resisting him even tougher.

"But I want to," Sebastian said, pushing forward stubbornly. "I . . . my mom and my dad never married, I grew up torn between two houses . . . and two races. Two cultures, even. The only place I ever felt like I wasn't out of place was the football field. So I focused on that. I still focus on that."

"You and your parents aren't close?" Beau, who'd gotten up to check on his phone, returned to the chair next to Sebastian's. He didn't reach out and touch him, but the weight of his gaze, reassuring and sympathetic, felt like a hug.

"Oh, I'm real close to my momma," Sebastian said. "But not my father. Not for a long time. But it's . . . it's still difficult. I might be older, but that somehow doesn't make it any easier to deal with."

"It wouldn't," Beau said with understanding.

"Do you know," Sebastian said, before he could stop himself, "that people actually thought your dad would kick you out of the house at seventeen, 'cause you were gay?"

"Yes," Beau said simply. "It happens to queer kids all the time, so I guess it could have happened to me. But my dad, he isn't like that. Not at all."

"I know," Sebastian said. Then laughed, feeling how uncomfortably close they'd gotten, even though they hadn't moved. Not one inch.

He realized then that he knew the answer to the question that Wade had asked two nights ago. *You wouldn't date him if you could?*

He would. He absolutely one hundred percent would. Even though Beau's father was his coach. And his momma would undoubtedly freak, thinking he was making her same mistakes. But he couldn't. So he dismissed the thought from his mind. Or he tried, anyway.

Reluctantly, Sebastian stood. "I gotta get going though. I just wanted to say . . . uh . . . thanks."

"Thanks?"

"For all this." Sebastian waved at the screen, still paused on the quarterback holding the football. "For the work you've done to help."

"It's my job," Beau said. But his voice was not nearly as steady as it could be.

There was something in it. Something Sebastian recognized, from that night.

A yearning.

God, they were so fucked, in such inevitable ways.

All he'd have to do, to break this painful stalemate between them, was take two steps, and then Beau would be right there, those dark blue eyes dilating with want as he gazed up at Sebastian. He remembered exactly how that had felt. The booze hadn't even been kind enough—or cruel enough—to take that image away.

But before he could, there was a knock on the door, and like Beau had been thinking about it, just the same, he flinched, then looked away.

"Oh," Paxton Kelly said, looking surprised to see Sebastian here, "I didn't realize you weren't done. I had a quick question if you have a moment."

"We are, so I do," Beau said. His voice was not quite steady.

"Yeah, we're done," Sebastian said. "I don't see your shadow, though. Where's Davis?"

Nope, you're absolutely not deflecting. Not one bit.

"On his way," Pax said.

Before Sebastian could get out the door, Pax caught his arm. "Hey," he added, "about the other night . . . I'm sorry."

"You're sorry?" Sebastian was confused, because as far as he was concerned, Pax didn't have a thing to apologize for. He wasn't going to apologize for . . . losing . . . was he? God, Sebastian really hoped not.

"You invited me to dinner—and it was nice, and thoughtful, and well"—Pax shrugged helplessly—"when I told Davis, he asked me why I hadn't gone."

Having been in the NFL for nine years and also knowing what Davis Abernathy had been through, Sebastian had a feeling he knew what was coming.

"I told him, of course, that I said no, we had a meeting, we had more work to do, because there's always more work," Pax said, "and he told me I was stupid. That I should apologize. And that next time, I should tell you that I'm in."

Yep, exactly what he'd predicted Davis might say.

"You know his city and his team and his *teammates* all shit on him, right?"

Pax shot him a look, his green eyes narrowing. "Everybody knows that. It's not a secret."

No, it wouldn't be. But Pax was so young, and he'd never played for a losing team, not by any metric, until last year. He'd been a golden boy, anointed as the next coming of football Jesus.

"Yeah, we all *know* it happened. But until your team trades for a quarterback who's not as good as you, who's rumored to beat his wife *and* his mistress, and then have a teammate's dad record a podcast all about how shitty of a quarterback you are, and how you never worked hard enough to win a Super Bowl—well, none of us really knows how that feels."

"How what feels?"

Sebastian smiled as Davis walked into the room.

"How it feels to have everyone turn on you," Sebastian said, holding out his hand and Davis gave it a quick shake.

He'd always liked Davis Abernathy, even when it had been his job to make sure his team lost.

"Yeah," Davis said wryly, "I wouldn't know a thing about that."

"This seems like a good gig, though," Sebastian said.

Davis nodded. "Nothing like being on the field, but . . ." He grinned, glancing over at where Pax and Beau had their heads together, staring at something on Beau's tablet, "but this is good, too. Really good." He paused. "You might think about it, someday."

"Coaching? Me?" Sebastian laughed. It was nearly impossible to make it as a coach if you weren't white. But he'd considered it, sure.

"That Rose kid could always use a few pointers from the best," Davis said.

"So everyone keeps saying," Sebastian said. He'd considered that too, of course, but not seriously. But the more he got a handle on his own new position, the more time and the more opportunity he might have to help Rose.

"For good reason," Beau inserted. "Brett's about to tear whatever's left of his hair out, trying to get him to cover."

"I'll check in on him next practice."

"See? We'll make you a coach yet," Davis teased.

As Sebastian left the office, he thought he could never be as satisfied with coaching as Davis was.

Didn't all his unfinished business keep him up at night? Didn't the way he'd been booted so unceremoniously from Seattle make him wish he could do it all over?

If Sebastian had been him, he never could have just up and retired, and then been happy to show up a few years later coaching guys who could've been his backups.

But he did. Genuinely happy.

It was weird, Sebastian decided as he walked towards the front of the building. He'd walked today, but was beginning to regret it because his legs were sore and tight. Maybe he should stretch out some first, before heading home. Take a few minutes in the steam room to loosen everything up.

The weight room, with its workout mat, was empty when Sebastian walked in. He shed his shirt, then his shoes, and headed, barefoot, to the padded surface.

He felt tight, but also anxious, like he could feel everyone's good-natured pushing creeping up on him. Like if he wasn't careful, it would overtake him.

James, his offseason trainer, had spent a lot of time teaching him how to stretch out his sore, overworked muscles, and over time, Sebastian had developed what he considered a nice routine, almost like a set of yoga poses, that helped both relax and center him, and unwind all the tenseness from his body.

When he'd walked in he'd had a lot on his mind.

Beau, at the forefront, and what on earth he was going to do about this tension between them that hadn't been alleviated by sleeping together, but only exacerbated. And then there was this new position, and all the stress and uncertainty surrounding it.

But when he finished, at least he'd managed to find a calmer, more reasoned perspective, and he no longer felt like tomorrow's practice, the last major practice of the week, would be enough to put him over the edge.

Sebastian gathered his shirt, stuffed his feet back into his shoes, and headed towards the steam room for a nice last bit of relaxation before he headed home. He could have just taken a nice long hot shower when he returned to his condo, but already, the Piranhas' facilities were beginning to feel more like a home than the somewhat lifeless penthouse.

Probably because he spent twice as much time here as he did at the penthouse.

It had felt like the right choice, a really solid decision, until Sebastian opened the door to the steam room, a rush of steam clouding his vision for a split second, and then he saw a single figure sitting naked on one of the cedar benches.

Beau looked up in surprise.

"You went home," he said.

Sebastian hesitated on the threshold. "Yeah . . ." he said.

He'd just managed to relegate the problem of Beau to a part of his mind where it wasn't overly bothering him.

And now here was Beau again, and he was *naked*. And *wet*.

Life, Sebastian decided, was so fucking unfair.

Sebastian looked utterly betrayed.

And Beau understood how he felt.

How could they have this incredible almost two hundred thousand square foot practice facility, and *still* end up running into each other all the time?

Beau supposed he should feel resigned to the cruelty of fate, but he didn't. Not even close.

"You gonna let all the steam out?" Beau asked, raising an eyebrow.

Sebastian rolled his eyes, and shut the door behind him, depositing his incredibly fine, incredibly naked ass at the furthest possible point.

Beau got it.

He was trying to be smart. Prudent. Put this unwanted sexual attraction behind them. But it was so inconvenient and so . . .

Nobody else left Beau Dawson at such a loss for words. Only Sebastian.

"I didn't know you came here," Sebastian said. The clear subtext being, *if I'd known there was a chance you'd be here, I'd have steered clear.*

"I ran too many miles yesterday," Beau said, "and was feelin' it a bit today. And I like to come here late at night, to think."

Sebastian nodded, his face barely visible through the steam. Beau almost told him to stop pretending that he *wanted* to sit so far away, and to come sit next to him. But if he did . . . well, Beau wasn't stupid.

He knew what would happen.

And even though it was such a distraction, one that he hadn't been able to shake, he wanted it to happen, anyway.

"I guess you probably do that, too, late at night," Sebastian said.

"Run too many miles? Yeah," Beau admitted. But he wasn't ready to say *why* yet. He'd known better, but he'd thought that if he punished his body enough, ran it into the ground until he had zero energy left, he might fall asleep without any thoughts of Sebastian creeping into his head.

It hadn't worked. And now he was paying for it in spades today.

For a minute, they sat together in companionable silence. Just them and the hiss of the steam rising through the vents.

Beau closed his eyes and tilted his head back, so he wouldn't be tempted to look at how gorgeous Sebastian looked in the dim lighting, moisture beading on his face, on his skin, dripping down lower, and then lower still . . . right where . . .

Stop it, Beau told himself firmly. *You set a boundary, and it was right, no matter how much you wish it didn't exist.*

He didn't even know if Sebastian was still interested after their night together. He'd been basically all business since the morning after—but then there had been that moment today, when he'd apologized and shared something of himself.

It wasn't anything he'd been obligated to do, and he'd done it anyway, and for a second, it had felt like they'd both only been a moment away from leaning in and kissing, obliterating the line they'd both established.

"I'm surprised that Pax and Davis let you off with *only* just one question." Sebastian's voice was hushed and dark, edged with something rough.

Beau opened his eyes, and to his surprise, even though he'd remained on the other side of the space, Sebastian was staring at him. Beau forced himself not to squirm at the thought that Sebastian might have been staring at him this whole time, gaze devouring every inch of his body.

It wasn't anything particularly special. He had decent muscle tone, he supposed, but he wasn't gorgeously ripped like Sebastian was, each part of him a work of art that deserved to be worshipped.

But still, Sebastian kept looking at him like every bit of him was exceptional, and Beau hadn't ever experienced that before.

Beau cleared his throat. "They were asking a JJ Watt question."

"I'm only surprised that didn't lead to three more," Sebastian said, his tone lazy and satisfied. "JJ Watt is a beast."

He sounded, Beau realized, just like he had after they'd fucked the other night.

And *that* didn't help. Not even remotely.

"Like recognizes like," Beau teased. "You're kinda a beast yourself."

The corner of Sebastian's mouth quirked up into a smile. "I guess we'll all see my new beast mode on game day."

"You get better every single day," Beau said, and meant it. Even meant the worshipful edge to his voice that he hadn't quite been able to help.

Sebastian's gaze was mesmerizing, and Beau couldn't look away. In fact, he couldn't *stay* away. Before he even realized what he was doing, he'd scooted a little bit closer. And then closer still. Until all he'd have to do is reach out and he could touch Sebastian's naked thigh.

God, his gorgeously muscled, *wet* thigh.

Beau slid his hands under his own thighs. Maybe that would remind him that he wasn't allowed to touch.

"You're tryin' to test me," Sebastian said wryly.

"Both of us," Beau admitted.

Sebastian opened his mouth and then shut it again. He eyed the ceiling, and muttered something under his breath.

"You're going to be the death of me. As in your father is going to *kill me*," Sebastian said, but he wasn't moving away. In fact, he was moving closer. His face, wreathed in steam, moisture dripping off his chin, was only a few inches from Beau's.

"What he doesn't know won't kill him," Beau said, his voice breathless.

"And yet . . ." Sebastian's eyes were glowing in the dim light, and yeah, he was definitely smiling.

Like he was looking forward to touching Beau again, even though he knew it might make everything harder.

"Actually . . ." He opened his mouth, hoping to clarify the situation again, and then never, ever speak of his dad again, but before he could even get the second word out, the door to the steam room opened again.

And Beau, despite what he had *just* been about to say, saw who it was and jumped back a good three feet away from Sebastian.

Okay, maybe his father wouldn't care, or at least he wouldn't be in a killing mood, but it was entirely different to be naked in the same steam room with him and Sebastian. *Together.*

Dread pooled deep in Beau's stomach.

"Coach," Sebastian said, his Adam's apple bobbing.

"Howard." His father turned his direction. "And Beau. You two look like you're deep into . . . something. What are you two discussing?"

"Uh, how Sebastian's gonna give JJ Watt a run for his money this Sunday," Beau said awkwardly as his father sat down.

So fucking awkwardly.

His dad tilted his head, considering this. "Brett did say you've been tacklin' better in practice." He hesitated. "'Course he also thought you couldn't tackle much worse, before."

"Oh that's just great," Sebastian muttered.

"You know how Brett is. Likes a textbook tackle," Beau said weakly. "And Sebastian didn't have much opportunity to tackle before. But he's making up for lost time now."

"Apparently." His father grinned. "You enjoyin' Brett's tackling clinics, Howard?"

"I don't think *enjoy* is the word I'd use, Coach," Sebastian said carefully, "but Beau's right. He likes a textbook tackle."

"Sloppy tacklin' don't get you nowhere," Asa said with a firm nod. "We gotta get back to the fundamentals. Brett's good with those."

"Our biggest problem," Sebastian said, "is that we aren't playing like a team. We're playing like fifty-two separate players."

"I've got some ideas about that," Asa said, grinning.

Beau was afraid he knew what his father was thinking of, and he was ready to tell him it was a terrible idea. That not everything translated well from collegiate to professional football, but Asa Dawson was an idealist.

He could already hear him saying, *but they're still football players, aren't they? They still play the same game.*

But when Beau looked over at Sebastian—all grown-up, adult man—he couldn't imagine him agreeing to participate in one of his dad's team-building experiments. He'd laugh. He'd scoff. Just like everyone else on the team.

"Well," Sebastian said, standing up, "I'd better let you think on those."

Beau was glad he was still sitting on his hands, because he might have done something stupid and reached out and grabbed him, pulled him back.

And if Asa wasn't sitting right there, his eyes lit up with interest as he looked at Sebastian, and then Beau, and then back at Sebastian, he might have.

It would have been a mistake, just like it would have been a mistake for them to touch each other again.

But at least it would have been a really fun, exceedingly enjoyable mistake.

"I . . . uh . . ." Beau said, scrambling for an excuse to follow Sebastian, who was already about to push the door open. "I should . . ."

"Wait a sec," his dad said, "there was something I wanted to ask you first."

Beau sighed and sat back down.

It was the right thing to do, to sit here and listen to his dad ask an almost completely irrelevant question about the offensive line and the configuration they'd decided on for this week's game, but that didn't mean that it didn't totally suck, watching Sebastian shoot him one last quick smile, and then disappear.

"That," his father said, relaxing back into the steam, "seems to be going well."

Beau forced himself not to tense. "What seems to be going well?"

"You makin' Sebastian Howard into a safety," he said.

"It's not been entirely smooth," Beau admitted. "There's some resistance still. There's lots of days I think he'd love to be back at corner."

"But he knows better," his dad said wisely.

His dad always knew everyone better than they knew themselves. Which was why it was probably inevitable that he'd find out that Beau had slept with Sebastian. He wouldn't even be angry, wouldn't judge, would just look at him and ask one simple question.

Will it get in the way?

And right now Beau could honestly answer that it hadn't. But if they kept dancing around each other like this, sex feeling like another inevitability, then Beau wasn't sure what his answer would be.

It could be great.

It could also be disastrous.

The number of potential pitfalls they faced was already high—Beau didn't need to add another to the list.

"He seems to," Beau said guardedly.

"And he trusts you."

Beau wasn't sure he'd go that far—but then Beau knew enough about sex and hookups to know that you didn't ask someone for what Sebastian had wanted if there wasn't some trust involved.

"He does," his father repeated, "I can see it."

Beau was afraid of what else his father was seeing, but he let it drop.

"Sure. It's easier if he does," Beau said.

"Don't give him a reason to doubt it," Asa said.

"Of course I won't." Beau was annoyed his father would even suggest that he might.

"That's a player, a *man*, who only gives his trust if it's warranted," Asa warned. "And then you'll have it til you break it."

"Right," Beau said, but hesitated. What was his father trying to say? Had he figured things out? Or did he only suspect and that's why he didn't want to say anything.

"Howard's a good man. And an even better player. You're helpin' him get there."

Beau didn't really disagree with anything his dad had just said, so he merely nodded.

"Keep on him, okay?" Asa said, and then to Beau's surprise, he got up. "I think I've got enough steam," he said. "Just needed enough to get my head on straight."

And Beau was left alone again, wishing, despite knowing better, that his father could have figured out how to get his head on straight without any steam at all.

Then he might have gotten to make another really bad—and really fun—decision.

Chapter Eight

Beau had lost count of the number of games he'd watched over his lifetime.

Even though every game began the exact same way, after that, no two were ever alike. It was a big reason why he never found football dull. He'd had friends in grad school who'd told him that he'd be bored within months, following a game where "men with more muscle than brains chased a ball up and down the field."

But to Beau, every single game was fundamentally different, required a unique game plan, and as every game progressed, a further unique set of course corrections. Those, Beau had learned at Tennessee and since, were what he was particularly good at.

He also assisted the coaches in developing each week's game plan, and helped the players to implement it.

But for the first two drives—offensive and defensive—Beau's main job was to watch and analyze what the other team had come prepared with. Ultimately he had to decide if it was worth sticking to the original plan, or if he needed to bend and adjust, with the hope of having better results.

Beau rocked back on his heels, watching with a frisson of anxiety as the Piranhas' defense got set for their first series of the game.

He should only care if Sebastian followed through on everything they'd discussed over the last week, while they'd been preparing for this matchup, but Beau knew that wasn't all of it. Not even remotely.

He wanted to see confidence in Sebastian's posture. He wanted to see him relish the challenge again. To enjoy his new position. To feel like he *belonged* again.

All of those things would make Sebastian a better player—or a player like he'd been a few seasons back. But there was more, too.

Beau wanted Sebastian to be *happy.*

And that, he knew, watching as Sebastian took the field, was a problem, because it had absolutely nothing to do with football. Not really.

"You think he's ready?" Brett asked, voice crackling over their comms system.

Normally, Beau wore his headset tuned to the offensive channel, on which Pax and Davis and Foreman discussed the plays and also what happened *after* running the plays.

But Beau had specifically requested to be tuned to the defensive channel this time around because despite all his work, Beau knew Sebastian was still uneasy, and he wanted every advantage when it came to helping him on the sidelines.

During the walk-through, his dad had pulled him to the side, clearly confused. "I thought you were on the offense during the game," he'd said.

Beau shook his head. "I'm switching to defense now, just for awhile, just to make sure the unit gels."

He could see that his father wasn't happy about this, but he'd also made a good point—after all, they had a rookie out there, and a player in the middle of changing positions—so he couldn't really argue. But because he was Asa, he did anyway.

"We need to score points," his dad had pointed out.

"Yeah, and we will." Beau could only imagine how Pax would self-combust if they didn't. And nothing Beau said was going to stop that eventuality.

His dad had tapped his fingers on his tablet impatiently. "I want you on the offensive channel."

"And I know I need to be on the defensive." Beau rarely argued with his father—for good reason. They were almost always on the same page.

But Beau didn't want to give in now.

"This matters to you." Asa didn't phrase it like a question. Instead it was a statement.

Beau had nodded. And that was that.

But it was also entirely possible that he'd given too much away.

How much longer was he going to be able to hide his obsession with Sebastian Howard?

Beau wasn't sure, but he had a feeling that the obsession was absolutely going to outlast his father's lack of awareness.

"Do I think Howard is going to go out there and give it his best shot?" Beau questioned back to Brett over his mic. "Absolutely."

Brett made a sound that meant he was less than convinced.

"He took the field like he owned it. Hasn't done that in one game since he switched to safety," Beau pointed out.

"That's like saying 'cause he's got an ugly girlfriend, he's a shit hitter," Brett yelled over the connection.

Beau grimaced. Brett was old-school, and in those days, yeah, you'd had to be super loud to be heard over the interference that everyone dealt with. But technology was so much better now, there wasn't nearly as much, and now Brett just yelled to yell.

You'll either get used to it or you'll be deaf, Beau thought with resignation.

Beau eyed the field, the play setup. "He's positioned well."

Brett hummed, sounding not entirely dissatisfied.

The Texans' quarterback caught the ball from the center, and dropped back, making a masterful pump fake, but Sebastian, whom Beau had spent the last week training for just this situation, wasn't fooled.

He leapt into action, sprinting to the other side of the field, helping Rose cover Hopkins, one of the Texans' most explosive receivers, and with the additional cover, the quarterback dumped off the ball to the running back, who was almost immediately tackled by one of the Piranhas' defensive backs.

"That's right, that's right," Brett said excitedly, nearing blowing out one of Beau's eardrums. "He's got it."

"He did that play," Beau agreed.

"He's got it. He's got *fire*," Brett announced.

Beau smothered his grin. "I think the expression is he's *on* fire."

"He's not on fire," Brett spluttered. "If he's on fire, I'd be worried."

Beau made a notation on his tablet of the next offensive formation, and watched as this time the Texans' running back zig-zagged through the defensive line, and this time it was Sebastian who tackled him, dragging him to the ground.

"Textbook, *fucking textbook*," Brett practically cried with happiness.

"Guess all that work paid off," Beau commented dryly.

"Oh yeah." Beau hadn't heard Brett this excited in years. "Oh. Yeah. Baby."

Beau rolled his eyes, but when the Piranhas' defense jogged off the field after only allowing one first down, he was slapping hands and backs and butts, giving out generous words of praise.

Sebastian came to a stop in front of Beau.

He still had his helmet on, but Beau could see his face through the black grill, and he was smiling as brightly as Beau had ever seen.

"That," Sebastian said, pulling his helmet off, "was *fucking fun*."

"Even Brett thought your tackles were textbook," Beau teased, following Sebastian to the bench, even though he'd promised his dad he'd keep an eye on the offense. But he had at least a minute or two while the punt team did their thing before Pax and the rest of the offense took the field.

"Yeah?" Sebastian downed a paper cup of Gatorade, and grinned again, impossibly even brighter this time. "Maybe he'll torture me less at practice next week."

"Always a possibility," Beau said. He should turn away. He should walk away. But frustrated, stymied Sebastian was hard to resist. Happy, satisfied Sebastian was impossible to deny.

"That first play," Sebastian said at the same moment as Beau said, "So, first play."

Sebastian laughed, so loudly a few heads turned their direction. Including, Beau realized, his father's.

It was rare that he ever tore his attention away from the field, but for a split second, he'd definitely felt his father's gaze on the pair of them.

"That first play," Sebastian repeated, dropping his voice down so Beau had to lean in to hear better, "I think he was totally gonna throw to that speedy-as-hell receiver, and then he *didn't* because I was in the right spot."

"The perfect spot," Beau agreed. "He knows Rose is a rookie, and he was probably hoping to exploit that. But you made it so he couldn't."

"He *wouldn't*," Sebastian crowed, clearly very pleased with himself.

They were in view of about a hundred people on the sideline, never mind all the cameras floating around, and God only knew how many viewers at home, so Beau felt safe. He reached out and patted Sebastian on the bicep, like he might any player who'd done a fantastic job. But the moment Beau's fingers touched Sebastian's smooth skin, overlaid on all that fine, firm muscle, he froze.

He'd forgotten what touching Sebastian felt like—like he'd just been plugged into an electrical socket.

Sebastian's face morphed into a mask. He'd clearly felt it too.

"I . . . uh . . . good job," Beau said, stumbling over his words.

"Thanks," Sebastian said, and turned away.

Dismissing him? Trying to refocus? Beau didn't know, but he escaped back to his normal spot on the sideline, just as Pax lined up for the first drive.

And if he saw but he didn't really *see* it, it was entirely not his fault. It was . . . well, it wasn't Sebastian's fault either.

It was that fickle bitch fate, who'd decided to make Sebastian the one person on the planet that Beau couldn't imagine resisting.

All the way through the first half of the game, Sebastian felt Beau's painfully brief touch on his bicep like it was a brand.

He didn't want to. It would have been a hell of a lot easier if even a simple, straightforward touch didn't rile him up like it did, but Sebastian was halfway to accepting it now.

He wanted Beau Dawson. And it seemed inevitable that Beau Dawson wanted him back.

The sex they'd already had hadn't changed a thing. He didn't want Beau less; he wanted him *more*.

Because now they knew just how good it was.

And how much better it could be.

He told himself, rubbing his arm with a towel even though there was nothing there, zero evidence that Beau had ever touched him, that if he focused on the game, he'd forget about the way it had felt.

But that didn't happen. Halftime came and went, and now they were deep in the fourth quarter, trying to prevent the Texans from putting together a game-winning drive.

The defense had come through this game, including, Sebastian thought, himself. He was finally in a groove, finding his rhythm, understanding his new place on the field, not just holding the center and making sure their receivers and running backs didn't get past him, but giving invaluable assistance to Rose and the other corner.

He could *see* his actions on the field making a difference in the way the rest of the defense played, attacking the ball instead of letting it come to them, and change was obvious from the score. The Texans were still trying to put a decent drive together because even though they were ahead by two, they didn't want to give the Piranhas' offense any chance to get the ball back and score.

Sebastian glanced up at the clock. Less than three minutes left. He wiped his face and shoved his helmet back on, jogging out onto the field.

They'd be able to run at least two plays before the two-minute warning. And then at least a handful after.

But all the defense needed was four plays, total.

If they couldn't get the Texans off the field, the game would be over before Pax ever got the shot he needed.

Evans, the inside linebacker and the captain of the defense, called the play, and Sebastian took his position, the world narrowing in until what remained was the turf, and his cleats digging into it, his lungs squeezing out each breath, and the quarterback, poised over the center, ready to catch the ball.

He counted off, and for a split second, his gaze flicked right to Sebastian, like he was checking his spot, and Sebastian leaned in, further, muscles braced to actually spring in the opposite direction.

The center snapped the ball, and the Texans' quarterback dropped back, pump faking really well, because he was the best in the league, but Sebastian had watched enough film with Beau to know better than to bite. "Always watch the fingers," Beau had reminded him so many times that he'd wanted to throttle the guy.

Except not really. He'd wanted to do something else. Kiss the words out of his mouth, maybe.

But Ben's fingers didn't flex, not the way they needed to if he was planning on actually throwing, and so Sebastian sprang to the other side, covering the tight end as he slid past Evans, and sat right in the open flat.

He jumped at the last moment, and batted the ball away.

"Good, good," Evans said, slapping Sebastian on the back as they jogged back to the line of scrimmage. "Next time, pick it off."

Sebastian grinned at him. "End the game right?"

Evans gave him a nod of approval.

The next play, it was clear they were going to go after Rose again.

Poor Micah. He'd been under siege the whole game, trying to cover two of the Texans' wiliest receivers, but he'd done a pretty good job. But they were clearly hoping that he was tired, or might make a rookie mistake in this big situation.

Sebastian sprinted after Rose and the receiver that he was covering, taking a pretty good route, better than Rose's, and at the last moment, he turned, angling his body into what he thought was a decent angle, and it was as easy as lifting his hands, and letting the ball fall right into them.

The moment it touched his fingertips, he gripped it, and switched all his weight forward, eyes scanning the field for players who might be able to stop him from running the ball back.

It turned out that he should've been looking behind him.

Because the Texans' receiver grabbed him, the very last second before he could sprint out of his grip, and tackled him to the ground.

Exhilaration blossomed through him, but it was tinged with regret.

Pax would get the ball at the wrong end of the field. He'd have . . . just two minutes to go the whole length of the field, trying to maneuver them into field goal range.

It was great he'd taken away the Texans' opportunity to score, Sebastian thought as he jogged back to the sideline after the defense finished their celebration, but it hadn't been enough.

And goddamn it, they needed a win.

It felt like an ugly premonition, crawling down his spine, as, out of breath and panting, he collapsed down onto the bench.

He felt Evans settle in next to him, slapping his back.

When he glanced up, he hoped that someone had brought him Gatorade, and they *had*, but it wasn't one of the assistants, it was Beau, and he was smiling.

"If we'd had a bet about how many balls you were gonna haul in as a safety versus a corner, I'd be winning," Beau said.

"Could've done better," Sebastian said, between heavy pants, taking the paper cup Beau offered.

Beau shrugged. "You did what you had to do to get the ball out of their hands. Maybe you didn't get the return you might've wanted . . . but listen, you did what you needed to do."

"Fucking right," Evans agreed, on his other side.

"Now, it's just on Pax to make it happen," Beau said.

He sounded optimistic and hopeful.

But Sebastian was already feeling the churn of failure.

And watching the last two minutes of the game, eventually getting to his feet and restlessly prowling along the sideline, wishing he'd done more, *wanting* to do more, he couldn't find Beau's optimism.

Sebastian watched as Beau's own positivity sank as the Piranhas' offense, supposedly so stacked with talent, had one miscue after another. Two penalties, including one ten-yard holding penalty negating a killer twenty-five-yard run by Kenyon.

It was slow-motion heartbreak.

By the time it finally ended on a last, painful Hail Mary pass, Pax chucking the ball into the end zone with all his strength in the final seconds of the game, only to have it be knocked away by one of the Texans players, Sebastian was in a fucking rotten mood.

Nothing was going to fix it, but what was absolutely going to make it worse?

Helen Gibson, the head of PR, grabbing him just out of the shower and telling him that she wanted him for the post-game press conference.

He never liked doing them, even when his team had notched a win.

And this one was going to feel particularly rotten.

"Why?" he demanded, as he pulled on a shirt, buttoning it with sharp, quick movements. He just wanted to get out of here. He wanted to . . . Sebastian didn't even know what he wanted to do.

Contemplate the complete failure of his career by himself, in total silence? Yeah, that sounded good.

He didn't even want a drink. That's how bad it was.

"You caught a game-changing interception," Helen said.

Sebastian shot her a disbelieving look. "It wasn't *game-changing*. We still fucking lost."

"Yes, well," Helen retorted briskly, "we haven't had you up on the podium yet, and you're one of the major stars of the team. So it's your turn."

"Great," Sebastian muttered.

"Five minutes," she said, turning away, probably going in search of Pax.

If Sebastian was Pax, he'd be hiding in a hole.

But Pax wasn't like that—Pax was a leader, and he'd get up there in front of the media and field all their questions about how he didn't do enough, how he wasn't good enough, even if it wasn't necessarily his fault.

If Sebastian had to do that every week . . . well, he just couldn't.

Which was why he was happy to admit that Paxton Kelly was a better man than he was.

Sebastian finished getting dressed, dread pooling deep in his stomach, and just as he was about to go looking for her, Helen appeared at the entrance to the locker room.

"Ready?" she asked, raising an eyebrow.

"No, not even remotely." Sebastian chuckled humorlessly.

"It won't be so bad. These reporters are on your side," Helen said as she led him through the hallways to the media room, located on the other side of the stadium facility.

She left him at the door, and ducked through it, double-checking that everyone was set.

He leaned against the wall, and closed his eyes. Trying to focus. Trying to think of how he was going to address these reporters' questions.

They were going to want answers. They deserved answers.

And Sebastian didn't think he had any.

He heard Helen announce from the microphone at the podium, "First, I've got Sebastian Howard for you, who caught the interception to end the Texans' last drive."

Sebastian sighed, and pulled himself up.

"Yes," Helen continued, answering a question he hadn't heard, "I'll have Paxton Kelly for you, too. You know I always give access to Pax."

Sebastian heard a noise and glanced up to see Pax in the flesh, standing there, his young, handsome face a complete fucking blank.

That, Sebastian discovered, was how he must be able to do this, week after week.

He kept it all inside.

"Sorry," Paxton said quietly.

It took Sebastian a moment to realize that he was apologizing and then another moment to realize *what* he was apologizing for.

Oh God, somehow it got worse.

"No," Sebastian said firmly, and even though he and Paxton Kelly weren't close, he reached out and pulled the guy into a quick, tight hug. He flinched at first and then relaxed. "No, you don't get to do that."

When Sebastian pulled back, there was surprise in Pax's eyes. "I don't?"

"No," Sebastian repeated. "No, you don't. You're doing your fucking best. And maybe you gotta go answer to those assholes in there"—he jabbed a thumb towards the media room door—"but you don't gotta answer to me. Ever."

"You sound like Davis."

"Davis," Sebastian said, "would know who you should and shouldn't answer to. And what you should answer for. Better than just about anyone, I'd imagine."

"Yeah," Pax agreed. He looked marginally more human now. Less like a robot about to face his inevitable destruction.

Helen opened the door, stuck her head into the hallway. "You ready, Sebastian?"

Sebastian nodded, and then turned back to Paxton. "Don't worry," he said, dredging up a grin from someplace he couldn't identify, "I'll make sure to make you look real good."

Paxton smiled back, the return to human form complete, and Sebastian focused on that as Helen led him up to the podium.

No matter what Helen had said about all the reporters being on "his side"—and that was a ridiculous concept anyway, because they were representatives of the city, and the city surely deserved better, didn't they?—it was still tough to stand up and face them.

Even the ones who looked sympathetic when they asked their questions.

The first ones were fairly simple and straightforward.

"How do you feel about your new position?"

"Good," Sebastian said, trying not to hold the edges of the podium with too much of a noticeable death grip. He didn't mind reporters one-on-one, but there was a whole room full of them. And they were all recording every goddamn word he said. "I'm really enjoying the new challenge. The transition has actually been easier than I thought it would be."

"Beau mentioned to me last week that he thought you'd be catching more interceptions as a safety than a corner. Do you think today's interception is a promise of more to come?"

"I sure hope so," Sebastian replied. "I just want to make plays that put the team in a position to win. That's why they pay me, and that's why I'm here."

When he'd first gotten into the NFL, his agent had pulled him aside and given him a rundown of what kind of stuff he should and shouldn't say to the media. He'd quickly learned that it was smart to follow Alec's suggestions, because if you didn't . . . well, Sebastian had seen it way too many times. And if he wanted to keep the media from prying into his life—both because of his family and his sexuality—then keeping his answers as bland as possible was the way to go.

"You aren't angry that you handed the ball to Paxton Kelly and he couldn't get the job done?"

All of the Miami media was new to Sebastian, but he made a note of this particular guy before he answered the question.

He was tall and blond, with what might have been an athlete's build under his polo shirt and khaki slacks, and had the kind of face that you either wanted to punch or kiss.

But Sebastian wanted to punch it, because he'd known too many of these pretty white boys in college. They were usually in a frat, and they were always insufferable.

"No," Sebastian kept his answer as short as possible. He couldn't have made it any shorter, anyway.

"No?" The guy raised one perfect blond eyebrow.

"No," Sebastian repeated.

"You gave him the ball and the win, and he fumbled it." The reporter shot Sebastian what he probably thought was a disarming smile, except that all it did was increase Sebastian's desire to punch it off.

"He didn't actually fumble the ball," Sebastian pointed out slowly, *"and* there's a lot more working pieces on the offense than Paxton Kelly. Pax is our guy. He's gonna keep being our guy."

There were two more questions, and then finally, Helen interceded and ushered him off the stage.

Maybe he should have waited around to see Paxton handle the reporters, but he'd already stomached all he could.

For a split second, he considered going to look for Beau, but what would he say? What *could* he say to make it better?

Nothing. There was nothing he could do or say. So instead of heading towards the office level, where no doubt Beau was already with his father, trying to break down what had happened at the end of the game, Sebastian took another turn and headed towards the exit.

He'd go back to his condo and . . . well, all he'd wanted to do earlier was contemplate the ultimate failure of his career.

That didn't sound any better, but he also hated the idea of having to talk to anyone about it either, so he took the least-fucked-up path, and headed home.

It was absolutely fucking cowardly, but Beau took his time after the game before heading to his father's office, where the rest of the coaching staff would gather to give their first quick and dirty impressions of the game.

A fucking disaster, that's my analysis, Beau thought as he finished up in the staff locker room, noticing that he was the only one still left.

His dad would be pissed.

But then his dad had a lot more to be pissed about tonight than Beau not being present so he could be subjected, along with the rest of the staff, to his patented "I'm so disappointed in you" face.

When he finally got up to the top floor, and turned the corner into the massive office that these days Asa Dawson was basically calling his home away from home, Beau was surprised to see that it was empty except for his father.

"Where is everyone?" Beau asked, flopping down into his favorite chair, opposite his dad's desk.

"Licking their wounds," Asa said succinctly with an underlying poison that Beau understood all too well.

"It was a rough way to lose a game," Beau agreed.

"Davis is blaming himself. Randy blames *himself*. But at least Brett seems pleased."

"Howard played great. Best we've seen so far at safety," Beau agreed cautiously. But none of that mattered if they couldn't move the ball when it mattered. To win games, you had to score points, not just keep the other team from scoring them.

"Yeah," Asa said with a heavy sigh. He still hadn't looked up from the tablet sitting on his desk. Beau didn't have to see it to know what it was. The final drive, repeating over and over in front of his father's face.

Reminding him that he'd failed.

"Rudy stopped by on his way out," Asa said. "Reminded me of why I was hired."

"Like you'd possibly forget," Beau muttered under his breath. The first time he'd met the owner of the Piranhas, Rudy Gonzalez, he hadn't been particularly impressed. Rudy had seemed to be more interested in the evenness of his tan than in his football team, but then he'd also given Asa free reign.

But that also meant that he had all the rope in the world to hang himself with.

Enough rope to hang Beau right along with him.

And that, Beau knew, was only fair, because while he might not be equally responsible for what happened with the Piranhas this season, he couldn't claim *no* responsibility.

After all, he'd been the loudest voice in his father's ear, pushing him to take this job.

"He's not wrong, though," Asa said calmly. "We came here to win games, and we haven't won any."

"It's going to get better," Beau said, desperately trying to hold on to his positivity. "We're going to win games. We were so goddamn close today."

"We were," Asa said. "And maybe we will. Maybe we won't. But it doesn't mean we're not going to continue to give our full effort."

"Hundred and ten percent," Beau promised.

Asa gave him a sharp nod. "Now go home, get some rest. Be here early tomorrow. We have a meeting first thing, because I want to go over every single fucking play of that fucking game."

Beau wasn't surprised. It was what he would have suggested.

They'd left opportunities on the field that they should have capitalized on, and the only way to find them was to go looking.

If they continued to lose like this—either by thirty points or by two—Rudy would fire them and replace the both of them with someone cheaper. Someone more expendable, and the Dawson experiment in Miami would be over.

And not only would they be unemployed, but Beau knew the stain, the undeniable taint, on his father's otherwise stellar record would haunt him. Because it would haunt Beau, too.

After he left the coach's office, he wandered around for a minute, not expecting to see many people left in the building, and he was right. They'd all cleared out.

Nobody wanted to stick around and think about what *might* have happened.

He nearly texted Pax to make sure he was alright, but then he put himself into Pax's shoes and realized he wouldn't want to hear from anyone right now.

He'd want solitude, so he could lick his wounds.

And there would be wounds. There was no doubt of that, because Beau felt like *he* had them, a deep sense of dissatisfaction and failure. It hurt to face them; all he wanted to do was forget about the way they felt.

The moment Beau had the thought, he should've dismissed it. But instead, he stopped in the middle of his tracks, in the middle of an empty hallway, and abruptly changed direction.

Maybe Sebastian wouldn't want to see him, but he wanted to see Sebastian.

Wanted to tell him good job. Wanted . . . well, Beau wanted so many things, none of which were really possible, but even the flashing red lights in his head didn't stop him from wanting them.

Or from going to grab them.

Chapter Nine

When he heard the door knock, Sebastian's first thought was *fuck it, they can just fuck right off.*

His second thought was . . . well, he wasn't proud of his second thought, but it existed all the same. Existed, and then he pushed it right back down again because seeing Beau right now would be the worst possible thing. His self-control was basically nonexistent, because he was feeling so goddamn sorry for himself, and if Beau showed up now, Sebastian already knew he'd use him to feel better.

They'd use each other.

So instead of getting up and tempting fate, he kept his butt in the chair on the open patio.

Tonight he hadn't poured himself a drink, because the idea of drowning his sorrows felt worse, somehow. A slow, slippery slope that he didn't want to start sliding down.

Sebastian tilted his head back and heard the knock again. Louder this time, and more insistent.

But still, he ignored it.

The number of people who would hang around and keep knocking were a very small list, and he could already eliminate Alec from it, because Alec had texted him earlier tonight, the message waiting for him on his phone when he'd gotten back to the locker room. He was in New York, at the Riptide game against the Giants, and since it was the Sunday night game, Sebastian knew it couldn't be him.

No, there was only one really likely possibility, and he was the reason Sebastian was torn between keeping his butt out here, out of trouble, and going to see what he wanted.

Stupid, his old coach yelled, *you know what he wants.*

But Sebastian stayed in the chair, long after the second round of door pounding ceased, and waited for the third set.

It didn't come.

Of course that was when he couldn't help himself. He shot up, practically jogging to the front door. What if he was too late? What if Beau had left already?

Even stupider, the coach yowled, *of course he left, you ignored him, told him you didn't want him.*

Sebastian yanked the door open, and to his shock, Beau was still standing there, holding up a hand, like he'd been about to pound on the door again.

For a long moment, they stared at each other, gazes colliding, not saying a word. Sebastian saw the anguish in Beau's eyes, and felt the echo of it deep inside.

Before he'd even made the decision, he'd already reached for Beau, wrapping his fingers around his forearm and tugging him inside. The moment the door shut, he didn't know who reached for who—maybe what happened is they reached for each other.

But Beau was in his arms, or he was in Beau's, he didn't know, but it didn't matter, because Beau framed his face with his hands and kissed him, hard and fast and resolute.

Like he worried if there was any room for doubt, he wouldn't actually do it.

Beau's kiss wasn't slow or sad—it was hot and fiery and passionate, and it burned Sebastian, consumed him, until one kiss melted into the next, each one increasingly needy, Beau rubbing his hardening cock against Sebastian's thigh almost helplessly as they kissed and kissed and kissed.

Sebastian finally managed to tear his mouth off Beau's. "Wait," he croaked. "*Wait.*"

But Beau was pulling off his glasses and then reaching for Sebastian's belt, palm sliding down his zipper, where his cock twitched against his touch.

"Why?" Beau asked, gazing up at him, lips red and wet and swollen. "Do you not want . . ."

He didn't even get the whole question out before Sebastian leaned down and kissed him again, firmly and with feeling. After keeping his hands to himself for a week now, it felt like a rush to finally be able to touch Beau the way he'd been craving.

"Then why do you want to wait?" Beau asked breathlessly after they broke apart again. His hand was still pressed against Sebastian's cock and the pressure felt so incredibly good that Sebastian was having trouble even following the conversation.

"I just want . . ." Sebastian took a deep breath. Trying to focus. "I just want to treat you right."

Beau grinned. "Trust me, you are. All of this is right."

"Even if it's wrong?"

"*Especially* if it's wrong." Beau sounded so certain, it was hard not to feel the exact same way. To let all the guilt and recrimination and worry go, and just *feel*.

"What do you want?" Sebastian asked, reaching out and cupping Beau's head in his hand, tangling his fingers into his dark hair and pulling. Just a little. Beau's pupils dilated even more, his face flushing with the rawness of it, and Sebastian wondered if there had ever been a chance they'd stay out of each other's beds.

"I want to make you feel good," Beau said roughly.

"Funny, I want to make *you* feel good," Sebastian teased. Letting his hand drift lower, and then lower still, until it cupped his ass through those khaki pants that shouldn't have been so goddamn sexy, but were anyway, just because of who wore them.

"Then what," Beau asked, tilting his head up, pressing more fully into Sebastian's touch, "are we waiting for?"

Sebastian didn't have an answer, so instead of telling Beau, he reached down and lifted him up, loving the way Beau's breath caught in his throat as he carried him into the bedroom, setting him on the edge of the bed.

He made quick work of his shirt, losing a few of the buttons in the process, and not really caring, until he glanced up and saw Beau's dark blue eyes glowing as he watched him.

"Slower," Beau said, as he finished slipping his own pants down around his ankles. Cupping his hard cock with his hand, Beau licked his lips. "Slower," he repeated, *"please."*

It shouldn't have been so hot, watching Beau touch himself. It shouldn't have been nearly as hot as touching Beau himself, but it was. Seeing the way he flushed pink, how he strained into his own touch, just because Sebastian was stripping out of his own clothes.

He knew he had a good body—it was fit not just because he'd always been fit, but because it was part of his job. But with Beau's gaze hot and heavy along his skin, prickling every nerve, he'd never felt it so viscerally before.

"This what you like?" Sebastian asked as he finished unbuckling his belt and slid his pants to the floor, leaving himself completely naked.

Beau's teeth dug into that lush bottom lip, and the heat in his gaze answered his question without a single word.

"I thought so," Sebastian said, and reached out, tucking a finger under Beau's briefs—the last bit of clothing he was wearing—and tugged them down, Beau's hard cock springing up now that he'd finally released it from its confinement. "I said I wanted to make you feel good," he said, and leaned down, flicking his tongue against the head. Beau hissed.

He was just about to sink to his knees and see what other noises he could wring out of Beau when he spoke up. "And I said I wanted to make *you* feel good," Beau said, a stubborn tilt to his jaw.

"Then . . . how about this?" Sebastian slid onto the bed and tapped his stomach. "Come 'ere, and we can make each other feel good."

Beau didn't need any further encouragement. He climbed onto the bed and then onto Sebastian, and for a second, Sebastian could only groan as Beau's hot wet mouth engulfed his dick.

It felt so goddamned good, he could just lie here and take every bit of it—but that hadn't been the point. Sebastian wasn't the kind of guy to only take and not give, anyway, so he reached up and tugged Beau into a slightly better position, trying to ignore the white-hot pleasure spiking through his veins as Beau continued to suck him in long, steady, *determined* strokes. Because that was Beau all over. He'd devote just as much careful attention to a blowjob as he'd devote to forming a game plan.

It was one of the reasons Sebastian liked him so goddamn much, he thought, letting Beau's cock slip between his lips, his hands reaching up to squeeze that gorgeously rounded ass that had starred in so many fantasies.

It would be so easy to let his mind wander . . . to fucking that delectable ass . . . because he really hoped that Beau might let him one day.

But that day wasn't this day, and he'd meant it. He wanted to make Beau feel good. Feel good enough to banish all those shadows from behind his eyes.

He tilted his head and began to suck in earnest, taking more and more of Beau's cock in, focusing hard so he wouldn't accidentally choke. He wasn't particularly experienced at this, but from the way Beau kept squirming on top of him and sucking his own dick with additional enthusiasm, that didn't seem to matter.

Sebastian slid his hands down, and with one, cupped and massaged Beau's balls, and with his other gathered some saliva, circling the spot that he'd dreamt about fucking.

Beau tensed and then groaned, loudly.

Sebastian took that as additional encouragement and gave him more, until he was finger-fucking him in rhythm with sucking his cock.

It was an endless feedback loop of pleasure. Every time he did something Beau seemed to like, he'd dedicate himself further, taking Sebastian deeper and longer and harder, until Sebastian lost himself in the feel and the smell of Beau all around him. And then it would begin all over again, until Sebastian felt like he was being strung out across a deep, impossible chasm, until he felt like if Beau wasn't grounding him, holding him down, he'd explode into a million glittering pieces.

Then unexpectedly, Beau went rigid, tearing his mouth off Sebastian's dick, and moaned *very* loudly into his thigh. "I'm . . ." he gasped. "I'm . . ."

Sebastian made an encouraging sound and wiggled his fingers in deeper, wanting to feel Beau pulse around him.

He didn't have to wait long—a second later, Beau was howling through his orgasm, shooting his come down Sebastian's throat.

Sebastian swallowed, working him through it, until he finally slipped out of his mouth, soft and satisfied.

For a long moment, Beau lay across him like a blanket, and Sebastian flexed his thighs, cock quivering, somehow even more impossibly turned on than he had been before. Having a front-row seat to Beau coming his brains out had been *that* hot. He really, really wanted to come, but he also wanted Beau to fully enjoy the aftermath.

But before he could say anything, suddenly, his cock was enveloped in that hot, greedy mouth again, and that was all it took before Sebastian lost it, pulsing in long, hot shudders, the pleasure stretching on and on until it finally began to fade.

"Fuck," Sebastian groaned as Beau sucked the rest of his orgasm out of him. "Fuck, fuck, fuck."

Beau laid his cheek against Sebastian's thigh, and somehow, even though he couldn't see him, he knew he was smiling.

"That good?"

"You know it," Sebastian said with a happy, relaxed sigh.

"It was absolutely my pleasure." Beau was flat-out grinning now. Sebastian could *feel* it. "And yours, too, apparently."

"Yeah." Sebastian's voice was rough. Both from the cock sucking he'd done, and also the unbelievable orgasm he'd just had. "Come up 'ere."

"Full of orders, aren't you?" Beau teased. But he rolled off Sebastian and crawled towards him, planting a kiss onto his cheek.

"Why don't we call them ideas?" Sebastian pointed out slyly as he wrapped an arm around Beau's shoulders and tugged him closer. "And it's not like you disliked the last one."

"True," Beau said.

For a long moment, they lay there.

Sebastian didn't know what Beau was thinking about, but it was something. He could practically hear his brain working in overtime.

"You know," he finally said, "the whole point of decompressing with an exceptional orgasm is to actually *decompress.*"

"Sorry," Beau said apologetically, turning towards Sebastian. "I just . . . I feel like it's my fault."

"It's your fault that Pax and the offense couldn't move the ball? You spend as much time with them as you spend with me, and that's a lot, because I'm there in your office all the time."

He was. And yes it was mostly for help on the change from corner to safety, but it was more than that too. He just plain *liked* Beau Dawson. Couldn't stay away from him. And it seemed the feeling might be mutual, considering where he'd come tonight when he'd been down.

"No," Beau said. He was silent for a long time. So long that Sebastian almost asked again, because he did genuinely want to know. And not just because Beau was currently in his bed, though that had at least something to do with it.

"I told him to take this job, you know?" Beau finally said in a rush, exhaling hard after. "My dad? I told him to do it."

"And now you think it's your fault that he's coaching a team that's started out the season with two losses and might have a lot more?" Sebastian remembered all the times he'd thought, *why did Asa Dawson compromise his reputation by leaving Tennessee and coming to the NFL?* Well, it turned out that answer was because his son had wanted him to.

"It *is* my fault," Beau said.

"No, it's not," Sebastian retorted, leaning on an elbow so he could look straight into Beau's eyes. "Yeah, you encouraged him.

But Asa Dawson isn't going to do anything that Asa Dawson doesn't want to do."

It was difficult to argue with that. After all, he was rather notorious for doing whatever the fuck he wanted.

"I worry that he took the job for me," Beau said. "To give me more opportunities."

"And if he did? He's a father who loves his son. There isn't anything wrong with that."

"You're being nice," Beau said, shooting Sebastian a look of frustration.

"No, I'm being honest," Sebastian retorted. "If you wanted me to be nice, you should've asked me *pre* orgasm."

Beau grinned at that, slapping him on the arm. "You suck."

"Actually, we *both* suck," Sebastian teased. "Come on, you know it's not your fault. And as depressing as that loss was—and it was really fucking depressing—the team's gettin' better. We aren't going to lose every game. You know that. If only because you and Coach Dawson wouldn't ever permit it to happen. You'll find a way to win. You always do."

Beau sighed. "That's true. And we will. Starting at six AM tomorrow."

"You're going to work at six AM?" Sebastian asked incredulously.

"Yep. Gonna do a play-by-play analysis. We did this sometimes at Tennessee, when things didn't work. Sometimes you need to look at the parts to see why the whole isn't working."

"Huh."

"I should . . ." Beau leaned over and began to tug out of Sebastian's grip. But he held firm. "I should get going. Get back to my own place. Get some sleep."

"Why can't you stay here?" Sebastian asked, before he could overthink it. Because he *wanted* Beau to stay. It had bothered him all week that the last time they'd done this, he'd essentially kicked Beau out, that Beau had kicked *himself* out.

He'd definitely been hesitant. Wary. Afraid. Maybe Beau had felt the same way.

Beau shot him a look. "Just because I have to get up at the ass crack of dawn doesn't mean you should, too."

"I don't care," Sebastian said bluntly.

Beau looked surprised by this. "Really?"

"Listen . . ." Sebastian sat up, deciding that if they were going to have this conversation, they were *really* going to have this conversation. Okay, he had no fucking clue *how* to have it, if he was being honest with himself, but at the very least, it seemed like a good place to start to take it seriously.

"I'm listening." Beau sounded concerned.

"I think we might be dating."

Beau's eyes widened at this statement. Sure, it had come out a little blunter than he'd imagined but . . . that didn't mean Sebastian hadn't meant it.

"We've never been on a date. We've fucked twice." Beau had obviously decided the best way to meet Sebastian's bluntness was with more of his own.

"Okay, I guess what I'm actually saying is that . . . I think we *should* date."

"You . . . you don't *do* that, though," Beau said slowly.

"Well, not publicly, no, but no, I guess not really ever. But I want to do this anyway. Even if we have to keep it under wraps. Because this . . ." Sebastian gestured between their still-naked bodies. "This is going to keep happening. And the last thing I want is for you to just come here for sex. Or for you to come here for sex when we lose."

"I didn't . . ."

Except he had. Twice. Sebastian was about to remind him of that fact when Beau snapped his mouth shut. "How do you know it's going to keep happening?" he asked instead.

"Because you light up when I touch you, and I light up when we're even in the same fucking room," Sebastian admitted. "That . . . that doesn't happen to me. But it happens to me with you. That's why I don't want to just fuck when we're sad and angry that we lost a game. I want to fuck when we're happy too. I want . . . I want to do more than just fuck."

"That's why I came here, though, because I can't be pissed off when we're in the same room," Beau protested. Sebastian would almost take Beau's protests personally, but he understood why Beau was pushing back on this.

It was a bad idea. Potentially catastrophic. But Sebastian wanted it anyway, and he was pretty sure Beau did too.

He just had such a big brain, always churning, always looking for different angles, and it would be bound to put up more than a token protest.

"Seeing me makes you happy?" Sebastian asked, raising an eyebrow.

"Yeah," Beau admitted. "Yeah, it really does. I don't know why, I don't get it, I can't . . ."

"You can't analyze it," Sebastian guessed.

Beau shook his head.

"I think you've just got to feel it," Sebastian said. Pressed a hand to Beau's chest. Felt his heart rate accelerate, even as his own did. That's what happened when they were together. It was natural.

It was maybe chemical. But it was something. "That's why we should go on a date."

"A real date?" Beau sounded unsure.

"A real date." Sebastian already knew where he wanted to take him.

Maybe it wouldn't be the fanciest date in the world, but it would still be a date.

Beau hesitated, but Sebastian already knew he would give in.

Because he wanted to, and because he couldn't stay away. Just the same as Sebastian couldn't stay away from him.

"Alright," he finally said. "We can go on a date. But . . . the moment this interferes with the team, or anything on the field . . . it ends."

"It won't," Sebastian promised. "I don't want it to, either. Your dad would probably gouge out my eyeballs or something."

Beau laughed. And just like that, Sebastian felt lighter—and happier—than he could remember.

Sebastian woke to his phone ringing.

Well, that wasn't technically true.

He'd woken up a few hours before, briefly and barely, as Beau had whispered his goodbyes and pressed a kiss to Sebastian's mouth, before slipping out into the pre-dawn.

But he'd fallen back asleep almost immediately after hearing the front door close, and he'd slept hard after, only waking up now to the obnoxious ringing of his phone.

Only one person had a ring like that—and he grabbed for the phone, picking it up on the fourth blast.

"Hi, Momma," he said, leaning back against the cream padded headboard.

"You haven't called in weeks," his mother, Chloe, said, her teasing voice just enough of a reprimand.

"But I *have* texted," Sebastian teased right back. "Not my fault that you're the worst texter in the world."

"I get busy, with dirty hands, and I forget, you know this," Chloe said. "But you could have always called me."

"Momma, it's the season, you know how it is."

"I sure do." She paused. Sebastian could picture her puttering around her little bungalow in Key Largo that he'd bought her with the money from his first NFL contract. No more long hard days at the bank and sneering customers, coming home with barely enough energy to keep up with an active, irrepressible boy, with none whatsoever to dedicate to her passion of hand-thrown pottery.

But now he could see her, standing at the sink in her kitchen with its bright turquoise walls, and he could even hear the light tinkling of the water, as she tried to scrub off the morning's clay from the pads of her fingers, from underneath her fingernails.

"You called because you're worried," Sebastian said, before she could say it.

It was always worse when she said it.

"I'm not *worried*. I know how you feel about winning, and I told you not to come back to Florida if you thought you wouldn't be winning. Money," she added reproachfully, "is not everything, Bastian."

"It's two games," Sebastian argued. "I've played for teams that've lost two games before."

Her silence was telling. She didn't think they could win any. That's why she'd called.

Screw the sports media; his mother, who'd spent endless Saturday mornings at practices and too many Friday nights in the stands at games, knew as much about football as they did.

Beau, Sebastian realized with surprise, would get along with Chloe like a house on fire. At least after she got over the fact that he might be making the same mistake she had. But he and Beau were different than Chloe and his father had been. His parents had never pretended to even like each other, not really.

Sebastian didn't know if that was the right path, though. Was that something you were supposed to do when you actually dated someone—introduce them to your parents?

Nathanial was off-limits. Sebastian hadn't even seen or heard from his father in ages, maybe even a decade, after the last time he'd told him to fuck off, that he'd be taking care of himself and his mother from here on out. But Chloe? She was an entirely different story.

If he was dating, she would want to know.

And she would absolutely want to meet Beau. But would Beau want to meet her?

Everything that had seemed very simple and straightforward last night when Beau was in his bed, suddenly, in the light of day, seemed more complicated.

"It's not as bad as you think it is," Sebastian said.

He could see her in his mind, tilting her head in front of the sink, a few of her braids escaping the crown of them, wrapped around her head, sliding across a bare, dark brown shoulder.

A queen who enjoyed sticking her hands into mud and clay more than anything else.

"If you have to tell me it's not so very bad, then it must be very bad," Chloe said sagely. "That new coach, he's not making trouble for you, is he? Because I can come up to Miami . . ."

Sebastian sighed and stopped her before she got a full head of steam. "Yes, he's from Tennessee, but he's not like that, Momma. I promise. He's not a racist asshole. Not by a long stretch. He's got plenty of respect for me."

"Does he know about you?"

Sebastian rolled his eyes. "You know nobody knows about me, Momma."

"You keep saying that, Bastian, but I'm telling you, people know."

"Why? Are you telling them?"

Chloe's silence was somehow more telling than even her words.

It was one of the things that he both loved and hated about his mother.

She knew him better than he knew himself.

"You don't have to hide for me," she said. "And not for him, either."

She barely ever used his father's name anymore. There was so much ugly history there, and regret, he couldn't exactly blame her.

He didn't like to say his father's name either.

"I'm not hiding for him."

Chloe hummed under her breath. They'd had this conversation enough times that he knew she didn't believe him. Not entirely.

"You're hiding *because* of him," she corrected gently.

"I am not." Sebastian wasn't; not anymore. He'd just gotten so used to hiding that it was second nature now. But he knew his mother, and knew she wouldn't be deflected. She was a force of nature, the way she battered at his arguments, at all his sensitive places that he would've preferred to keep hidden. So he dangled out the one thing that might grab her interest instead. "Actually," he said, "I'm dating someone, so that's hardly hiding."

"Oh, really," she teased. "Who is it? Some nice cute Cuban boy?"

"I . . . uh. . . no. He's actually . . . well, he's actually the coach's son."

She was silent. "You're dating the coach's son?"

"Yes." It was reckless. It was stupid. And she was going to tell him that. "Though I guess technically not *actually* dating, since the first date hasn't happened yet, but it *will*."

"You seem determined," Chloe said, her voice completely free of inflection. "You like this boy."

Sebastian dug his fingernails into his hand. He already knew what she was going to say. "Yes."

"You know all I want is for you to be happy," she said carefully, "but . . . he would be so different from you."

And unspoken in his mother's voice, he heard what she didn't say, *look how that turned out with me and your father. We hated each other, and then we fought over every inch of you for years. You nearly turned away from us, you were so angry about it.*

"Momma, it's just dating. We aren't getting married."

"I suppose . . ." Chloe sighed. He knew what else she wasn't saying. *It was just a few dates for me and your father, too, but then you came along, unexpectedly, and complicated everything.* But she didn't have to say the warning, because it wasn't like he was going to be accidentally impregnating Beau.

At least there was that.

"Don't worry, Momma, there won't be an unexpected blessing out of this."

"I know," she chided. "I just worry, that's all. But I *am* glad you've found someone. I worry you're so alone there, in that big penthouse, with all those windows and all that glass . . . it doesn't feel like a home. It feels like a freakin' crypt."

He wanted to tell her again that it was a good investment, but he knew it wouldn't matter. Chloe was endlessly pragmatic, but some things were more important to her than even common-sense business decisions, like the importance of family and home.

Even during the hardest of their years together, she'd always provided a cozy, comfortable home for them. It hadn't always been as full of family as she'd have wanted, because many of her relatives hadn't been able to forgive her for Sebastian. But eventually, she'd created a family for him out of friends. Distant relatives. Until there were a dozen people he could call and they'd show up on a moment's notice.

When Nathanial had tried to take him away from that home, she'd fought like a demon to keep him where she thought he belonged.

For a long time he'd resented that fight, but over time, he'd come to understand that in her way, she'd been trying to give him what she thought he'd needed.

"I'm sorry you don't like it, Momma."

"What does your boy think about it?" she asked archly.

Sebastian told himself that he shouldn't be surprised that she'd come back to Beau again. "His name's Beau, Momma," he said, "and I think he likes it."

"I bet your Beau likes that *you're* in it," she teased.

Sebastian laughed. "You're not wrong."

"I knew it," she said smugly. "I might be old, but I know how it is. How it *still* is."

She wasn't old at all; in fact, he knew she was still so beautiful that men frequently turned and stopped in their tracks, stunned by her as she walked by, completely aware but totally uninterested.

"You should come up for a game," Sebastian said. Specifically did not add anything about meeting Beau, because that was a fraught possibility that he was still on the fence about, but it *would* be good to see her.

"Y'all gonna win a game for me if I come all that way?"

"All that way? Momma, it's less than two hours."

"I'll think about it, I'm in the middle of a few important pieces," she said briskly. "Maybe if you can win a game or two first."

He knew she didn't give a rat's ass about the Piranhas winning games—she only cared because she knew *he* cared.

"I'll see what we can do," Sebastian said dryly.

"You also see that you take that boy of yours out on a nice date," she said.

"Don't worry, I know how to show him a good time."

"Sebastian Glenmore Howard!" she exclaimed.

"Not *that* kind of good time," he said hurriedly, though he supposed that was *also* true.

"Treat him like a gentleman," she warned.

"I promise, Momma."

"Good." He could see her nodding in approval. "I just want you to be happy, you know."

"I know," he said. "Love you."

"I love you, too," she said, after saying goodbye, leaving Sebastian thinking about what she'd said.

Despite everything that had happened, and how angry he'd been as a teenager, and then a young man, he'd never been able to believe that she didn't want him to be happy or didn't love him fiercely, desperately.

It was one of the reasons why she was still a part of his life, and his father wasn't.

Because his father hadn't wanted to own his half of him because he loved him and wanted the best for him, he'd wanted to stake his claim because Sebastian had his blood, the *Howard* blood, in his veins, and he considered that too valuable to waste.

Now his father couldn't possibly claim that Sebastian's existence was a waste, because he'd ended up rich and famous in his own right, but before? When he'd been a punk-ass kid, with a chip a mile long on his shoulder, with a mother whom Nathanial Howard wished would just go away?

That had been an entirely different story.

CHAPTER TEN

BEAU LEANED BACK IN his chair, rubbing his tired, gritty eyes, wishing that he wasn't still seeing the imprint of play after play running through his brain.

But after ten-plus hours of staring at the television monitor, analyzing every single goddamn play of the game, he knew he'd be seeing them in his dreams tonight.

"Well," his father drawled, the word lengthening under the weight of his Southern accent—always stronger when he was tired, "that was enlightening."

"Was it?" Beau couldn't help the retort that slipped out.

He wouldn't have said it in front of the other coaches, but they'd long since slunk off to their individual offices to try to process what they'd just seen. At least he *thought* he wouldn't have said it in front of them, but he was so goddamn tired, he didn't know for sure.

And that was only partly because they'd spent the last ten hours reviewing and analyzing and over-analyzing every play of the game. It was also because he hadn't gotten nearly enough sleep the night before.

That was all Sebastian's fault.

Asa glanced over at him. "You didn't think so?"

Beau looked at the pages and pages of notes he'd made. "I think it's easy to look at all this, and decide to change everything."

"You don't think we should."

"I think we just need one thing to bring the team together, to get them into unison. I don't know what the one thing is, but it's out there. Something to gel the offense. Something to gel the defense. Something to gel them both together, give the team an identity."

"Yeah," Asa said moodily, "special teams sure didn't lose this game."

He wasn't wrong. The two field goals they'd kicked had been spot on, and the coverage on both punts and kickoffs had been sufficient if not necessarily brilliant. At least, on top of fixing everything else, they seemed to have found a kicker they could count on. Trading away Vaughn for Dylan Leonard had been a good move, in the end.

"We lost the game as a team," Beau pointed out slowly. "What we need is to *win* as a team, too."

"Some changes seem obvious, though," Asa said, sorting through his own notes. "Get Rose and Howard on the same page. Try to get the ball out of Pax's hands faster. Coach him to take what we can get. Establish the running game, and then stick to it."

"Yeah, we're puttin' too much pressure on Pax," Beau agreed. "He's gonna blow up."

"I think so, too," his father said. "I'm gonna talk to him and Davis this week."

"You think . . ." Beau hesitated. He heard Tristan's teasing conspiracy theories running through his head, and it wasn't like he *believed* they were true, but maybe there was something there, after all. Something they could use. Or something they could fix. "You think Davis is doin' right by him?"

His dad looked up in surprise. "You don't like Davis?"

"You know I like Davis a lot," Beau said. "I'm worried Davis' experience has added extra pressure to Pax."

"Should we bring in someone else? Another assistant?"

Beau had been considering suggesting that very thing, thinking that maybe another voice in Pax's ear might not be a bad thing, but the moment his dad said it out loud, he reconsidered.

Davis was currently loyal to them, and loyal to Pax, because they'd treated him better than the rest of the NFL had. What if they did the same thing? Would it sour their relationship? Would it, even worse, sour his relationship with Paxton?

That was a risk they couldn't afford to take, not so early in the season.

"Naw," he said, "I think I'll just spend some more time with both of them. Give another viewpoint, sometimes."

His father nodded. "I trust you on this," he said. "You know people, Beau. You can see right in their heads, figure out how they think, and how they could think *better*."

Analysis of people and plays, and then strategic deployment of that analysis—that was why he was here in Miami, and why he knew various other teams around the NFL were paying more attention to him now than they ever had.

Everyone wanted to know if Beau was Asa Dawson's secret weapon.

He wasn't, not by a long shot. That was all Asa, who had, as far as Beau was concerned, one of the greatest football minds of a generation, but he'd learned at his father's feet. And it turned out that they were just different enough that Beau was usually useful to have around.

"I'll keep an eye on that situation," Beau promised. "But I think . . . I think Pax is gonna figure his shit out. He's a solid QB . . . if he can get out of his own way."

"Same as Davis was," Asa said with a heavy sigh. "I worried that they would be too similar, that they'd end up internalizing the same way, and we'd have a problem."

"You don't think . . ." Beau started to say it before he remembered that he was still in his father's office, and they weren't in their living room. His father was still wearing his coach hat; not his dad hat.

"What?" Asa asked when he hesitated. "What don't I think?"

"You don't think they're . . ." Beau could hear how stupid the question was in his own head, but he spit it out anyway. "You don't think they're involved, do you?"

"Paxton and Davis?" Asa laughed. "What gave you that crazy idea?"

Beau had been dumb enough to ask the question, so he wasn't going to throw Tristan under the bus for suggesting it in the first place.

"No reason, really, just a weird thought, probably 'cause I'm so fucking tired," Beau said.

"I'm runnin' a football team not a dating service," Asa said firmly. "Wade and Tristan, that's another story, 'cause they're both players, and they know to keep their relationship off the field. But Davis is a coach, he's got authority over Pax. He wouldn't cross that line. Especially with his past."

Beau nodded. He didn't necessarily disagree with his father, but he'd also been around football teams long enough to know that sometimes things happened even when they weren't supposed to.

"Well," he said, leveraging himself out of his chair with a groan, "I'm gonna go grab some dinner and start putting together some game plan suggestions."

He absolutely did not ask about what his father would think of him and Sebastian. He was not a coach, and he had no real authority over Sebastian, even though he was a player, just like Paxton was.

Davis held an official title. It was his *job* to get Paxton ready for each week of football. He had a place in the hierarchy.

And Beau? Well, he didn't. Not really. His official title was "Special Assistant to the Head Coach." Meaningless, really. Asa gave him all his power, but Asa could also take it all away.

But Beau didn't ask, because he didn't want to tip his father off, and also because *God*, it was so new, this thing between him and Sebastian. It might not work out. In fact, Beau was almost sort of counting on it, because Sebastian was successful and hot and confident, and Beau was . . . well, he was confident, too, just *less* confident than Sebastian, and he was absolutely less hot. So the chances of them going on more than a handful of dates were mediocre at best. Beau was already trying to prepare himself for the possibility that he might only get one.

But then, Sebastian had admitted that he didn't do this often.

Maybe it wouldn't fizzle out. Maybe it wouldn't end in disaster.

If it didn't, Beau thought as he walked down the hall towards his office, what the fuck were they going to do then?

His mother's warning echoing in his ears, Sebastian waited til it was almost five, because Beau had told him all about the undoubtedly lengthy meeting he'd be in all morning and probably into the afternoon, and then he'd texted Beau.

Dinner tonight?

Beau responded back almost immediately. **Normally sure, but it's been a long-ass day. Don't want to fall asleep on our first date. Wouldn't be a very good look.**

Sebastian considered this. He didn't want Beau to fall asleep on their first date either, but then . . . he also couldn't deny that he wanted to see the guy.

You just saw him this morning, as he was heading out the door, that voice reminded him dryly. *How desperate do you want to look?*

Normally, Sebastian *might* care how desperate he looked, but with Beau, things were different. *He* was different.

So instead of immediately suggesting a different day, Sebastian instead texted back: **You still at the office?**

Beau: **Unfortunately, yes.**

Sebastian: **IN your office?**

Beau: **I don't know where this is going, but yes. I was thinking about ordering some dinner, but that requires energy.**

Maybe he couldn't *see* Beau, not like he wanted to, but that didn't mean he couldn't do him a solid.

Sebastian: **Don't worry about it, I got you.**

He made a quick phone call, and then hung up, sending Beau one last text. **They'll be there in fifteen, don't leave your office.**

When Beau texted back, Sebastian could practically hear the trepidation in his voice even though there were only words on his screen. **Alright. I guess I'm trusting you.**

Sebastian was confident enough that he just sat back on his couch, the TV turned to ESPN, the sound low in the background, and waited.

Sure enough, thirteen minutes later, Beau texted him again. **This really great guy just brought me a HUGE (and I mean HUGE) Cuban sandwich. I took a bite and nearly cried, it's that good. THANK YOU.**

Sebastian couldn't help himself. He grinned and typed back. **You're very welcome. It was my favorite sandwich place, back when I was in college.**

Beau didn't reply back for a few minutes, but Sebastian figured he was eating and he couldn't be mad about that. The season was *long*, and Beau did so much work, til such crazy late hours, that he needed to keep his strength up.

Sebastian had never really worried about anyone before, but he found he was already starting to worry about Beau—and he didn't like it much. It made him feel . . . weird. Shaky inside. Unsure.

And those were not normal Sebastian Howard feelings.

Then Beau texted back, and the rush of *additional* feeling was also new and different, and yes, a little bit scary. But it also felt goddamn good. Made Sebastian feel like he was alive, and before this, he'd just been going through the motions for way too damn long.

Instead of texting, to Sebastian's surprise, Beau called him.

"Did you butt-dial me?" Sebastian asked when he clicked the accept button on his screen. "I thought all millennials hated talking on the phone."

Beau laughed, and there was that feeling again, rushing through him. Making him feel like he could run ten miles or bench-press an elephant.

He'd made Beau Dawson laugh, and if that was the only thing he accomplished this today . . . it was a good day.

"I'm actually heading back to my condo to hopefully fall asleep without seeing yesterday's game in my dreams," Beau said. "I dropped off the other half of that enormous sandwich in my dad's office. I hope he eats it."

Sebastian felt a frisson of unease worm its way through all those feel-good emotions. "Did you tell him I sent it?"

Beau laughed again. "I'm a millennial and now I'm also stupid," he teased. "I get it."

"That's a no, then."

"That's a no," Beau said. "Told him I ordered it from some place you recommended though." He hesitated, and Sebastian could practically hear his mind turning. "He works a lot. Too much. Doesn't eat unless I make him, which is why I dropped it off for him. That's . . . you're not mad, right?"

"Of course I'm not mad. It's a huge sandwich. I could eat a whole one back in college, and it'd last me all day, but now?" Sebastian chuckled. "I doubt I could finish it, either." He made a mental note that next time he sent Beau food—because he already knew this wouldn't be the last time he did it—he'd send some to Coach, too.

"I think you're saying that just to make me feel better, but I'll take it," Beau teased.

Beau wasn't entirely wrong.

But Sebastian wanted to do this right, goddamn it. Even though he didn't really know *how*.

A little bit of effort, he could hear his mom saying with that look of hers, with the arched brows and the pointed gaze, *is worth a hundred times doing it perfect and right*.

"Should I expect that we're gonna get our asses kicked tomorrow?"

Beau laughed. "Yeah, probably, a little."

"It's okay, I can take it."

"You sure about that? You think you can take it, and still take me out afterwards?" Beau asked.

"You want to go out tomorrow night?" Sebastian asked, surprised. He'd been just about to suggest it, but he hadn't been sure what Beau's schedule was. If he'd be spending the next seven days, sixteen hours a day, in his office.

"I think I can get away for a few hours," Beau said. "At least," he added in a teasing voice, "if you promise to feed me again like you did tonight."

"I can do that," Sebastian said. He heard a door opening and closing. "You home?"

"Yeah," Beau said, exhaling in a rush of breath. "Finally."

"Go get some sleep. I'll see you tomorrow?"

Beau yawned. "Yeah, I'm just about to drop. Just wanted . . . just wanted to talk to you before I did. And say thank you. So thanks . . . again."

"You're very welcome," Sebastian said quietly.

It occurred to him after Beau had hung up that maybe people didn't do nice things for him enough. That maybe he'd spent years being unseen, only viewed as an extension of his famous father.

Sebastian didn't know what that was like—his experiences with his father weren't much better, only different—but he resolved as he turned up the volume on the TV that he was going to make sure that Beau knew that one man not only saw him, but couldn't tear his eyes away.

It was just a date.

That was all.

A date.

You shouldn't be so nervous, Beau chided himself as he stared at the mirror in the staff locker room. He'd taken a shower and changed into jeans and then debated for the next five minutes what shirt he should wear. Sebastian hadn't said where he was taking him or what the dress code was. It would be someplace private, Beau knew that much, because while Beau might be out, Sebastian wasn't.

Does it matter if he's the only one who sees what you're wearing? Beau wondered.

But the truth hit him hard and fast—Sebastian was the *only* one who mattered. He could give a shit about anyone else.

With that in mind, Beau discarded the Piranhas polo shirt, his daily uniform, and instead grabbed a dark blue button-up, because it matched his eyes, leaving a few buttons undone and rolling up the sleeves in deference to the Miami heat.

He gave a half-hearted swipe through his messy dark hair, hoping he might be able to marshal it into some kind of order. But it was useless.

It's okay, Beau thought as he turned away from the mirror. *He knows what you look like. He's seen you naked—twice. And he still wants more.*

His phone, that he'd stuck in his back pocket, buzzed, and he grabbed it, checking the screen. **You ready?** Sebastian had texted. **I'll meet you at the south exit.**

Beau had worried a little that Sebastian would be ridiculously circumspect, insisting they meet in some private location before they went to some other private location, and he was relieved that Sebastian wasn't taking it *that* seriously. If anyone saw them meeting at the south exit, it wasn't like players and coaches didn't hang out all the time. Look at Pax and Davis—they spent ninety-nine point nine percent of their time together. And then there were all the players who ended up living together, like Logan and Dylan.

Don't overthink this. Don't be nervous. Don't worry. It's all gonna be fine, Beau thought, giving himself a last-minute pep talk as he headed towards the south exit.

And the moment he turned the corner and saw Sebastian standing by the double doors, one of those infectiously charming smiles blooming on his face the moment he spotted Beau, he knew it would be okay.

It was going to be better than okay.

"Hey," Sebastian said. "I drove and parked just over in the players' lot."

"Great," Beau said, walking through the door as Sebastian opened it for him.

As they walked to Sebastian's car, he didn't reach out and touch him—his hands were actually shoved in the pockets of his jeans and Beau theorized it was because he *wanted* to—but there was such a proprietary way he looked at Beau as they walked through the parking garage, his gaze returning to skim over him again and again, like he couldn't quite bring himself to look away. And Beau discovered that he didn't really mind that Sebastian couldn't reach out and take his hand right now, because the way he was looking at him? It was more romantic than any hand-holding that Beau had done—but then, that bar was embarrassingly low.

Nobody had ever tried to *romance* Beau before. He didn't know if that was what Sebastian was going for, but just the thought that he could, that he would *want* to, made Beau's heart beat a little bit faster.

The garage was still about half full of cars, but it was empty of people, and when they reached Sebastian's car, a low-slung Audi convertible, painted in oil-slick black, he opened Beau's door for him.

Nobody had ever done that for him either, and considering how protective Sebastian was over his privacy, Beau was surprised.

"I . . ." After settling into his own seat, Sebastian turned to Beau, the look in his honey-brown eyes sincere. "I know this won't be perfect. I know you're . . ." Sebastian cleared his throat. "It might not be a *public* date, but I want to do right by you."

"Listen," Beau said, reaching over and squeezing Sebastian's knee through his jeans, "it's fine. The fact that you give a shit about that, and nobody ever really has before, that means a whole fucking lot."

Sebastian's fingers drifted over Beau's, his thumb giving a slow, deliberate caress to the underside of Beau's wrist, making his heart and his pulse stutter. "I'd like to kick all their asses," he said softly. "For not treating you the way you deserve."

Beau wanted nothing more than to lean over and press a kiss to Sebastian's mouth. He'd known from the first moment they'd met that his lips were completely, utterly, painfully kissable, but now? Now that he knew how perfect they were, on his own, on his body, around his cock? It was nearly impossible to resist.

But at the last moment, before he leaned in that last final inch, Beau remembered they were still in the Piranhas players' parking lot. Anyone could walk by. Anyone could walk by, look into Sebastian's car and see them.

And while Beau was less worried about the fallout, he wasn't about to completely disregard Sebastian's perfectly legitimate concerns about keeping their relationship private.

"Let's go," Sebastian said, the edge of his voice rough, like he'd had the exact same thought process as Beau. For a wild half second, Beau almost expected him to drive them back to his building, and lead him up to his penthouse, and into bed.

God, he absolutely fucking wanted that. But he already knew how incredible and all-consuming sex with Sebastian was.

Now he was curious to know what a date with Sebastian Howard would look like.

Seemed Sebastian wanted to show him, because when he pulled out of the garage, he took them in the opposite direction of his building, deeper into the city of Miami.

While Sebastian drove, they talked about the day's practice.

"It wasn't nearly as tough as I'd been expecting," Sebastian said, sounding surprised.

"You *did* catch the interception that gave the offense a chance to win the game," Beau reminded him. "The problem isn't with the defense."

"Not entirely," Sebastian argued. "But we're still not on the same page. Not like we should be."

Beau shouldn't have been shocked that Sebastian had noticed the disconnect—after all, he'd played in the NFL for almost ten years now. He knew what good teams, teams with good rhythm and pacing and communication, felt like. And he'd know the opposite, too.

"I'm," Sebastian continued, "going to work more with Rose this week."

"You like him?"

"Like him? Let's say I'm willing to help him. That's as far as we're going." Sebastian threw him a hot look, as he pulled them into a strip mall parking lot. Beau was flustered enough from the way that look reminded him of every single time Sebastian had stared at him before kissing him that it took him a second to register where they'd parked.

"This is . . ." Beau trailed off. Should he lie and say it looked nice? It looked like a freaking strip mall. Suddenly, he was wishing he'd thrown on a t-shirt. Now he was going to look painfully overdressed.

Maybe he'd overestimated this whole thing.

Maybe this wasn't really a date. It was just . . . what? A meal before sex?

Beau ordered himself not to feel disappointed, but it was hard.

"Just trust me," Sebastian said as they climbed out of the car. "I know it doesn't look like much, but this is my favorite place in Miami. Better than any rooftop bar or ridiculously expensive steakhouse or even some of those seafood places down by the water."

"Okay," Beau said, as Sebastian led him towards one of the more unassuming storefronts. "Sushi?" he asked as Sebastian opened the door.

"Yeah, I hope that's okay? I realize I didn't ask . . ." Sebastian trailed off, looking suddenly just as nervous as Beau had felt in the locker room.

"It's better than okay," Beau said. "Sushi is my favorite, and we didn't get nearly enough of the good stuff in Knoxville."

"Well," Sebastian said, suddenly grinning as they ventured into the darkened restaurant, "prepare to be amazed."

A tall Asian man, with bleached blond tips on his long, feathered hair, turned towards them, and when he saw Sebastian, his smile widened even further. "You're back already," he said, and to Beau's surprise, the two men embraced. "And you brought another friend."

"Yeah, you got a dark corner we could hang out in?" Sebastian asked.

The man nodded. "Of course, of course, I've got you." He showed them to a spot, nice and private, in one corner of the restaurant.

"Sake, and an order of those amazing spicy dumplings," Sebastian ordered as they sat, and then looked over at Beau. "What about for you? You want sake or something else?"

"White wine? Something dry, maybe?" Beau asked.

The man nodded, and a second later he was gone.

"You know him," Beau guessed as Sebastian leaned back in his chair.

"Yeah, Akio and I go way back, back to when I was in college. I came here all the time. Even worked here for a little bit."

"You worked . . . *here*?"

Sebastian grinned. "You sound surprised. You should know better than to assume that every badass football player grew up with a silver spoon in their mouth. Sure, we had scholarships, but we still had to eat. Still needed rent money."

"I should have," Beau admitted. But he hadn't wanted to ask. Because Sebastian had been so sensitive about his past and his family, the last time it had come up. Sebastian had volunteered a bit more information when he'd apologized, a few days later, but Beau was still wary of saying the wrong thing or asking the wrong question.

"Yeah," Sebastian said, and then hesitated, like he wasn't sure if he should say more, but then he plunged ahead anyway. "I told my father to fuck off a little too soon, needed a bit of cash to get me through to the draft, and Akio was happy to help out. I was a fucking terrible waiter, but he didn't mind. Probably because I knew the menu better than he did."

"You came here that much?"

"It's cheap and it's good. That's one thing you can rely on football players finding out—not only the most efficient way to get us fed, but the *best* way to fill us up."

Beau nodded, hesitating. What he wanted to ask was why he'd told his father to fuck off, but that felt potentially dangerous, and not exactly the kind of thing you talked about on a date. Instead he shared his own experience. "There was a diner in Knox that the players liked to go to. Huge plates of food. Cheap, filling, and also happened to be the best breakfast I've ever had."

Sebastian nodded, toying with the paper wrapped around the chopsticks.

"You probably," Sebastian said with a somewhat resigned sigh, "want to know why I told my father to fuck off."

"I mean, sure, yeah, I'm curious," Beau admitted, "but if you don't want to talk about it . . ."

"My parents went out on exactly two dates. That's how long it took my dad to get under my mom's skirt." Sebastian recited this emotionlessly. "And then I showed up, unexpectedly, nine months later. They weren't married. They didn't even *like* each other. Probably because they were so fucking different. My mom . . . she fought for me, because she loved me. He just fought for me because he thought I was a thing he should have possession of." Sebastian's mouth curved into a wry smile. "Last semester of college, he showed up and tried to take fucking credit for everything. For me. For my success. For how high they kept saying I'd be taken in the draft. For everything. And I punched him in the face and told him to fuck off."

Beau supposed he should be surprised. Sebastian had told the bare bones of this story before, when he'd apologized about not wanting to talk about his family. But he'd shared more now, even though he clearly didn't like doing it, and Beau felt the weight of his confession settling onto him.

Maybe this wasn't the kind of thing you normally shared on a first date, but it was the kind of thing you shared with someone you cared about—with someone you thought you could *really* care about, someone you thought you might have a future with—and Beau realized, his heartbeat accelerating, that Sebastian might actually feel about him the same way Beau felt about Sebastian.

They were in the private corner, nearly hidden away from the rest of the restaurant, so Beau didn't hesitate, he reached out and slipped his fingers into Sebastian's hand, squeezing it. "That must've really sucked, growing up like that."

"It did, sometimes. And other times, I was fine. It wasn't . . ." Sebastian took a deep breath. "A lot of other people had it a lot worse."

"Doesn't mean I can't be sorry," Beau said gently and Sebastian smiled.

"I'm sure you get really tired of people defining you by either your dad or your sexuality," Sebastian said. "Or *both*."

"Both," Beau said wryly. "Especially the people who try to be all sympathetic and understanding, and inform me that I don't have to keep trying to win his approval just because I'm gay."

Sebastian's jaw dropped. "People say that to you?"

"Not a lot, and less now, but yeah. It's happened." Beau had wanted to punch *them* in the face, but that was much harder to do when someone was *trying* to empathize, even when they were doing it in the worst possible way. "They just never expect that I work in football because I love it."

"And that you're good at it?" Sebastian raised an eyebrow. "'Cause you are. You're like . . . absolutely fucking brilliant, you know? I can think of a dozen times you pointed out something in a game plan or on film that I used in the game. I'd never have found any of that on my own."

"Thanks." Beau shrugged awkwardly. "But it's just what I do. It's what I'm good at."

"You're fucking amazing at it," Sebastian said, squeezing his fingers. "I just hope this is okay."

Beau was touched that he'd be so concerned. "The place looks great and I'm excited to try the food," he said.

Sebastian shook his head and his expression turned pained. "That we're out together. You're white and I'm, well . . . well, I'm not."

Beau stared at him. Shocked. "You think I give a shit about that?"

"No, not really, but . . ." Sebastian laughed, humorlessly. "I thought I should ask."

"Like you'd be good enough to fuck, but not to date?" Beau shook his head emphatically. "No. A thousand times no. No, it does not bother me. Not in the least. I do not give a crap. It wouldn't matter if you were alien and had blue skin, okay?"

Sebastian nodded, looking relieved, and to Beau's surprise, seemed to relax a little more. Like that had been a question that had been bothering him, and he hadn't been able to keep it in anymore.

When Akio arrived with their drinks, Sebastian didn't tug his hand away, even though Beau let go so he could. So clearly Akio was a good enough friend that he knew the truth.

Akio dropped off their drinks, and their appetizer, and Sebastian let go of his hand, stripping his chopsticks of their paper coating, flicking them apart with an expert motion.

Beau was slightly less competent with his own chopsticks but he still managed to scoop up one of the dumplings, and as he chewed it, he understood exactly why Sebastian had wanted to bring them here.

"Incredible, right?" Sebastian said, grinning at him as he swallowed.

"Seriously incredible."

"And yeah," Sebastian said casually, like he didn't want to make a big deal out of it. "Akio knows about me."

"But not many people do."

Sebastian shrugged noncommittally. And Beau realized that this was going to be the second conversation that they probably shouldn't be having on their first date—and instead, he changed the subject. They could talk about more than just football and their personal issues, right?

Because if they couldn't, Beau wasn't sure where this was going.

He loved football, of course—he wouldn't do what he was doing if he didn't—but while he'd always imagined having a partner who both supported and gave a shit about football, he wasn't stupid enough to think that was all they should have in common.

"So, what's your favorite kind of roll?" Beau asked. Sushi. It wasn't much in common, but it was *something*.

Sebastian glanced over at him, the corner of his mouth quirking into a grin. "Are you changing the subject?"

"Might be?" Beau confessed, taking a sip of his wine. It was good, much better than he'd imagine getting at some strip mall sushi joint.

But then, not much about this evening had gone as he'd expected.

Sebastian leaned forward, forearms resting on the table. Beau had to force himself to focus on the man, on his magnetic gaze, and *not* on the rippling muscles of those forearms. Sebastian Howard was really fucking gorgeous, and he tugged at every single bit of Beau. Even the parts that screamed loudly that he might be a crazy stupid risk.

"You don't like that I'm not out, not like you," Sebastian said flatly.

"Actually, no, I don't care about that," Beau said, surprised, though if he thought about it, was Sebastian's concern really that much of a shock?

"Even though you've done all this before?" Sebastian waved in his general direction. "And I haven't."

"I'm not . . . you don't have to do anything you're not ready for. I'm not sure *I* was ready when I came out," Beau said. "I don't mind doing what we're doing. This is your timetable, not mine."

"And if the timetable doesn't exist?" Sebastian asked, arching an eyebrow.

But Beau wasn't going to fall for that. He knew him well enough now to know when Sebastian was testing him. Sebastian Howard was driven to the point of obsession and honest to a fault. Maybe he wouldn't come out while he was actively playing, but that didn't mean he intended to hide forever.

Someone like Sebastian would never want that.

"It exists," Beau said firmly. "And it's yours, and yours alone, okay?"

"You really mean that. You're not . . . you really don't give a shit."

Sebastian had been bluntly honest enough that Beau told himself that he could meet him there. "I just want you," he said. "However that works."

"And *that's* something we have in common, not just what our favorite sushi rolls are," Sebastian said, grinning.

"Hey," Beau said, grinning right back, "I was *trying* to stay on best 'first date' behavior."

"I don't give a fuck about that. I just want you, too," Sebastian said.

And Beau realized at that moment that not only did Sebastian's gorgeous looks take his breath away, but his gorgeous *brain* did the exact same damn thing.

He was fucking breathtaking, inside and out.

Chapter Eleven

Sebastian never liked it when he wasn't on the field for the most important play of the game. He knew it wasn't always defensive—it hadn't been defensive the week before, when he'd intercepted the Texans' ball and then Pax and the offense hadn't done anything with it, ultimately losing the game on a Hail Mary pass that hadn't gone anywhere—but that didn't mean that Sebastian didn't hate it.

He wanted to be on the field, he wanted to be making the plays, he wanted to be the force that pushed his team towards victory. Standing on the sidelines, watching as other players took their shot at glory, had always been hard, and it had never gotten any easier for him.

It was definitely not easier now, especially not with the memories of last week's game and its completely unsuccessful drive running through his head as he watched Pax and the rest of the offense take the field.

"You shouldn't look so worried."

Sebastian glanced over and saw that Beau had appeared next to him.

"I don't look worried," Sebastian claimed.

Beau shot him a fond, amused look. "You look like you're gonna vomit," he said. "And you look just about how I feel. If we lose again . . ."

"Don't even say the word," Sebastian nearly yelped in panic. "You're gonna . . ."

Beau raised an eyebrow. "I'm gonna? Were you saying I was going to *curse* us? God, Howard, you are a superstitious football player after all."

Sebastian glowered, even though it was tough to maintain that particular expression. That *friendly* kind of expression. Because every time he saw Beau, every time they talked, every time they were even in the same goddamned room, he wanted to grin like a lunatic. He wanted to touch him. He wanted to kiss him. He wanted to do a hell of a lot more with him.

He was so happy, but he had to keep it locked down tight, or else it was going to escape in giggly bubbles right out of him, and *someone* was going to question his permanent heart eyes.

And probably that someone was going to be Asa Dawson.

"I'm a football player, aren't I?" he grumbled. "We're all fucking superstitious."

Beau nodded thoughtfully, his eyes on the field as the ref blew his whistle, getting positioned for the first play of the drive.

"You think Pax can do this?" Sebastian asked. He knew what he wanted to believe. He knew what he wanted Beau to tell him.

It was weird being so goddamn happy every time he was with Beau, and yet so goddamned stressed, each and every time he walked into the Piranhas' facility. The second loss had hit the team hard, and even though they were rallying, as best as they could, there was an undercurrent of fear everywhere. Sebastian could practically taste the question in the air, between every speech that every coach made, between every rep in the weight room, between every greeting the players made to each other.

What if we suck so much we lose every single fucking game?

It was unlikely, because it wasn't like they didn't have talent, and it was *hard* to lose every game of an NFL season, but the possibility lingered, the monkey on their back, still hanging on for dear life.

"Oh, he can do it," Beau said confidently.

But Sebastian was learning him better, from late nights in his bed, and the two late-night dinners they'd squeezed in since their first date, and he could recognize the worry in his eyes now.

He was thinking the exact same thing as everyone else.

What if we lose every game?

And while that would be horrible and awful for Sebastian, it wouldn't destroy his career, not the way it might torpedo Beau's.

"He's gonna do it," Sebastian said, wishing he could strip his gloves off and reach down and grip Beau's hand. Squeeze it reassuringly.

They watched as Pax threw a quick out to Tristan, and with his speed and agility, he made the most of it, dodging around two defenders, sprinting right past the corner for a solid thirty-yard gain.

"Better blocking that play," Beau muttered as he glanced down at the tablet in his hands.

"Logan pulled well," Sebastian agreed.

"The line is finally gelling," Beau said, eyes narrowing as he gazed out at the field, waiting for the next play. They had a minute and a half to go another forty-five yards, til Dylan was in field goal range. It wasn't impossible, but then they should've been able to score on the final drive in the last game, too.

Just because it could be done, it *should* be done, didn't mean that it happened.

"I know you've put in a lot of hours with them this week," Sebastian said, dropping his voice down, until he was sure that only he and Beau could hear. "*Long* hours, where you could've been doing a lot of other, much, *much*, more fun things."

Beau chuckled. "Yeah, I know. I missed doing them, too. But if we win this game . . ."

Sebastian understood. It was part of why he was beginning to see why they fit together like two puzzle pieces, despite all their differences.

He didn't resent Beau working hard, because he worked really hard, too. But when they came together, and work finally took a back seat . . .

Sebastian yanked his attention back to the game. He did not need to be thinking about what he and Beau were going to do tonight, and hopefully tomorrow, when they finally had a few precious hours to themselves.

When nobody else was trying to steal his guy's attention away.

"We're gonna win this game," Sebastian said, trying to find the confidence. He looked down the sideline, at where Dylan had cloistered himself towards the end zone, warming up, kicking the ball into a small net. "He's solid. Rock solid. Pax just has to get us into position."

Beau nodded in agreement. "I just . . ." He suddenly grinned, turning to Sebastian, and there were the heart eyes, in *his* face. "Is it wrong that I want us to fuck when we aren't both pissed off about the team losing?"

Sebastian laughed. "No, no, I'd love to fuck in celebration for once. Would be nice."

"Exactly," Beau said with a chuckle.

"Well, Pax better get on that," Sebastian said.

They hadn't discussed telling anyone; but Sebastian already knew that eventually they would. He didn't want to keep their relationship a secret from his teammates, and especially from teammates he considered friends.

Guys like Tristan and Wade and Dylan and Logan. Maybe even Pax. Yeah, some of them knew he and Beau had slept together, but they didn't know it was so much more than just sex.

But first, they needed to win this goddamn game.

Pax's next pass dropped to the turf, just out of the range of Johnson's hands.

"Damnit," Beau hissed.

"It's fine, it's fine," Sebastian said, more for himself than for Beau.

But instead of looking increasingly frantic like he had in last week's game, when passes hadn't been caught, and they hadn't been moving the ball, Pax still looked calm and confident as he set the offense for the next play.

Out of the corner of his eye, Sebastian could see Davis pacing on the other end of the sideline, arms flapping as he called into Pax's headset in his helmet.

"I think he wants this as much as Pax does," Beau said, following Sebastian's gaze.

"No, no way, nobody wants it as bad as Pax," Sebastian said softly, remembering Pax's face before last week's press conference.

And like he was proving Sebastian right, the ball snapped into Pax's hands, he dropped back, and he threw a gorgeous dime, right into Wade's hands. He stiff-armed the corner trying to cover him, sending him to the turf. Wade turned up field and got the first down, and even a little more, fighting with his big, strong body for every single inch.

"Yes!"

They both turned to see Davis punch the air in celebration, a wild grin on his face as Pax called the Piranhas' second to last timeout.

"Just . . ." Sebastian checked the first down marker as they reset the field. "Thirty-five yards to go?"

"Doable," Beau agreed with a nod. "I'm gonna . . ." He gestured to where Coach, Davis, and some of the players were milling around near the sideline, putting the final touches on the last few plays before the game ended and hopefully they won.

"Sure," Sebastian said, even though he didn't really *want* him to go. He didn't want to watch the rest of this alone—it was nerve-wracking and made him unbearably anxious, mostly because he couldn't be on the field, directly impacting the play—but he understood that Beau had a job to do.

And that he was damn good at it.

So he was left to watch, as the timeout ticked to an end, and the offense took the field again.

To Sebastian's shock—and apparently the defense's too—the first play the Piranhas ran was a running play. And because nobody had expected it, Kenyon got a solid twenty-yard run in.

The offense ran up to the line, wanting to save the last timeout for—*hopefully*—Dylan's field goal attempt, and they ran another play, Pax dropping back and letting the ball fly, right into Tristan's hands.

He'd clearly been working with Kenyon, because he did a nice spin move, danced around another defender, and with only thirty-five seconds left on the clock, went down five yards into Dylan's field goal range.

The sideline as a whole erupted into a savage cheer. They could taste the victory, it was that damn close.

Dylan just had to nail the kick, and they'd win, *finally*.

Coach called the last timeout, and as Dylan jogged onto the field, Sebastian glanced over to see Micah Rose walking up to him.

They hadn't talked much—except nuts and bolts of football. When they were on the field together, he'd occasionally offer suggestions, but Sebastian hadn't spent the time with him that he knew he should.

Rose had talent. It was raw and unformed, but it was there.

"I hate this part," Micah said.

Sebastian nodded in agreement. "Not being on the field for the most important play of the game? Yeah, it fucking sucks."

"I never even want to watch," Micah added. "But I know that doesn't look good."

"We're a team."

Micah shot him a sideways look. "Are we though?"

"We're goddamn tryin' to be," Sebastian said.

"Maybe if we win . . ." Micah trailed off.

But Sebastian shook his head emphatically. "A team's not about winning. A team's about having each other's backs. About giving a shit about each other. And . . ." Ugh, it hurt to admit this. "We need to spend more time in practice together. Not just the team. You and I."

Micah raised a black eyebrow. "Really?"

"You want to learn to be better, or not?"

Micah considered him for a long moment. "Yeah," he finally said, right as the final timeout drew to a close, "yeah, I guess I do."

"Good," Sebastian said with a nod. "Then we'll make it happen."

"I still," Micah added with a quick smile, "really want to win this fucking game."

"God, don't we all," Sebastian said with a commiserating grin.

"Couple of the guys were talkin' about going out, either win or lose, but man, it's gonna be a party if we win," Micah said.

Sebastian watched as Dylan lined up, his form calm and ready, his face expressionless, totally wiped of any emotion.

He knew enough about kicking to know that you had to approach every single kick the exact same way, like they all meant the same thing.

But Dylan had to know, deep down, that this one meant more.

The ref blew the whistle and Sebastian's heart lodged in his throat as the ball snapped to Zach, the holder, and then Dylan nailed it, right through the uprights.

"Yes!" he yelled out, punching the air with his fist as he and the rest of the team swept onto the field, surrounding Dylan, every single player wanting to revel in the moment.

They'd fucking done it.

Finally.

"This ball could go to the entire team," Coach said, holding it up in his hand, sending a cheer through the entire locker room. "Y'all all worked so goddamn hard. The defense put us in a position to win. I can think of a half dozen players who played their asses off, keeping a powerhouse of an offense off the field, and giving our own offense a chance to score and win. And score we did, Dylan nailed the hell out of that kick, like nothing was on the line, when everything was. But Pax, he's our guy, our quarterback, and he led us today. This ball has to go to him."

He tossed it towards Pax, who caught it neatly, staring at it like he could barely even believe it.

As he flicked the ball from one hand to another, a hush settled over the locker room. Sebastian had played for three other quarterbacks, but never a rookie as raw as Pax. Never for a quarterback who was learning on the fly, discovering how to be a leader one game at a time.

Pax was—but he wasn't alone, either.

It seemed that Paxton understood that, because he turned to Davis, who was hovering slightly behind him, pride shining in his eyes.

"I can't tell you what this win means," Paxton said, "or what your belief in me means. I'm gonna make sure it's never misplaced. I'm gonna lead this team, and I'm gonna lead us to a place that nobody ever thought we could go. But I thought it, and . . ." He hesitated, glancing behind him, and Sebastian felt his breath catch, because there was something in Pax's gaze when he looked at Davis, and it was there, too, in the way Davis gazed back at him.

"I couldn't have done it without my right-hand guy," Pax said, gesturing towards Davis. "He keeps me calm. He keeps me focused on what's really important, and most importantly, he's a friend and he's a support at the best moments and during the worst."

Davis smiled back, and fist-bumped Pax, another cheer going through the crowd of players in the locker room. But there was something in the way his eyes still lingered on Pax that made Sebastian do a double take.

Well, shit, Sebastian thought, because that was only going to be misery and ugliness for those two. Players didn't date coaches, even secretly. They just didn't do it at all, because it was a terrible conflict of interest. A little less for those two, because Sebastian knew that Davis had less power than most coaches, but still . . . the heart would want what it would want. No matter what was wise or safe or appropriate.

If Beau had really been a coach, Sebastian didn't know what he'd have done.

They'd been so drawn together, it had been impossible to resist the irresistible.

But Davis would know better. He'd been through too much to do anything else. He'd keep his feelings—and his hands—to himself, but Sebastian couldn't help but pity the pair of them. He'd really believed that Tristan was talking out of his ass when he'd suggested the possibility, but maybe now Sebastian wished that he had been. Because this would suck.

Maybe he'd have never noticed if he wasn't knee-deep in the honeymoon period himself. Maybe that's why Tristan had noticed, because he was seemingly permanently stuck in heart-eyes mode with Wade. But Sebastian hoped that nobody else would put two and two together and get four.

"You're quiet."

Sebastian glanced up to see Wade standing in front of him. He'd already showered and dressed, but Sebastian was only half done, a towel wrapped around his waist.

Sebastian wasn't sure what to say . . . he *was* goddamned thrilled. Nothing could take away from that.

But he was also tired, even though the season was just beginning. He'd put so much of himself out there on the field today, hoping that it might be enough to tip the balance and get them a W.

It had been, but now as he pulled on a shirt, he wondered if he'd given too much.

"A bunch of us are going out," Wade said, gesturing to where Tristan and Pax and a handful of others were standing. Dylan. Logan. And Beau. "We gotta celebrate this historic win."

"Historic?" Sebastian raised an eyebrow. "We only lost two games in a row. That's it. *Two*." Yeah, it had felt like a hundred, but two losses wasn't the end of the world, at least now that they'd gotten that first amazing win.

"Yeah." Wade grinned. "But it's *my* first NFL victory. Same for Tristan. We gotta mark it somehow."

"First of many, I'm sure," Sebastian retorted dryly.

He'd been hoping that he and Beau could slip out to his condo, maybe order some food in, have their own kind of very private celebration, but if he tried to pry Beau away now, the rest of the guys might suspect that the thing with him hadn't been just a one-night thing.

He was definitely not ready to tell them yet.

It was still too new. And he hadn't figured out what the hell he was going to do about Coach.

"So, you comin' or not?" Wade wondered. "It's not gonna be a real celebration without the Sea Bass there."

Sebastian rolled his eyes. He already knew what he was going to say. He'd been toast the moment he'd seen Beau standing with the other guys.

"Sure," he said. "I'm good for a few rounds, at least."

Wade grinned. "Awesome."

He finished dressing and then wandered over to where they all stood, near the door out of the room, chattering excitedly. About the win, about the night to come, where they should start, and where they should go next.

"We're going to Hibiscus," Sebastian announced. "That's the only place to go tonight."

Tristan raised an eyebrow. "That old place?"

He wasn't wrong; it *had* been around for awhile, but Sebastian had always liked it. It wasn't new and wild, and maybe that was part of its attraction.

"They've got a new rooftop bar," Sebastian said. "Just opened. The manager keeps going through my agent, trying to get me to show up. Make a splash."

"Oh, we're gonna make a splash," Tristan said, rubbing his hands together.

"I thought Hibiscus was old and overrated," Sebastian teased him.

Tristan rolled his eyes. "For you, Sea Bass, I'll even get excited about Hibiscus."

"Then it's settled," Sebastian said, turning away for a moment. He made a quick phone call and then sent a text.

"We've got two cars coming," Sebastian said when he turned back to the group. "Nobody's gonna get a DUI on my watch."

He'd also texted Alec to let the club manager know they'd be arriving, and they were just heading as a group to the parking lot where the cars were set to pick them up when his phone buzzed.

As he read the message, Sebastian could nearly hear Alec's dry-as-hell delivery.

He's beside himself with happiness. You're going to make his whole night. PS: congrats on the win.

Sebastian smiled and tucked his phone back into his pocket.

Trying to be casual, he sidled up next to where Beau was walking, hoping that if they were together now, they might get to ride over to the club together.

"Great win," Sebastian said with a grin, swinging his hand with just enough force that it bumped against Beau's upper thigh.

"Great *team* win," Beau replied, his smile just as bright.

"Does it feel good to have your first NFL win under your belt?" Sebastian asked.

"First of many," Beau vowed. "I tried to convince my dad to take the night off, but he's so excited and energized, I bet he doesn't leave his office again until tomorrow morning."

"Does he do that all the time?" Sebastian asked.

Beau shrugged. "Too much," was all he would say about it. "But at least this time it's because he's happy and already planning for the next win, and it's not because he's angry we lost again."

Sebastian nodded in agreement, but secretly he wondered if that really mattered, if the end result was the exact same.

"Glad you got out of there, at least," Sebastian said, bumping him again with his fingers, letting them linger for a split second, hoping that the others were too busy chatting to notice.

"I wouldn't have missed this," Beau said, gazing up at him as they came to a stop next to two large black SUVS.

"See," Sebastian said, dropping his voice down, so nobody else could hear, "I was hopin' for more of a private kind of celebration. Just you and me."

"That," Beau said, beaming with his own version of the heart-eyes that Sebastian was despairing of ever hiding, "is an excellent plan for the end of the evening."

"Last stop of the night, my place?" Sebastian suggested softly.

Beau nodded. "And I don't have to be in until noon tomorrow . . . the joys of actually winning a game. So maybe even a late brunch?"

Sebastian leaned in, smelling a whiff of Beau's soap along his neck. It wasn't anything special, but it made him hot anyway. Everything about Beau did. "As long as it's in bed," he said in a low voice. "You can have anything you want."

Beau's eyes widened, pupils blowing out, and Sebastian suddenly wasn't sure they'd even make it to the last stop of the night.

But then Tristan yelped with excitement, telling them to get a move on, he was ready for the dance floor, and everyone laughed.

"Come on," Sebastian said, pulling the door open on the second SUV and beckoning Beau in—absolutely not staring at his ass in those tight jeans as he climbed in. "We better get going or else Tristan is gonna start a nightclub right here."

"Don't tempt me!" Tristan called back.

Beau had been out to clubs and parties with players before—he was often their age or even younger than them, and so he often got invited. But he'd never been out with Sebastian before, and it was an entirely different experience, sweeping into a club at the right hand of Sebastian Howard. He led the group, Pax and Tristan and Wade behind him, Dylan and Logan and Davis bringing up the rear.

It was a good group, and they were all in good moods, though Beau had sensed that Sebastian hadn't initially been a fan of going out tonight.

But he'd ended up planning the entire thing, and so far it had run like clockwork.

The manager met them at the door, clearly looking thrilled that Sebastian and a whole group of Piranhas players had just arrived at his club.

"Welcome to Hibiscus," he said, and led them upstairs, to a private area, right at the edge of the dance floor, to the left of a waterfall feature, lights from Miami Beach sparkling around them in the darkness.

Tristan and Wade immediately left for the dance floor, dragging Dylan with them. Logan settled down on one of the low couches, with Sebastian next to him, and Beau watched as Davis and Pax walked over to one of the bars.

"This place is great," Beau said, taking a seat on Sebastian's empty side. He hoped it wasn't too obvious. But Sebastian apparently didn't give a crap how obvious it was, because he slung an arm across the back of the couch, not technically touching Beau's back, but the proprietary look on his face told the whole story.

"Yeah, seems like you're really enjoying it," Logan teased.

He glanced over at Sebastian. "They might have . . . guessed that we hooked up," Sebastian finally admitted. He looked almost apologetic.

"Yeah, except that he said it was a one-time thing, and clearly . . . it's not that way at all," Logan said.

Maybe Beau should have been angry that Sebastian had told some people, but he wasn't the one who felt like their relationship had to be some kind of state secret. It didn't bother him at all that Sebastian hadn't kept it a secret. Of course he'd said it was a one-night thing . . . and they both knew better.

But at one point, that's what it had been.

Until they couldn't help themselves.

"It might've started as a hookup, but it's more than that now," Beau admitted. He glanced over at Sebastian, who looked both nervous and pleased. "We're figurin' it all out."

"Happy for you two," Logan said. He reached over and fished a beer out of the cooler built into the central table they were sitting around. "Cheers," he said, flicking off the cap with an expert motion and tipping it in their direction. "I'm glad you're not letting the rookies take all that sweet romance for themselves."

"What about you?" Beau wondered, grabbing a beer for himself. He glanced over at Sebastian, who nodded, and he picked up a second one for his guy.

"What about me?" Logan said wryly. "Relationships suck, not that I think I'm supposed to be telling y'all that."

"They're hard, if you're not out," Sebastian said softly.

"Can be," Logan agreed. "Though at least here is better than in Minnesota. Couldn't have even gone out like this there. They're locked down tight, afraid of anything changing. Afraid of alienating any of their fan base."

"Are they that close-minded?" Sebastian asked. "In Arizona, they didn't seem to care either way. I wasn't the only queer guy in the locker room, and a few of them—Henry, Andreson, and God, what was that guy's name?—just did whatever the fuck they wanted. It wasn't for me, not back then, but I knew it was at least a possibility, if I wanted it to be."

"What stopped you?" Logan wondered.

"Timing," Sebastian admitted with a shrug, "and the idea of having my private life dissected for the public eye always made me feel a bit queasy."

Beau had never asked why he'd stayed in the closet. But he was glad Logan had asked—because for him, it wasn't such a loaded question. But Beau wasn't particularly surprised by the answer Sebastian had given. He was an intensely private guy, who clearly didn't like how a lot of fans thought they *owned* a piece of an NFL player.

"You," Logan said, glancing over at Beau, "lived in the South. You know how it is."

Beau considered this for a moment. Had it been hard? At times, yes. Right after he'd come out at seventeen, when the news had raced through the collegiate and professional football worlds like wildfire, so many people who thought they'd known how his father was, because of his accent, and where he'd lived his life, had believed they'd known how he would react.

What they had never realized was that Asa Dawson had known about Beau for years. It had never been a secret in their house, and his father had never made him feel like he wasn't perfect and amazing, just the way he was.

But that wasn't the way a lot of the South was, and Beau had been forced to confront a *lot* of those ignorant assholes over the years.

"I do," Beau said. "But Knox wasn't actually that bad. They're a more progressive city. That's . . ." Beau cleared his throat. This was hard to admit, because so many people thought they knew the legend of Asa Dawson better than they knew their own histories, but these were friends. "That's actually why we moved there in the first place. Why my dad took over the team at Tennessee. He wanted to stay in the South, but he didn't want me to be . . . well, he didn't want me to be judged."

"Your dad's a good guy," Logan said.

Sebastian hadn't said a word. Had just looked at Beau—looked straight through him, like he *knew* him, like he cared about him so much that he'd wrap him up in cotton wool if he could.

But Beau was real good at protecting himself.

He met his guy's look straight on. Strong. Challenging. He hadn't been that afraid little boy in a long time. And yes, his father had helped him become the confident man he was now, but he'd always made sure that Beau could always stand on his own, too.

"The best," Beau agreed. He could sense Sebastian's tenseness, like everyone here was judging him, even though nobody was.

Or maybe he can't stop judging himself.

So he changed the subject. "So that still doesn't explain why you're not dating anyone," he said playfully to Logan. "All I'm hearing is excuses. I thought good linemen didn't make excuses."

Logan laughed. "You got me there. How 'bout, I just haven't met the right guy yet. I hear that once you know, *you know.*" He nudged Sebastian, a mischievous smile blooming on his face. "Isn't that right?"

Logan's teasing seemed to loosen Sebastian up, finally, and he smiled.

"Yeah," he agreed, and the look in his eyes as his gaze moved to Beau made his heart beat faster in his chest. There was want in that look—so much fucking want—but it was more than that. Affection, care, and Beau didn't want to think it could be love, because he was terrified of believing it was if it *wasn't*, but it sure looked like it.

Logan must've agreed, because he chuckled. "Nope," he said, "you're definitely not lettin' the rookies have it all." He nudged Sebastian with a big, beefy thigh. "Come on, don't let them have all the fun."

Beau hadn't been about to suggest dancing, because Sebastian dancing with him, even in a private club, might be enough to help people connect two and two together, but there wasn't a reason *he* couldn't go dance with Tristan and Wade and Dylan.

He stood up. "I'm not," he said, setting his beer bottle down, and as he walked towards the dance floor, he could feel Sebastian's eyes on him.

Watching him.

Considering him.

Wanting him.

Tristan and Wade and Dylan had made a loose triangle on the dance floor, and while Tristan was moving his hips like he'd been born to do it, Wade was bouncing around mostly like an idiot, and Dylan looked like every white man who'd ever attempted to dance.

Beau figured he'd fit right in. He slotted himself in between Wade and Dylan, slapping Dylan's hand as he held it out in a high five.

They were celebrating, because they had a fuck ton of things to celebrate. They'd finally won a game. His career wasn't over. And he hadn't destroyed his father's career, either.

Beau threw his hands in the air, bumped hips with Dylan, and let the endorphins pumping their way through his bloodstream carry away all his worries.

Those were for tomorrow. Tonight was for *this*.

Chapter Twelve

Sebastian wanted to be mad at Logan for encouraging Beau to dance—for making him *want* to join him.

But it wasn't really Logan's fault, was it?

It was his. For being so goddamned afraid.

Nobody ever announced they were straight; why did he feel like he had to announce he was gay before he danced with Beau?

He could just do . . . whatever, and he never had to say a word.

Logan had moved on to his second beer, but Sebastian felt keyed up, *anxious*, and he got up, deciding that he'd find something stronger at the bar.

Pax and Davis were at one end, heads dipped together, deep in conversation, their drinks forgotten in front of them, and for a split second, Sebastian almost thought about interrupting them, but that wasn't why he'd come over here.

"What can I get you?" the bartender asked after he'd walked over, stopping in front of Sebastian.

"Rum . . ." Sebastian hesitated. He doubted they had the sipping rum he preferred, and he didn't want to take shots and get drunk, so he added, "And Coke."

"Sure thing," the bartender said, and as he began to mix the drink, Sebastian glanced out onto the dance floor.

Beau was still out there, flushed, hair mussed, his hips moving like his life depended on it, and Sebastian felt the inexorable tug towards him.

How could you want something—*someone*—so much and still be afraid? Sebastian didn't know, but he was. As much as he didn't want to admit it, even to himself.

"Here you go, sir." The bartender set his drink in front of him. "And can I say congrats on a great game? Not quite as good as last week's interception, but you guys finally got the big W."

Sebastian smiled, pulling out his wallet, and stuffing a hundred-dollar tip into the jar on the counter. Not just because the guy had congratulated him, but because he knew how tough it was, working these kinds of gigs.

"Thanks," he said, taking a long sip of his drink. It was perfectly mixed, with a nice splash of lime. "This is great."

The bartender smiled. "Great drink for a great player," he said. "No matter what position you're playing."

And it wasn't like Sebastian hadn't believed it was true. He knew he could be impactful just by *being* on the field. Beau had said it enough times, and it wasn't like he hadn't believed him but . . . it had an entirely different impact coming from someone who didn't want anything from him.

Not his performance, not his money, not his body.

Not even his heart.

He took another long drink, watching Beau as he laughed with Dylan. Wanting, more than he knew what to do with, to walk over there and put his hands on Beau's hips, pull him in. Make him burn the way that Sebastian burned every time he looked at him.

He took his time finishing his drink, watching and waiting until Beau was flushed red from exertion, and he came wandering over as the song transitioned to something slower, sexier.

Beau knew it too, knew he'd been watching, because his eyes were hot as he walked up next to him.

"Hey," he said.

Only a single word but it was all there, in his eyes.

Beau Dawson and his enormous brain could say a million words with just a look. With one word.

"Want a drink?" Sebastian asked, holding up his mostly empty glass.

"Nah," Beau said, "just some water. I'm really not much of a drinker."

"I just wanted something to take the edge off," Sebastian said, flagging the waiter down. "Can we get two bottles of water, please?"

The bartender reached into the fridge under the counter and set them down on the bar. If he recognized Beau, it didn't show on his face.

"Thanks," Beau said with a grateful smile. He turned back to Sebastian. "What edge?" he asked, his tone playful.

Sebastian shot him a look. "You know what kind of edge," he said. Then lowered his voice. "The edge where I've been wanting to fuck you for hours now."

Beau's eyes widened.

Maybe he might have suspected the truth before, but he *knew* now.

Sebastian took a long drink of water. Hoping it would make him a little less thirsty.

It didn't work.

Sometimes no matter how hard you worked, you couldn't get that extra step back.

And no matter how afraid you were, it was impossible to fight the inevitable.

"Come on," he said, his voice low and rough sounding as he held out a hand towards Beau. "Dance with me."

Beau looked surprised.

No—he looked *shocked*.

"You want to dance with me? Like *dance* with me?"

Sebastian nodded.

"Oh. Uh. You might . . . I can't guarantee . . ." Beau tripped over his own words, trying to say the thing that Sebastian already knew.

The thing that Sebastian had decided didn't matter anymore. He knew the exact moment desire won out over fear.

He'd never make public speeches. He'd never give interviews about his sexuality. He was far more likely to just say *no comment* every time someone asked. But he was done hiding, especially when hiding meant only watching as Beau moved his body to the music without him.

He wanted to be right there, next to him.

Logan had really known what he was talking about when he said everything changed with the right guy. Beau made him want to be a better man, a man who was less afraid.

"Doesn't matter," Sebastian said firmly. "I want to dance with you. You wanna dance with me?"

Beau stared at him for a second longer. Nobody, Sebastian thought, would wonder what was going on between them if they could see the look in his eyes. They were full of so much wonder and joy and pride—and maybe something else, something that Sebastian wasn't quite ready to identify yet, that still terrified him, but in the best kind of way.

"Yeah," Beau said finally, his own voice not quite steady. He reached out and took Sebastian's hand, squeezing it. "Yeah, I wanna dance with you."

It was only a few steps to the dance floor, and only a few steps further to where Miami spread out beneath them like a carpet full of stars.

"This," Beau said, as Sebastian didn't waste a moment pulling him right against him, "is perfect."

Sebastian, sliding his hands down Beau's hips, tugging him closer, couldn't disagree.

"Hey!" Tristan exclaimed as he and Wade and Dylan must have realized who'd just joined them. "I didn't know . . ."

Wade shot his boyfriend a look. "You totally did," he said dryly.

Tristan shrugged. "But . . ."

Sebastian didn't let him finish the sentence. "We are now," he said firmly, and then he turned all his attention back where to belonged. Back to Beau.

He'd been half hard from just watching Beau move, but now, pressed together, Sebastian could feel every shift of his body, and his arousal ratcheted up until his fingers pressed hard into Beau's hips.

"You," Beau said breathlessly as one song segued into another, "are really good at this."

"My mom might've worked two jobs, but she was never too tired to dance at night in our kitchen with me," Sebastian said in a low voice, meant just for Beau to hear.

Beau tilted his head, gaze fixed on Sebastian's face. "I know what this means," he said.

Sebastian smiled. "That I want to dance with the guy I'm crazy about?"

Beau rolled his eyes. But the snarkiness in his expression quickly morphed to lust as Sebastian rolled his hips—and his hard cock—even more insistently against Beau. "I think," Sebastian said, "what it means is that people can say whatever the fuck they want to."

"You don't care?"

Sebastian dipped his head, lips only a fraction of an inch away from Beau's. "Do I *look* like I care?"

Beau wet his lips. Somehow made them impossibly even more kissable. Sebastian's control, already hanging by a thread, fractured even further. *God*, he wanted this man.

"No," Beau said softly. "No, not even a little."

"Good." Sebastian flashed him a smile. "Then it won't matter what they think when we leave together in a minute."

"Oh, we're leaving?" Beau arched an eyebrow.

"We," Sebastian said, trailing a hand down Beau's back, coming to rest right above where the curve of his ass began, "are definitely leaving. Unless . . ." He let his hand slide just a little further, and he heard Beau's sharp intake of breath. "Unless you want to stay?"

"No, no." Beau's voice went high and breathy, and Sebastian could feel the hard, hot line of his cock pressing against his hip. "No, we should go."

Sebastian turned to where Tristan and Wade were dancing, only a few feet over. "We're leaving," he said succinctly. "I'm assuming y'all can figure out how to get yourselves home?"

Tristan laughed and Wade nodded. "We're good," he said. "Have fun."

"Oh, I think we will," Beau said, shooting Sebastian a positively evil grin as he led them off the dance floor.

Tristan was still cackling as he called out behind them. "Be safe, you two crazy kids. Use protection!"

There was something incredibly sexy about Sebastian's single-mindedness as they'd exited the club, he'd found them a cab, stuck them both in it, and gave the driver his tower address in a terse, short voice.

And then proceeded to touch Beau in every way he could without getting kicked out of it, getting arrested for public indecency, *or* kissing him.

Those big, capable, calloused hands were everywhere. Roaming across his stomach, his chest, his arms, worming their way behind him, leaving trails of fire along his back, stopping right where Beau wanted to be touched so goddamned badly.

"What," he gasped as quietly as he could, "are you trying to do?"

"I'm trying," Sebastian said, leaning close enough that Beau was *sure*, absolutely fucking positive, that he was going to finally kiss him, "to make you want me as much as I want you."

Beau choked as he pulled back just a fraction, not actually kissing him after all, but the way he was looking at him was as good as a kiss. Or a brand.

It burned that hotly.

"Only a couple more blocks," Sebastian said, like he was the one who was being driven crazy—when of course it was Beau, and he'd never asked for any of this.

Except he'd craved it. Even though he'd never dreamed that it would actually happen.

Finally, just as Beau thought he might actually splinter apart, or do something really embarrassing, like orgasm without actually having his dick touched, they pulled up in front of Sebastian's building.

He was a little gratified to see Sebastian's fingers shaking, as he pulled some bills out and practically threw them at the driver.

"I think," Beau said, as Sebastian's hand pressed to his back, nearly pushing him towards the front door, "that you might've over-tipped him."

"Brat," Sebastian murmured as his big strides covered the marble floor in the lobby. He pressed the elevator button. Then jabbed it. Again. And again. And again.

"Impatient, much?" Beau teased again.

He should've been afraid of how much Sebastian's eyes flashed at his words, but before he could have any chance to regret it, the elevator *finally* showed up, and Sebastian was pushing them inside it. He barely waited for the doors to shut before plucking Beau's glasses off his face, his body pressed relentlessly against Beau's, and then his mouth was on his, and everything went gloriously, perfectly blank.

He didn't hear the elevator dinging as they passed by each floor, or the final ding as they hit the top floor and Sebastian's penthouse.

All he could hear was Sebastian's panting, the little groans he kept making as Beau's fingers dug into his shoulders, the desperate mewls coming out of his own mouth.

The elevator dinged again, more insistently this time, and Sebastian broke the kiss just in time to push them out into the foyer.

"Shit," Sebastian said as he unlocked his front door, not sounding like he regretted a moment of what they'd just done.

Then they were behind Sebastian's door, and they were doing it again, kissing like their lives depended on it.

"Wait," Sebastian groaned, tearing his mouth off Beau's for half a second. "We need . . . bed . . . not the floor. Not again."

"Is this another one of those *treat me right* things?" Beau asked archly, trailing a hand down Sebastian's chest, popping buttons as he went, revealing all that delicious light brown skin, perfectly muscled and all fucking his. He pressed a hand to Sebastian's fly and loved feeling his cock twitch against even the barest touch.

"It's an . . . *I need to get you naked fucking now* thing," Sebastian growled, and suddenly Beau was in the air, over Sebastian's shoulder as he carried him into the bedroom. Depositing him on the bed, Sebastian grinned. "That's better," he said, shrugging off his shoes and then his shirt.

"I don't know if it really is," Beau teased, licking his lips as he watched Sebastian tug down his jeans. "Might be better if you came over here."

Sebastian didn't. Not right away. But the detour he took to the nightstand, grabbing lube and a condom, made his pulse flutter. He tossed them on the bed, and then turned back to Beau, dangerously sexy intent in his eyes.

"Like this?" Sebastian asked, returning to his spot in front of Beau, and taking a single step closer, his hard cock bobbing in front of him. Beau licked his lips.

"Closer," Beau insisted, sliding to the edge of the bed, toeing off his shoes, and reaching for the hem of his t-shirt. But Sebastian closed the gap between them, closing his fingers over Beau's own.

"Let me," Sebastian said in a low, tight voice. "I *want* to."

Beau's mouth went dry. He sounded so desperate, and he'd never heard something so sexy in his whole damn life.

How had he ever gotten this lucky?

He wasn't sure, but he wasn't going to say no to anything Sebastian wanted—but that didn't mean he couldn't tease him a little more first.

"Bet you've wanted to do this all night," Beau said, voice muffled by his t-shirt as Sebastian tugged it over his head.

Sebastian's eyes glowed as they met Beau's again. "Actually," he said, leaning in, brushing a single heart-stopping kiss across Beau's mouth, "I've been wanting to do *this*."

And he dropped to his knees, tugging at the zipper of Beau's pants, dragging them down his legs.

"Yeah," Beau exhaled breathlessly. "Please."

There was nothing hotter on earth than how gorgeous Sebastian looked, muscles bunched on his shoulders, straining against his own self-control, as he leaned in and gently, delicately licked up his cock still trapped in his briefs.

"You want this?" Sebastian's voice was dark and deep, utterly debauched.

"Yes." Beau's own was strangled. Desperate.

Then he was pulling down the last barrier, and Beau groaned as his hot, wet mouth enveloped him, tongue rubbing along the sensitive underside of his cock as he swallowed it all the way down.

Pleasure buzzed in Beau's brain, and then a thumb slid up his thigh, just as wet, and brushed up against his hole.

"You want this," Sebastian asked, nuzzling the side of his cock with his cheek. "Tell me you want this as much as I do."

"I do, I do," Beau gasped as that thumb slid, inexorably, further in, sensation skittering along his nerves.

"Good, 'cause I can't wait to be inside you," Sebastian groaned, his tongue slipping along his cock, adding to the sensations rocketing through him.

Beau had only done this a few times—he'd never felt driven to do it with any of his short-term hookups, because he'd wanted there to be trust and understanding before he committed to it.

But with Sebastian it felt like there was *only* trust and understanding.

With Sebastian, he couldn't wait until he was buried so deep inside him he wasn't sure where he ended and Sebastian began.

Sebastian slid another finger inside of him, joining his thumb, and Beau cried out as he stretched him, gently, carefully, leaving Beau wild with how much more he wanted.

"Come on," he begged, more than ready to forego the rest of the prep. The pleasure was intoxicating, pulling him right to the edge, leaving him teetering. He was not going to come before Sebastian even got inside him but if he kept doing that clever thing with his tongue, swirling it over the head of his cock?

Beau didn't know how he could possibly keep from exploding.

"Want it to be good," Sebastian crooned, his voice rough.

Beau laughed, because it was already so much fucking better than he'd ever felt before.

"God, Sebastian, it fucking is," Beau said, unable to stop giggling as Sebastian finally slid his fingers out. "Just . . . goddamn it. Do it."

"If," Sebastian said, leaning over, grabbing for the condom, landing a messy kiss on his lips, "if I'd known you were this fucking eager, I'd never have let you drag me to that club." He tore the package, and was rolling it on as Beau tried to pull him in with his legs.

"Oh, you liked it," Beau teased, and Sebastian reacted so beautifully—like he always did, to every single bit of Beau's tormenting. He leaned in, kissing him hard, Beau's mind going blissfully blank right until he felt Sebastian begin to push inside him.

He gasped right into Sebastian's mouth, as the pressure increased, until Beau thought he might scream with it. But instead, the pressure subsided, and slid relentlessly into pleasure as Sebastian began to thrust.

"Oh, *God*, just like that," Beau cried as Sebastian hitched his legs up, hitting a new and exquisite angle.

"Beau," Sebastian panted, his eyes finding Beau's own. He felt *seared* by the emotion in them. "God, *Beau*."

Beau almost couldn't bear it. The pleasure was crescendoing through him, and the look on Sebastian's face was searing, so fucking beautiful that he only had to reach down and brush his hand over his cock, and that was all it took before he went flying, his orgasm rocketing through him.

Sebastian cried out, his fingers curling around Beau's knees, but he didn't look away, gaze glued to Beau as he rode out his own orgasm.

Pleasure slowly eked out of Beau, until he just felt soft and warm and loved.

You shouldn't even think it, he warned himself.

But it was impossible not to when Sebastian was *still* looking at him like that. When he'd not entirely discarded the closet, but he'd still stepped a little bit into the light—and all because of *him*.

This wasn't just a series of quick fucks.

This was *something*.

And even though the last thing Beau should be thinking of was his father, he couldn't help it.

You're not going to be able to tell him. He might not be mad, but he's going to be . . . disappointed. Or something. And you can't deal with that. Not after all this time.

"You good?" Sebastian asked softly as he pulled out.

"Never better," Beau said honestly.

He would figure out the thing with his dad at some point. But not tonight.

Tonight, everything was perfect.

Chapter
Thirteen

Beau's phone blared out, startling him from sleep, the ring-tone—and the fact that it was ringing at all—telling him exactly who it was that was calling this goddamn early. He let it ring again, and then once more, but finally, reluctantly rolled out of the warm cave of Sebastian's arms, and grabbed it from the nightstand next to the bed.

"*Whaaa,*" Sebastian mumbled, still half-asleep.

"It's . . ." Beau glanced at the screen even though he *knew* who it was. Nobody else's phone number was programmed to ring despite his *Do Not Disturb* settings.

It rang again and Sebastian made a grumpy noise behind him. Because Beau had left or because the phone kept ringing? Or both?

Beau gave in to the inevitable and answered it. "Hey," he said.

"Beau," his father barked over the line. Sounding way too excited, and way too awake for whatever-the-fuck time it was in the morning.

Light had begun to filter through the curtains in Sebastian's bedroom, but he could tell it wasn't exactly *late* into the morning, and Coach had told them all last night that they'd have the morning off. He'd been promised *brunch in bed* by an incredibly hot man.

"Yes, I'm here," Beau said, rolling his eyes, swinging his legs over the edge of the bed. Sebastian's minimalist penthouse, with all its metal and plastic and marble wasn't so bad, except in the morning, when the floors were really fucking cold.

"I knocked on your door," he barked into the phone. "You didn't answer."

"Yeah, because it's really fucking early," Beau grumbled. He wasn't against telling his father that he hadn't slept in his own bed last night, but he also knew he'd want to know *who* he'd been with, even if it was none of his business.

"We need to talk," his father said, all impatience. "Open your door."

"I would, but I'm not actually there," Beau said, giving in. He glanced back and saw that Sebastian was awake now, and he was intently listening to their conversation.

He knew exactly what Sebastian was worried about, but he had no intention of telling his father who he was with.

"Oh?" The question was unspoken.

"No," Beau said forcibly, "no, you don't get to ask."

He wasn't looking at Sebastian anymore, but he swore he could feel his gaze intensify.

"Alright," his father drawled. "I won't. Even though I want to. But we need to talk. I had an idea."

"Don't you ever turn it off?" Beau asked, even though he already knew the answer. He didn't. Never. Not even after a win. Not even if they won sixteen games. He'd never turn it off. It was what made Asa Dawson so good. What made him the freaking best.

He just laughed. Then said, "Meet me at that little diner, between our building and the practice facility, okay?"

Beau bit back a groan. He was supposed to have *naked brunch* today.

"Beau?"

"Fine, yes, I'll meet you."

"Ten minutes," his father barked, and then hung up.

"He," Sebastian said, coming up behind him, putting a big warm hand on Beau's bare shoulder, "actually never turns it off. Does this happen a lot?"

"Not a lot . . ." Beau started to say, then chuckled under his breath. "Okay, more than I probably want to admit to. But when neither of us has any other kind of life, it isn't so annoying. But now . . ."

"Now?" Sebastian questioned.

"Now," Beau said, taking a deep breath. Taking a risk. Because they hadn't actually talked about this specifically. "Now, I'm going to have to set some boundaries with him. Because it's not just me anymore."

"No," Sebastian said, curling his hand around his shoulder and tugging him back, until he was resting in his arms. "No, it's not just you anymore. He's gonna have to learn how to share."

Beau laughed. "He's not going to like that at all."

"That's okay," Sebastian teased, "because *I* like you."

"I like you, too," Beau said. *Maybe even more than just like, but you're not ready to hear it, but that's okay, because I'm not sure I'm ready to say it. Not quite yet.* "I better get ready."

He pulled away, standing up and wondering for a split second where the fuck his clothes had gone.

"You want me to call you a car?" Sebastian asked, stretching, and nearly stopping Beau's progress as he gathered up his jeans, his shirt.

"No, I can walk. It's actually closer to here than it is to my place," Beau said.

"If you're sure," Sebastian said, and there was an edge of concern—not really *worry*, exactly, but care, like he gave a shit how Beau got around—and it warmed his heart.

"I'm absolutely sure," Beau said, leaning over and pressing a quick kiss to Sebastian's mouth. "Now go back to bed, and enjoy sleeping in for both of us, okay?"

"Okay."

Beau finished getting dressed, then detoured to the bathroom. He'd started keeping a toothbrush here, and showering and changing in the staff locker room—but he wouldn't be able to do that this morning. At least not before he saw his father.

He ran a hand through his hair, and decided this would have to be enough.

It definitely looked like someone else had had their hands in it all night, and that wasn't far from the truth.

He gave Sebastian one last kiss goodbye—this one was not just a quick peck, either—and then he took the elevator, waving hello to Luis as he passed the concierge desk, and then emerged into the Florida sunshine.

It took five minutes to walk to the diner, which meant he was about five minutes past the ten minutes that his father had set.

When he walked into the diner, Asa was already sitting at a booth, a cup of steaming coffee at one elbow, hair still damp at the temples from a shower, his regular daily uniform of a polo shirt and pressed khaki shorts on, a frown on his face.

"You're late," he said. "Where were you coming from?"

Beau grinned. "Hi, Beau, how are you? How was your night? Did you have fun celebrating the win? Thanks for meeting me on such short notice and *only* being five minutes late."

Asa rolled his eyes. "Fine, fine, you aren't going to tell me."

"Bingo," Beau said, picking up the menu even though he already knew what he wanted.

"It's just not like you," Asa complained a minute later.

"No, you like it when I'm at your beck and call," Beau teased. He would be a lot more frustrated, but he *had* been at his father's beck and call—that was what he was used to, and that was as much Beau's fault as his father's—and it was going to take time for them both to adjust to the new way of things.

"I do," he muttered.

"But that's going to be changing," Beau said gently.

His father stared at him. "So this wasn't just a . . . one-time thing? What do y'all call it now? A *hookup*?"

Beau rolled his eyes. "You are not ancient, despite how much you insist on pretending otherwise. And no, it wasn't a *hookup*. It's a . . . well, I guess it's a relationship."

"And you won't tell me who it is," Asa stated.

"Not yet," Beau hedged. He wasn't sure when Sebastian would feel comfortable telling his father. He wasn't sure when *he'd* feel comfortable telling his father. He wouldn't go as far as forbidding it, but he wasn't going to be happy about it either, because the chances of this spilling onto the field grew higher the deeper they got involved.

And Beau had a feeling they were getting *very* deeply involved.

Thank God the waitress showed up then, and they ordered, and when they left to grab Beau's coffee and put their food order in, Beau was able to change the subject.

"So what was so pressing that you had to call me at seven in the morning?" Beau asked, arching an eyebrow. "We were supposed to get the morning off."

"You *do* have the morning off," Asa claimed. "We're just father and son, having a nice breakfast, good cup of coffee to start the day . . ."

Beau grinned. "That's absolute bullshit and you know it, you're not even wearing your dad hat right now," he said. "You've got the coach hat firmly affixed to your annoying head."

"Fine, fine, okay, yes, though I *did* have it on earlier, when you didn't want to talk about your . . . *hookup*."

"You mean my relationship?"

"Yes, that," Asa said. "But you didn't want to talk about it, so I'm going to respect that."

"Uh-huh," Beau said, not believing it for a second. He got his insatiable curiosity from somewhere and it wasn't his mother.

The waitress appeared with his coffee and he took a long sip of it, black. Shuddered a little, because it was strong, but it was also seven in the morning, and he'd been up most of the night with Sebastian, and he could use all the help he could get.

"What I wanted to talk to you about was this idea I had. I was watching some college games . . ."

"On your night off? After we won?"

Asa rolled his eyes. "Yes, unlike some people, I didn't have a . . . *hot hookup* last night."

"Okay, you were slumming it, watching college ball," Beau said. "What did you come up with?"

"Remember that thing we did, way back at the beginning?"

Beau considered reminding his father that at the beginning in Tennessee, he'd been *thirteen* and not actually on his coaching staff. But then, that hadn't necessarily been true, either. He'd been unofficially on staff, spending more time in the practice facility than he did their house, and helping his dad, analyzing plays even back then. Pointing out different strengths and weaknesses.

"What thing?"

"It was maybe second year? We had a really disjointed team. Lots of freshmen. Not a lot of veterans returning," Asa said, "and we had to bring the team together. So I came up with that idea of a warmup routine. To get everyone on the same page, and to remind everyone that they *were* on the same page."

"Yeah," Beau said. "But you're not going to be able to get a team of NFL veterans to do jumping jacks in unison."

"Why not?"

Beau laughed. "Because it's . . . Because it's ridiculous? Because they're grown men and not basically children pretending to be adults? And they're not going to be led through a warmup that you choreographed for them?"

"It'll work," Asa insisted stubbornly. "The *point* of it is getting everyone on board. Because if they buy into *this*, they're gonna buy into the rest."

"And how are you going to make that happen?"

"Easy." Asa grinned. "You're gonna help me."

Beau groaned. "Hell no. I'm not going to help you." Except he already knew that he would. And not just because his father was also his boss and the coach. Because if he *could* convince the players to buy in, Beau could see how it would help. Hadn't he sat in his father's office only a week ago and said, *if we can find something that gels them together . . .?*

This was the thing.

As much as he really didn't want it to be.

He could already see the team coming together, becoming *one* team from a bunch of disparate parts—and this being the thing that would do it.

"Ugh," Beau groaned again. "I hate it when you're right about this stuff."

"They like you, they respect you, if you tell them it's gonna work, they'll do it."

"Yeah, but they can't just go through the motions," Beau warned. "If they do, it's not going to have the effect you want."

His father shrugged. "You can convince them. You convinced Sebastian Howard to play safety. You can do anything."

"Is this supposed to be a fatherly pep talk or an Asa Dawson pep talk?"

"Both?" His father had the nerve to look sheepish.

"You're buying breakfast," Beau said. "And as far as I'm concerned, if I do this for you, you're buying breakfast for the next hundred years."

It was a silly requirement—they were both wealthy, and Beau could afford his breakfast if he wanted it—but he couldn't ask his father to permit the one thing he truly wanted. Because that would mean confessing that he was involved with Sebastian.

But it wouldn't hurt, Beau decided, to hold that in his back pocket. It was always good to have Asa Dawson owe you a favor.

"So you'll do it." Asa sounded very pleased.

"Like you didn't know I would," Beau grumbled.

"I wasn't sure, honestly, because this is a different kind of thing than we normally do. You're right, those guys at Tennessee, they were kids masquerading as adults. These guys *are* adults. It's different. Different than how I imagined it would be, and it wasn't like we didn't prepare for it to be different."

It was the closest Beau had ever heard his father come to admitting that their success in the NFL hadn't been automatically preordained.

"We did," Beau agreed. But it had been a risk.

A risk he'd encouraged his father to take.

He'd only been thinking about the upside if the team was a success. Not the possibility that they might not be, and what his father might pay for that.

"I think this'll work out just fine," Asa said, smiling. Pleased. Because he'd figured out the problem *and* the solution.

Beau didn't want to feel guilty. He wasn't *precisely* guilty about Sebastian, but that, along with what he *should've* known, *should've* felt before . . .

What he should have expected.

Beau couldn't deny that it *was* guilt. Not anymore.

"Listen, I should've . . ." Beau took a breath. Nervous, suddenly. He was used to being right. Used to being deadly effective. Used to being his father's secret weapon. "I shouldn't have told you to take this job."

Asa leaned back in the booth, his dark eyes twinkling, his expression amused. "Oh, you think you convinced me to take it, huh, and it's going to destroy my career?"

Beau shot him a look. "It could, and *yes*, I did convince you to take it."

"Son," Asa drawled, "nobody convinces me to do anything I don't want to. I'm a stubborn sonofabitch, you know that. Your mother certainly knows it. I was glad you wanted me to take it only because that meant you might come with me. That's all."

"No, I *told* you," Beau insisted.

Asa held up a hand. "We're not doing this. I'm putting my father hat on now, and I'm tellin' you so you know it, loud and clear. I took this job because I wanted it, and because Gonzalez paid me that ridiculous amount of money."

He knew his father had been rich before. Tennessee, after all his success, hadn't exactly been stingy with their contracts. But yeah, he'd known the Piranhas money was a *lot* of money. Nothing paid like the NFL. And desperate NFL owners who needed wins? They paid better than anyone else.

"What if all those football nerds who idolize every move you make knew you'd taken the job for money?"

His father rolled his eyes. "I didn't *only* take it for the money. I also wanted to prove I could do it. Everyone always says college coaches can't make it in the NFL. It seemed as good a time as any to prove them wrong."

"So you're still glad you did it?"

Asa grinned as the waitress arrived with their food. "Boy, the season just started. Don't tell me you're ready to give up already."

The last thing Beau had expected to be doing on the Monday after their first win was sitting in his office at not quite eleven in the morning, watching old videos of the first Tennessee teams that his dad had coached. Trying to put together a warmup routine that would bring the team together but wouldn't emasculate them at the same time.

Beau leaned back in his chair, watching as another video played on the big screen on the opposite wall. He'd been young when his dad had implemented this. By the time he'd officially joined the Tennessee staff, during his freshman year of college, Asa had long since let the routine die.

What he hadn't realized, because he'd been too young, too green, to really understand the depth of his dad's undeniable genius, was that not only did this warmup routine bring his team together, it was undeniably intimidating to the opposing team.

They'd jog onto the field, dividing loosely into the different position groups, starting their individual warmups—and then the Tennessee players would arrive, and move in unison, as one terrifyingly efficient army.

Beau tapped his fingers on the desk. His father had used a variety of songs back then, mostly AC/DC, but he wasn't totally pleased with the choice.

He made a note on the pad in front of him. They'd need to find a different song, and then make sure they could use it.

"What on earth are you watching?"

Sebastian stood in the doorway to Beau's office, his workout clothes on.

"Uh," Beau said, fumbling for the remote, pausing it so the Tennessee orange and white jerseys frozen in a blur of movement. "Research."

Sebastian raised an eyebrow. "Coach called you out of bed at seven in the morning to come down here and watch cheerleading routines?"

Ugh. This really did not bode well, if Sebastian had seen a brief look at the screen and come to that particular conclusion.

"What are *you* doing out of bed and here?" Beau asked, not answering Sebastian's own question. He wasn't going to say that Sebastian would be the *hardest* person to get on board, but he was definitely going to be one of the most resistant players. Because of that, Beau was going to have to take a different approach with him. A *Sebastian-only* kind of approach.

"Well," Sebastian said, walking closer and also dropping his voice, leaning practically right over the desk and making Beau wish very badly that they were not in his office, but somewhere else. Somewhere private. "*Someone* abandoned me this morning and the bed was really lonely without him. So I thought I might show up and get a few reps in. Maybe bother that guy a little."

It was impossible not to smile. Beau didn't even try to resist it.

"I'm glad you came, because as it turns out, that guy's pretty happy to see you too," Beau said.

Sebastian grinned. "You think you could escape for an early dinner?"

Beau thought about the work he had to do before tomorrow, and the coaches' meeting that they'd be having in a few hours, and decided that *yes,* he would make the time for an early dinner with Sebastian.

"I think I can swing that."

"Well." Sebastian shot him another one of those ridiculously charming smiles, the ones that left Beau slightly breathless. "I'll see you in a few hours, then. Don't miss me too much." He blew Beau a kiss—so quick that Beau almost missed it, but he'd still done it.

It might not be a real kiss, not on the cheek or on the lips, but the feelings were still there. Sebastian was still thinking, *I want to kiss him*, and Beau decided that was what really mattered.

As soon as Sebastian had turned the corner, passing out of view, Beau turned his attention back to the screen, starting the video playing again.

But before he could continue his list of steps he'd have to take to implement this new idea, his phone rang.

He considered silencing it and letting it go to voicemail but then he saw the name on the screen, and groaning, he reached to answer it.

Somehow his father always managed to conjure his mother's presence into being, and today was no exception. He'd mentioned her at breakfast, and here she was calling.

"Beau," she said brightly after he'd answered. "I thought I might catch you at a free moment. Monday morning after a win. Congrats, by the way. I'm sure you and Asa are very relieved."

Beau knew just how lucky he was that she and his father had divorced so amicably. There'd never been any fights, just a gradual distancing, growing worse by the year, until one day they'd sat him down and said they'd always be friends, but they'd learned that's what they were better as. Friends.

Then Lynn had moved to New York, and had, Beau knew, fully expected him to follow her when he went to college. But he hadn't. He'd stayed in Tennessee and stayed at his father's side.

She'd been a little resentful after that, but they talked enough and he always spent a few weeks there after the end of the football season.

She took him to horrible art galleries that he wished he enjoyed and he took her to baseball games that she slept through.

"Did you watch it?" Beau asked, switching the phone to speaker, and muting the TV, restarting the routine.

He knew better than to ask, but there was always a chance she'd tuned the TV to the game and then proceeded to do something else entirely.

"Oh I checked the score. Your father was worried about it, so I made sure to see how it went," Lynn said.

It should have made Beau feel guilty that *his father* talked to her more than he did, but he was busy, wasn't he?

Of course it wasn't like Asa didn't work absolutely ridiculous hours, too. *He*, Beau thought with frustration, *somehow always manages to find the time.*

"It definitely came down to the wire but Dad made sure we had a great kicker and he came through when it mattered," Beau said.

"It certainly seemed like your father was going to will the team to a victory," she said wryly. "Which is just like him."

"How's your art coming?" Beau asked, changing the subject because even though she'd ostensibly called to congratulate them on winning their first NFL game, his mother could only stand to talk about football for about two minutes, and they were rapidly nearing that mark.

"Oh, *wonderful*," she enthused. "I've been working on a new mixed-media piece—yarn, and some oils, with metal chunks I picked up in the alley behind my townhouse—and Gladys, she's been dropping by every few days to see the progress, and I think she's going to display it in the gallery."

"That's great." Beau meant it too. She was so much happier up in New York, working away on her pieces, than she'd ever been down in the South, trying to be the football coach's wife.

It made Beau wonder how they'd ever gotten together, or how they'd ever thought they could be happy enough together to get married.

But Beau also knew people changed. They grew up, and they became more of who they could be.

Beau didn't think he was even the same man he'd been a year ago in Knoxville. He'd gotten complacent. A little too used to success. Way too dedicated to work.

"I'm glad," Beau said suddenly into the lull, "I'm glad you moved to New York."

"Really?" Lynn sounded surprised. "I always supposed . . ." She laughed self-consciously. "I always supposed that you were angry at me for leaving."

"No," Beau said honestly. "It was the right decision. Like it was the right decision for me to stay with Dad."

"You two always did understand each other," she mused. "I was surprised, at first, that you didn't want to come to New York, but I get it now. And how is Miami? Different than Knoxville, I'm sure."

"It's good." Beau hesitated. "Even better, actually, 'cause I met someone."

"Oh?" She immediately sounded intrigued. "I suppose you're not going to tell me who it is." Unlike Asa, she clearly knew he wasn't going to spill. "Especially if it's a player."

He knew they talked, but would she tell his father about his boyfriend? Beau wasn't sure. Besides, Asa had probably already worked out that he was dating a player because he wouldn't tell him who it was.

"It's a player," Beau said. "He's . . . he's really great."

"Is it that cute Logan Banks?"

"Mom," Beau teased. "I thought you didn't watch the games."

"Oh, I don't," she said. "But I follow everyone on Instagram, and he gives me a kind of vibe."

"It's not Logan," Beau said. "I'm not going to tell you who it is because you won't be able to stop yourself from telling Dad."

"True," she said. "But he's nice? He treats you good? He's not . . . using you to get ahead?"

"The opposite in fact," Beau said dryly. "I think he resented me at first, and he absolutely resented my position. Definitely all the power I had over him."

"But you've worked it out?"

"Oh yeah, long time ago. He . . . well, he figured out I was right." Beau couldn't help but grin at that.

His mom laughed. "I bet that was fun."

"I'm pleading the fifth," Beau said.

"I'm glad," she said, "really, really glad you met someone, Beau. You sound happy. You work much too hard. You're just like your father that way."

He knew.

His mother had only been saying it for years—and he'd never even needed her pointed comments to know it was the truth.

"I know," Beau said. "But the idea is . . . well, I'd like to find a better balance. He makes me want to do that."

"Good," she said. "And if your father bitches, send him to me."

Beau laughed. "I can deal with him, Mom. Really. But . . ." Beau considered. Before his mother had fled to New York to be an artist, she'd been a professor of psychology. It was how his parents had met. She'd been a graduate student and his father had been an assistant coach. "I could actually use your advice on something else."

"Sure," she said.

"I need to convince someone who won't want to do something that they really want to do it."

There was no other way to describe it: Lynn cackled. "Please tell me," she said between chuckles, "that this is not about your father."

"It's not," Beau said. "But it's one of his ideas, and I think it's gonna be tough implementing it. *But* if I can get certain players on board, that'll make it easier for the others to accept."

"The problem is getting the certain players on board, then." Her voice turned sly. "Is one of these problematic players your boyfriend?"

"He might be," Beau hedged.

"That'll actually help," Lynn said briskly. "He'll be primed for it. Just perform a little reverse psychology."

"That's it?"

"Tell him," Lynn said, "that something terrible is going to happen. That he'll hate it. Will he hate it?"

Beau considered. "I don't think he'll *like* it."

"Then tell him he'll hate it. Reiterate it over and over. When you actually present the real situation, everything will look *less* bad."

"You really think that's all I need to do?"

"If you can sell it, yes," she said. "But you really have to sell it, and that's why it'll be easier since you're involved."

Beau nodded, considering this angle. He could do it. Sebastian would be super pissed, until he realized with relief that what Coach wanted wasn't so terrible after all. It was doable.

"Good luck," Lynn said. "And text me, let me know how it goes."

"I will."

"Love you and don't let your father work himself into an early grave," she said.

"Love you too," Beau said, hanging up.

Then he began to scribble on the notepad, his brain suddenly overflowing with ideas. He'd even had the inspiration for a song to use.

He really, he decided as he began to plan out how he was going to approach this, needed to talk to his mother more.

CHAPTER FOURTEEN

BY THE TIME BEAU had showered, gotten dressed, and was sitting with Sebastian at the little taco place he'd suggested they try for dinner, he'd planned out not only the nitty-gritty parts of the routine, he'd worked out how to present it to the players.

Sebastian would be the first nut to crack, and he would start tonight.

Asa was adamant during their earlier coaches' meeting that they start implementing it in practice tomorrow, so tonight was the only time that Beau had to get his boyfriend on board.

And that, he already knew, was not going to be easy, but with his mother's advice, he thought there was at least a decent chance of him getting Sebastian to agree to at least *consider* it.

"How was your workout?" Beau asked after they each ordered a Corona with lime.

Sebastian eyed him. "It was a workout," he said. "Nothing special. But I think I should be asking you what's got you so preoccupied."

"Sorry," Beau admitted, "it's been a wild day."

"You gonna tell me about it?" Sebastian asked as he dug a chip into the salsa verde the waiter had brought, along with their drinks.

"Actually, yes," Beau said.

Sebastian glanced over at him, clearly surprised. "You are? You didn't seem to want to talk about it earlier."

"That was earlier," Beau said with a shrug. "And it's not like I didn't *want* to tell you, I just wasn't ready yet."

"And you're ready now."

"Yeah," Beau said. Paused. "But you're not going to like it."

Sebastian laughed. "Oh, honey, I didn't really think I would. But I've been on board, haven't I? You convinced me to play safety, and I don't hate it. Not like I thought I would. I can even see why you thought it was a good idea. I guess what I'm saying is . . . I trust you. I trust your ideas. Even the crazy ones."

"Except this isn't one of my ideas," Beau retorted lightly, scooping out some salsa. It was fresh and tasty with just the right amount of spice. "It came directly from Coach."

"And that's worse?" Sebastian asked, raising an eyebrow.

"My father can be a wild card. He's unconventional. This is one of those kinds of ideas," Beau said. "He wanted something to bring the whole team together, to remind you guys that you *are* a team."

"And having us run stairs or do burpees or bear crawls til we can't move isn't good enough?"

Beau broke the chip in his fingers apart into several pieces. "No."

"Well, you'd better lay it on me," Sebastian said, "now that you've filled me with sufficient dread."

Beau laughed. He should have told his mother that Sebastian was too smart to be fooled by any kind of basic psychological trick.

"Do you remember about fourteen years back, when my dad first started coaching at Tennessee?"

Sebastian shrugged. "I didn't follow it all that closely," he admitted. "I was in Miami then, in college, and we didn't play Tennessee."

"But surely you guys would talk about the entire team warming up in unison," Beau said.

Sebastian's gaze narrowed as the waiter arrived with their fish tacos. "Yeah, of course, now that you remind me. It was like this ridiculously choreographed thing." He froze. "Wait a damn second," he said, "that's what you were watching earlier today, in your office. Not cheerleaders but players . . ."

Beau nodded, and Sebastian shot him a look.

"What, it's a good idea," Beau said mildly. "It would bring you guys together. And you know how intimidating it is for the opposing team to bust out something like that?"

Sebastian leaned back in his chair. "You know I love fish tacos and you've nearly ruined my appetite, so this better be an idea you feel pretty damn strongly about."

Beau knew better; nothing could dent Sebastian's appetite.

"You don't want to intimidate the shit out of a team before they even take the field?" he asked archly.

"You mean like that rugby team . . . what's their name . . . they do this, and the Samoans do a variation as well."

"That's more of a sacred chant, this is . . . less religious. Less of a ceremony. More fifty-three of you warming up together."

"But same idea," Sebastian said, spearing a piece of blackened mahi-mahi with his fork. "Same conclusion. It's a declaration of intent."

"Yes." Beau should have trusted that Sebastian would get it. He was smart. But he also abhorred looking stupid, and if the team couldn't pull this off, if it didn't go well . . . that would be inevitable.

"You're starting this soon. Tomorrow?" Sebastian guessed. "Or else you wouldn't be telling me tonight."

"You're right, annoyingly," Beau said, nodding. "It's all set."

"You using music?"

"Yeah," Beau said, picking up his taco. "We used AC/DC at Tennessee, but I wanted this to feel different. I think you'll like it."

"I don't know, I'm kinda picky about music. Also kinda picky about how I warm up," Sebastian warned.

"But you're gonna do it."

Beau stated it, he didn't ask.

Sebastian sighed. "Yeah, yeah I am. I trust you. I know you wouldn't send us out there to look stupid. You're sending us out there to win."

"We won by the skin of our teeth yesterday," Beau said. "We can't count on the situation swinging our way like that every time. We need to win dominantly."

"And you think this'll help us do that, so I'll do it," Sebastian said.

"You guys are all talented. The game plans are solid. I think winning games is a lot about confidence and also about imposing your will on the other team, versus letting their will being imposed on you. It's about an attitude when you take the field. And this sets you up for that."

Sebastian nodded, and Beau could see that he was considering the argument.

Not for him. He'd already agreed do it. But Beau knew he was considering how best to frame it for the other players. The players who'd say to all the coaches' faces that they were on board, but behind their backs would laugh at what they'd been asked to do.

"Come on," Sebastian finally said, "let's eat. Then maybe we can figure out where we left off this morning before your dad interrupted us."

Beau grinned. "I like the sound of that."

"Then," Sebastian said, lowering his voice, until it was the low, rough murmur that never failed to make him hard, and was already working wonders now, "you'd better eat your tacos."

Less than an hour later, they were back at Sebastian's penthouse, but instead of heading to the bedroom, they'd barely managed to make it to the couch before he couldn't resist Beau's mouth a second longer.

He collapsed onto it, pulling Beau into his lap and their kisses had turned hotter and then hotter still, until he felt like he might burn up with the passion of them.

Beau rubbed insistently against his thigh, his cock a hard line in his jeans, as he whimpered into Sebastian's mouth. It was so good, so completely, totally, wonderfully perfect that Sebastian *almost* didn't want to stop or move or change anything about their current situation. But his own cock was straining against his shorts, wet and twitching with every single movement that Beau made.

"God," Beau panted into his mouth as Sebastian gave in and snaked a hand in between them, rubbing against Beau's dick insistently. "Feels so good."

Sebastian wanted nothing more than to hear him make those sounds today, and tomorrow, and for the next hundred years.

"Come on," Sebastian coaxed, wrenching open the button on his jeans and pushing down the zipper, getting them just open enough that he could wrap his hand around Beau's cock. "Oh yeah, baby, just like that."

Beau groaned and suddenly his fingers were twitching against Sebastian's cock, nimbly sliding into his shorts, and pleasure shot through him in a dizzying rush.

Tipping his head against Sebastian's, Beau's eyes screwed shut, precome making the slide just a little easier. But Beau seemed to like it a little rough, and Sebastian gave him all he could take, pushing him inexorably towards his orgasm, just as Beau worked him towards his own.

A minute later, Beau was moaning, pulsing in long, shuddering spasms as he came, Sebastian following only a few seconds later, letting the orgasm empty out all his worries, his cares, his anxieties.

For a long moment, neither of them moved, Beau still curled up on his lap.

"I needed that," Beau finally said, softly.

"Me too," Sebastian said, and pulling off his t-shirt, wiped up their messes and tossed it to the side. It was still warm in the growing dusk, and he had Beau's body heat anyway. Best way to keep warm.

Beau didn't seem like he wanted to move, and Sebastian decided he was okay with that, leaning back against the soft edge of the couch, enjoying the quiet for a moment.

At least he was trying to.

One question had apparently survived his orgasm and kept pestering him, refusing to let him relax in peace.

"You were worried about telling me what Coach wanted to do," Sebastian stated, rather than asked, breaking the silence that had fallen between them.

Beau shifted a little, but didn't move.

Didn't answer right away either.

Finally he lifted his head, his blue eyes shadowed with worries that Sebastian wished he could alleviate—but knowing that he couldn't. Beau had taken on those burdens because he wanted them, and it wasn't Sebastian's right to take them away. But he could make sure Beau knew that he could always trust him.

That he'd always have Beau's back. No matter what.

"Yeah," Beau admitted. "I was worried. It's . . . it's a lot to ask. Those guys at Tennessee, they were different. Younger."

"Don't you dare say hungrier," Sebastian inserted with a soft chuckle.

"I wouldn't." Beau's expression was still serious. "You're hungry. Everyone else on the team's just as hungry. Maybe more hungry. I worry about Pax and the hunger he's fed."

"You mean, the hunger Davis feeds him."

Beau's expression turned cautious. "Davis has a justifiable ax to grind with the NFL."

"Pax has got a level head. He can take care of himself."

Beau was quiet for a moment. "I *was* worried about telling you. I guess I shouldn't have been."

"That's what I'm tryin' to tell you," Sebastian said. "You don't need to worry about me. I . . . I got you."

"You got me?"

Sebastian was uncomfortably aware that he was not doing a good job of this. "I'm yours. And you're mine. Not just here." He gestured around the penthouse. "But on the field, too. You tell me something, I'm gonna believe it. I'm gonna do it. Because you told me. And I trust you, Beau, more than I trust just about anyone else on earth."

"Because I'm good at what I do," Beau said.

Sebastian nearly groaned in frustration. He was *really* not doing a good job with this. But in his defense, he'd never done it before.

"Yes, but not just that. Because . . . because I care about you. And I know you care about me too, and because of that, you'd never step over the line. So if you tell me something, if you *ask* me to do something, I'm gonna trust that it's legit."

Beau's gaze softened. It was so warm, grazing along Sebastian's bare skin. "Who knew you were such a romantic."

"Nobody before you, that's for sure," Sebastian said, huffing a little in embarrassment. But hoping that Beau understood.

"That's why I believe you," Beau said simply, and leaned in, kissing him.

The next day, practice began as almost every practice did.

But just as everyone was jogging onto the field, and about to separate out into their different positional groups, Sebastian watched as Coach blew his whistle and clapped his hands, gathering the rest of the staff to him. Beau was there, too, wearing his Piranhas hat backwards—something that Sebastian had considered stupid at one point and that now sent butterflies scattering through his insides. He was right next to his father, clipboard and tablet in hand.

"Y'all, let's have a quick meeting," Coach called out, his voice rising effortlessly. He was wearing what should have been a nearly brand-new Piranhas visor cap, his dark hair, sprinkled with just a hint of gray, thick underneath it. But the cap was sweat-spotted and worn, looking like he'd owned it for years, even though this was his first year coaching.

He didn't know how old Coach Dawson was, but considering Beau's age, and his own looks, he doubted he was over fifty.

Still a guy in his prime.

And married, the way that Beau was headed, to the job.

Maybe that might've bothered another guy, but Sebastian loved his job too, and he knew when he eventually retired, he'd never be able to truly leave football behind. Maybe he'd end up on ESPN or in the broadcasting booth, or even on the sidelines, coaching, but he knew neither of them was going to change what they were doing.

Sebastian didn't mind; he just wanted to be the guy that Beau came home to in five years. In ten. In fifty.

He'd never felt this way before, and he wasn't sure he'd done a real good job of explaining it to Beau last night, but he couldn't deny it, at least to himself, any longer.

"What's up, Coach?" Pax asked, shading his eyes, as the players milled together.

"I asked Beau to help me with a way to bring this team together," Coach said. "We had a real good win on Sunday. We needed that. I don't know about y'all, but winning one game only makes me wanna win a whole lot more."

There was a rumble of approval that moved through the crowd of players and Sebastian realized that Coach hadn't miraculously come up with this idea just now. It seemed much more likely that he'd thought of it before this, and he'd waited until just the right time to deploy it. When they'd won a game, and everyone was going to be hungry to win more.

"Right now, we've been warming up with our different positions," Beau said, speaking up, his voice carrying just like his father's. Was it heredity, or was it a learned skill? Sebastian didn't know, but it was impressive. "But we're gonna change that. At least the beginning of the warmup."

Sebastian watched, not just Beau, but the rest of the players, as Beau demonstrated, his slim but athletic build going through the warmups he'd choreographed together. There seemed to be mostly confusion, but confusion—and not outright derision—was good.

Then Beau said, "And now we're going to work on doing that, all together."

"What?" Rob Jeremiah, the left tackle, called out. "You want us to do like . . . a fucking routine? On the field?"

"Have you ever seen the All Blacks?" Coach inserted casually, but his eyes were gleaming. Bright. Taking in every single bit of information and processing. Sebastian wasn't surprised that he'd made the same connection that he had. He'd been planning this for longer than twenty-four hours. No matter what he'd told Beau. "They're a rugby union team from New Zealand. They do a similar ceremonial performance before each and every game of theirs. We aren't doing it for ritual purposes but it accomplishes the same goal. Brings us together as a team. Reminds us that we have each other. And that we're confident. Also reminds the opponent of those very same things."

"It's intimidating," Beau continued, picking up where his father left off. "It's intimidating as all hell, if we can do it right. So let's do it right." He clapped his hands, waved above his head, and the music changed, a relentless bass line starting.

It wasn't a particularly hard group of warmups—basic exercises really, easy to do to the music, and easy enough to string together. The purpose of it wasn't to get ready to play physically, Sebastian realized as they ran through it once, and then twice, then a third time, it was to get ready to play emotionally.

On the third round, he found himself glancing around him, watching others, making sure their movements were tuned to his own, and also, because he couldn't freaking help himself, making sure that nobody was just going through the motions. Beau was right, this was the kind of thing everyone committed to, or else it fell apart.

The offensive line seemed to be committed, but then Logan was the leader of that group—and if he did it, then they'd all do it. And Logan was a surprisingly smart guy, who'd get what they were trying to do. And sure enough, every time they went through the routine, Logan did every jumping jack, every stretch, every lunge.

Pax was too, but then Pax was getting increasingly fanatical. Sebastian knew Beau was worried about him, and he was beginning to think his guy wasn't exaggerating.

Rose was to his left, and to Sebastian's surprise, he was definitely half-assing it. Probably thought he'd left this kind of shit behind in college.

But he wasn't the only one. Kenyon looked bored and Sebastian caught a handful of eyerolls.

It wasn't really his place to interfere with Kenyon—he was offense, so he was absolutely Paxton's responsibility—but Rose? Oh, Sebastian could deal with him. Publicly enough that it might shake Kenyon back in line.

Beau broke them up into their sections, asking them to practice the routine a few times more on their own, making sure everyone knew it. And then they were free to continue on with practice.

"But," Beau warned, "we're gonna do this first thing every practice. And at the game this weekend. So be ready."

There were a handful of half-hearted groans, but Beau gave one last pointed look at each of the offenders before retreating back to the other sideline where Coach stood.

Coach Brett led them in another set of more specialized warmups, and then they moved on to tackling.

Sebastian had always gone through the motions when it came to tackles, because he didn't tend to use most of the techniques the same way the other guys did. He'd had his own set of unique, specialized moves that he'd cobbled together in his experience as a corner.

But when he'd moved to safety, that hadn't been good enough for Coach Brett, who'd taken one look at his tackling in the first game and had decided that he needed a total fucking overhaul. It made sense; the last time he'd really worked on tackling had been in high school, when for some bizarre reason his coach had decided he should be a linebacker. That hadn't lasted more than a week once he'd gotten to Miami. They'd made him a corner, and he'd believed that he'd stay a corner forever.

Change is good, Sebastian told himself as he huffed out a breath as Coach barked at him to try a different angle, *you just fucking hate it, that's all.*

"Better," Coach Brett called out. "You've got that fire, Howard, you just gotta direct it."

Fire, Coach Brett's utmost compliment.

Maybe this wasn't quick, but he *was* slowly getting the hang of it.

By the time Coach was satisfied though, he was tired. And he still had to deal with Rose, who was on the back end of the field, running routes with Tristan.

Having endured that particular hell, he knew the only saving grace was that Rose was probably more exhausted than he was.

Sebastian watched as they ran a few more plays, guzzling one cup of Gatorade, and then another, trying to catch his breath.

When they wrapped it up, Sebastian jogged over.

"Rose," he called out.

Micah raised his head. "What?" he barked.

"Come on," he said gesturing to an open, empty section of the field. "Let's work on your technique."

Micah had agreed to work with him, but now as he slunk over, he seemed less than thrilled at the possibility.

Maybe he already knew Sebastian was gonna kick his ass.

"The reason Tristan's losin' you every time is because you're turning around at the wrong time," Sebastian said, demonstrating in a few quick steps. "You gotta turn around a half second sooner. And your angles could use some work."

"Tristan's losin' me 'cause he's too fucking fast," Micah grumbled under his breath.

"Yeah, and he's not the only one. You think you can cover Davante Adams or DK Metcalf with sloppy technique? No way, man, no way. It's not gonna happen. You're gonna get embarrassed out there, and then *I'm* gonna be embarrassed." Sebastian met his eyes with a cold stare. "And you really don't want to embarrass me. I also don't wanna have to do your job for you, either. So let's see a few more routes."

"Who am I gonna cover?" Micah challenged.

Tristan, Wade, and a few of the other receivers were already on the opposing sideline, chatting with Coach.

"Me."

Micah laughed, which was just the first of his mistakes.

Sebastian didn't say a word, because he wasn't going to need to say a single damn one.

They lined up, and this time, Sebastian took a particularly tricky pattern of ins and outs that he'd seen Odell Beckham Jr. run a handful of times.

Micah kept up with him through the first, and then the second, but not the third, because he turned, just as Sebastian had warned him, just a fraction late, and Sebastian pushed through, pumping his legs with a last burst of speed.

He slowed, and then came to a stop, ten yards downfield. "That," he said, panting, "was an easy fucking pass."

Micah glowered. "Maybe. Maybe not."

"I was ten yards off of you, it was an easy fucking pass," Sebastian reiterated. "Catch *and* run. Maybe even a touchdown."

Sebastian watched as Micah tried to rein in his temper.

He didn't want to piss him off, because anger was a deterrent to progress.

But he also really wanted to piss him off, for daring to roll his eyes at Beau.

It wasn't really a question of which path he was gonna take—only how far he was gonna take it.

But maybe they could get in a little practice first.

"You gotta turn earlier," Sebastian repeated. "If you'd turned when I said, you wouldn't have lost me."

"It feels . . ."

Sebastian understood, nodding. "But you gotta be proactive, not reactive. Let's try it again."

They didn't just do it once.

They did it half a dozen times, Sebastian varying his route each time, blowing by Micah, as he struggled to get his timing just right.

Finally, at the end of the last set, Micah leaned over, breath coming in short gasps. "Fine, I'm turning at the wrong fucking time," he huffed, clearly really annoyed. Not quite as pissed off as Sebastian had hoped, but he decided that was probably a good thing. A better thing. If Micah was going to learn from him—if he was going to teach him the way Beau wanted him to—then anger was only going to get in the way.

It just wasn't as fucking satisfying as it could've been, that was all.

"You sure are," Sebastian said with a chuckle. "You know what else you're doin'?"

Micah shot him a hot glare. "No?"

"You're rollin' your eyes. Just goin' through the motions. That's not what we do here."

"You're just as new as me," Micah said, rolling his eyes again, which only pissed *Sebastian* off. "How do you know what the Piranhas do?"

Sebastian took a handful of steps closer. Not threatening, not exactly. But enough that Micah hopefully got his drift. "The Piranhas want to win. I want to win. I think, despite your punk-ass attitude, you want to win, too. If we do nothing, if we roll our eyes and pretend that we're too fucking cool to do what the coaches say, then all we get is nothing. That what you want?"

Micah was clearly reluctant, but he did shake his head.

"Right. I didn't think so. 'Cause I will absolutely kick your ass from here til next year rather than accept nothing."

"You think you could?" Micah challenged right back.

He really was a stupid punk-ass kid. Sebastian sighed. "Don't even try to test me, man. Just *don't*."

"Everything okay over here?"

Sebastian looked up to see Beau jogging over.

Of course he'd been watching, and of course, he'd noticed, just as Sebastian had, Micah's lack of commitment to the new warmup routine. And he was probably coming over here now so that Sebastian didn't do something stupid and kick Rose's ass.

He might be sorely tempted, but he wouldn't.

Maybe ten years ago, when he'd been Rose's age, *maybe*. But he'd learned that it wasn't worth it a long time ago.

"Everything's fine," Sebastian said, shading his eyes. "Just doing a little extra coaching. Making sure Micah's timing is down."

"It's off?" Beau looked surprised, which surprised Sebastian, because not much got past Beau—but then he'd never actually played corner. It was a *blink and you'll miss it* kind of thing he was trying to educate Rose on.

"Just a hair," Sebastian said as Micah tried to protest.

"It looked off to me," Beau said slowly, "not on film, but when you were blowing past him just now." He shot Sebastian a look—and he knew Beau well enough to know exactly what that look meant. *You're pushing and I don't know why.*

"Yeah, no fucking kidding," Micah complained.

"Well, keep at it," Beau said, which was definitely not what Micah had wanted to hear. "Sebastian ran the best corner routes in the NFL. If anyone's gonna teach you to nail that timing, it's gonna be him."

Sebastian could feel the anger emanating from Rose—he wanted to roll his eyes again, so badly he could taste it. But he didn't.

Was it because of his veiled threats? Or because Micah wasn't stupid enough to provoke the special assistant to the head coach?

Sebastian didn't know, but he was glad, because he *really* didn't want to kick Micah's ass.

He glanced over at Micah. "You wanna go again?"

"Tomorrow," he said. "I'm worn out from Tristan and then from you, not letting me fucking take a breather."

"We'll do it before practice, then," Sebastian said firmly. "Make sure you're ready for our warmup, too."

The look Micah shot him was assessing. Like he was re-thinking not just his opinion of Sebastian, but the situation they'd found themselves in. "You really give a shit, don't you," he stated, rather than asked.

"All the shits," Sebastian said with a chuckle. "I wanna win games, don't you?"

Micah nodded.

As Sebastian jogged towards the locker room, ready to clean up and get some ice on his sore muscles, he thought that was a job well done.

Two birds, one stone.

He'd help Rose become a better corner, and make sure he stayed in line, too.

Right before he hit the locker room, Beau joined him.

"I was almost sure," he said, under his breath, "that you were gonna kick his ass."

"Really?" Sebastian asked innocently, even though Beau wasn't entirely wrong.

Beau rolled his eyes. It was cute coming from him. Adorable, even. "You don't often get that hard-ass look on your face. You know the one."

"Good news for me is I don't have to," Sebastian teased.

"I don't know about that," Beau retorted. He grinned. "It was pretty hot. Or it would've been, if I hadn't been worried I'd have to break you two up."

"Shouldn't have to worry about him tomorrow," Sebastian observed as they entered the locker room. He collapsed down onto the bench. He was fucking tired as hell. All Coach Brett's tackling drills plus the extra work with Rose had wiped him out. "I took care of that, too."

Beau smiled. To keep that look on his face, Sebastian would gladly go back out onto the field and run a dozen more drills. "You noticed that too, huh?"

Sebastian shot him a cocky grin. "Baby, I notice everything."

Chapter Fifteen

Today, Beau thought with trepidation as he watched the players run out onto the field of the opposing team, was the real fucking test.

Would they take the momentum they'd generated from their first win and win again? Would the warmup routine, even performed on a different team's field, bring the Piranhas together? Or would they stumble, against a pretty good Raiders team, and lose all the progress they'd made?

Beau didn't know, and anything Beau didn't know made him nervous.

"You ready for this?" His dad walked up next to him. There was a crease between his eyes that Beau wasn't sure he'd seen disappear in at least a week. You'd think winning the last game and finally getting that victory they'd wanted would make him less anxious, less nervous.

But Beau was there to attest that didn't happen.

All winning did was make you want to win more.

"Ready as we'll ever be," Beau said. "You take care of the music?"

"They said they'd play it but who knows," Asa said wryly. "It's the Raiders. They're a bit of a loose cannon, always. We warned them, might have to do it without music."

They had, yesterday during the walk-through in the hotel. His dad had been fairly confident he could convince the Raiders to play one song during the warmups, but again, it *was* the Raiders. Who knew what they'd actually do.

"They're ready," Beau said, though he didn't feel nearly as confident as he sounded.

"Yep," Coach said, gazing out onto the field.

Beau looked down at his tablet, cycling through the game plans, reassuring himself by looking at the opening drive they'd planned out. It was solid. It was *better* than solid. Pax was confident too, looking more and more relaxed in the pocket.

Maybe he'd worried too much about the effect that Davis' history would have on him. Maybe they were actually better for each other than he'd thought. He hadn't had as much time as he'd wanted to spend with them this week, but it was still on his list.

At some point during the season, he'd be able to focus on the offense, and hopefully quarterback play.

When he raised his head, he saw Sebastian looking right at him. A little risky, maybe, considering his dad was standing right there, too, but he was, as usual, absorbed with something in his pad, and he probably wouldn't notice.

Beau gave a little salute and Sebastian grinned, the brightness of his smile obvious even from fifty yards downfield.

"Beau," his dad said, but before he could say anything else, the music changed and, like magic, the bass line started, blaring across the field.

And every Piranhas player froze, and exactly as Beau had designed it, began moving as one team.

"Look at that," Asa said, awe in his voice. "It's fuckin' working."

Beau stared out at the field. It wasn't perfect—not everyone was totally in unison—but it was close enough, and he could hear the rising murmur going through the crowd. And the glares that the Raiders' players were throwing their way told the rest of the story.

He didn't mean to, but Beau realized two things when it was over. *One,* he'd been holding his breath nearly the whole time, as he tapped his stylus on the side of his tablet with the beat. When the music finally faded out, he felt breathless but also exhilarated. And *two,* he realized the roar lifting through the stadium wasn't the crowd, wasn't the Raiders' players, it was the Piranhas, and they were shouting, a long, loud cry of confidence and success.

"That," Coach said, turning to Beau, "is exactly what I had in mind. Great job."

Beau nodded at him. His father had never been afraid of praise, but he was also stingy with it, saving it for moments that were deserved.

And this, he thought, was definitely deserved.

As the team took the field, he could feel a different electricity in the air, a charged determination. Everyone moved differently, with assurance and certainty.

When Pax took the field for the first offensive drive, he stared right into the teeth of the Raiders' defensive line and he didn't even blink.

Beau wasn't naive enough to believe that doing some jumping jacks to a song was enough to change the way a team played. They'd been heading to this spot with each consecutive game. But the warmup routine had helped solidify that drive, turn it from fifty-three individual ambitions into one overriding *team* ambition.

The offense played solidly, putting together a drive that ended in a field goal. But they didn't return to the bench looking like they'd settled; they came back *energized*.

Ready to tackle the next opportunity they'd get.

Davis Abernathy wandered over his direction after he'd gone over the last drive's plays with Pax.

"You know, I thought you were a little crazy."

Beau grinned. "How'd you know I'm not?"

"Well," Davis said, "jury's still out, maybe. But it worked. That crazy goddamned routine worked."

"It worked because everyone wanted it to work," Beau said. "Including your guy."

He didn't want to see it.

But there it was anyway. Beau might've missed it but he was looking for it. A split second when Davis' expression froze at Beau referring to Paxton as "your guy." It had been less than a second. But he'd seen it, and now he couldn't forget it.

Beau had meant it in the strictest platonic sense—after all, Davis was the quarterbacks coach and Pax was the starting quarterback—and he hoped, *God he hoped*, that it wasn't like that, but he could tell. For a moment, Davis' mind had gone somewhere that was not strictly platonic.

Even though he kept meaning to, Beau resolved to spend some more time with them in the next few weeks. Because if something was going on . . . well, he was just going to assume it wasn't. Because it'd be a clusterfuck.

"We're both committed to this team," Davis said.

Beau nodded. Trying to clear his head. "He's turning into a good leader, and that's what we need. We're like the island of misfit toys. Rookies, also-rans, veterans looking for a fresh start. We got 'em all. There's so much talent here. Some of it obvious, some of it buried under a ton of crap. But it's there. Just a matter of gettin' it all on the same page. At the beginning I don't think some of us were in the same fucking book."

"Pax is tryin'," Davis said. "Tryin' his damn hardest to make it work."

"And he's doing it. What I'm trying to say is . . . he didn't have to buy into this, but when he did, he brought most of the team with him."

"Of course." Davis smiled. "He knows what he's gotta do. Win games. Bring the team together. Be a leader."

Hearing it all laid out like that, made it seem like it was easier than it was. But Beau knew it wasn't.

Some of the most experienced quarterbacks in the NFL didn't know how to do any of those things.

As the game progressed, Beau made notes, picked out plays, pointed them out to players, but the whole time, it felt entirely different than it had the last three games. He felt electrified, like he'd been plugged into a socket, because the team's energy was palpable. And it didn't quit, not even in the fourth quarter, when the Piranhas were leading by ten, and the Raiders were attempting to score.

Sebastian was flying around the field, seemingly everywhere at once, making play after play, frustrating and stopping the Raiders' offense, until they finally came to a halt, forced to kick a field goal.

With two minutes left, and up seven points, Pax led the Piranhas' offense back on the field, and put together a solid drive, leading to another Dylan kick, right as the time expired.

Beau couldn't stop the wave of exhilaration that crested through him, or the savage fist pump. They'd done it, *again*, and even better this time. This was, even more than last week, a fantastic team win. Everyone had contributed. The defense had made key stops. The offense hadn't sputtered out. And special teams? His father, who was never wrong, hadn't been wrong about Dylan Leonard either. He was rock solid, kicking in important moments like he was still just warming up on the sideline.

They, Beau realized as the players swept him along into the locker room, might have a really good thing here.

It wasn't the first time he'd thought it.

But it was the first time he truly believed it.

Sebastian relaxed—or tried to relax—into the seat on the Piranhas' plane.

They still had two hours left before they reached Miami, and despite the long hot shower, and hours on this goddamned plane, he still felt keyed up. Full of adrenaline.

It had been a good win, for sure, something that the team had needed, especially to follow up last week's win, but he'd never felt like this before.

Logan, across from him, opened one eye. "You squirm one more time, I'm gonna come over there and make sure you're incapable of squirming. Okay?"

"Sorry," Sebastian said quietly, aware that most of the plane was asleep or at the very least chilling.

Unlike him, whose body *wouldn't*. No matter what he did.

He was afraid he knew what the problem was. And he was afraid that the solution wasn't possible.

Because he wasn't going to go grab Beau from his spot with the coaching staff, and convince him to go to the tiny-ass bathroom with him and get each other off.

They'd only had sex after the games three times. That's it.

But somehow Sebastian had gotten used to it. Craved it. Craved *him*.

You can't have him right now. Soonest you can have him is hours from now. And that's if he doesn't shut the door in your face, because it'll be two in the fucking morning and it's crazy that you want to fuck and not sleep.

But, Sebastian considered, he could at least go talk to the guy. He pulled out his phone and sent off a quick text.

You awake?

He sat there for another moment longer, staring at the screen, tapping his fingers against it.

"Really, man, go take a chill pill or jack off in the bathroom or something," Logan said, this time not even bothering to open one eye.

Sebastian didn't blush. He refused to let himself.

"Uh, yeah, sorry," Sebastian murmured awkwardly.

He glanced down. Still no response from Beau. He could be busy. He could be asleep. Or his phone could just be on silent?

He decided he might as well head to the bathroom, because on the way to the one in the front was where the coaches typically sat, Beau with them.

He could just . . . check to see what Beau was up to.

What he was doing.

If he was awake.

Definitely not if he wanted to go to the bathroom *with* him.

He stood, and as he walked towards the front, he passed Wade and Tristan, both asleep, Tristan's head on Wade's shoulder, and his own heart spasmed.

He didn't want to get his ass kicked. Especially not by Coach.

But there was a part of him that couldn't help wanting that. Wanting to not hide anymore, to acknowledge how he felt about Beau, and not have to keep it under wraps all the time.

But Coach would not only kick his ass, he might find himself unceremoniously traded to a different team—and the last thing Sebastian wanted was to give up the Piranhas. Not now. Not when everything was gelling. Not when Micah had asked him for help, and was beginning to look better. Not when he was actually *enjoying* playing football again, finding a joy in his new position that he'd never imagined. And not when he'd found a new group of friends, who had his back.

Coming clean to Coach about Beau would almost certainly mean losing all that, and would mean starting over, too. But he was getting to the point where he wasn't sure anymore which was worse.

That, Sebastian thought as he navigated through the dark, quiet plane, *is really fucked up*.

But it was true.

He couldn't deny it anymore.

He finally reached where the coaches sat, and sure enough, the only one awake was not Beau. It was Coach, watching something on silent on his tablet.

Sebastian hovered a second too long, the desire to be honest warring with the practicalities of his situation. And that was long enough to catch Coach's attention.

He glanced up at Sebastian.

"You need something, Howard?" he whispered.

Sebastian shook his head, and then realized he'd been standing here like he did.

You do, you need to be honest, but you're fucking terrified of what being honest means.

"Uh," Sebastian mumbled, "uh, I just wanted to say you were right about the routine thing. It worked great."

Coach stared at him. Unnervingly. Then, Sebastian's heart clenched in his chest as Coach glanced over to the seat next to him. To where Beau slept, propped up on the window.

"Turns out," Asa said wryly, "I'm right about a lot of things."

And then, Sebastian swore he wasn't imagining things, he looked right back at Beau again.

Oh shit. He knows. He knows. He knows.

"But," Coach continued, "sometimes I'm wrong, too. Guess we're going to have to take each thing as it comes, huh, Howard?"

Sebastian gulped and nodded sheepishly.

Then turned tail and practically jogged back to his seat.

Freaking out every moment of his return journey.

Logan opened both eyes as he flopped into his seat.

"Maybe you don't know how to do it right," he said. "Beau could probably help you with that."

"Beau's *asleep,* and . . ." Sebastian swallowed hard. How had Coach found out? Had someone told him? He would've sworn that none of the guys who'd been at the club that night would. Logan was loyal, and he'd absolutely vouched for Dylan. Pax wouldn't, because he'd been too busy staring at Davis, who couldn't help staring back.

Tristan and Wade?

Wade wouldn't. And Tristan wouldn't *mean* to, but he was a talker, and liked his gossip. But still, Sebastian found it hard to believe that he'd slip up about something this important because Tristan was absolutely solid, a great guy. And an even better friend.

And, more importantly than anything else, they all understood what it was like to be in the closet.

They wouldn't expose Sebastian. Not on purpose.

Doesn't matter how Coach knows, Sebastian thought, heart still racing uncomfortably, *he just knows. And I'm gonna have to do something about it.*

What, he didn't know.

"We'll be landing soon," Logan said. "For the love of God, try to relax and sleep a little, okay?"

Sebastian nodded, but he knew he wouldn't.

There was no fucking way he was going to be able to relax now.

Sebastian's panic didn't exactly recede, but by the time the plane landed, he had a plan.

It was not a very complicated plan.

Talk to Beau. He'll know what to do.

He knew his father better than anyone else, and he'd know what they should do about it, how he needed to thread the needle to confess the truth *and* stay here, in Miami.

Because anything less, Sebastian had realized over the last hour of terror, was unacceptable. He didn't want to give up Beau, and he didn't want to give up this incredible opportunity.

This team had believed in him—*Beau* had believed in him—when nobody else did. When he'd felt so alone, trying to play a position that only he'd believed that he could still play.

Beau and the coaching staff of the Piranhas had shown him a different way, and it was already paying off.

But if they dumped him off, traded him for pennies on the dollar, Coach punishing him for fucking around with his son, he'd never get to see where all the tantalizing possibilities were headed.

He'd never get to see what he was really, truly capable of.

The bus took them from the airport back to the practice facility. And yawning, Sebastian watched as everyone went their separate ways, getting into their cars, ready to head home after a long-ass day.

He watched as Beau exchanged a few words with his dad, and to Sebastian's surprise, Asa went back into the facility, and Beau pulled up his phone, probably, Sebastian figured, to call an Uber to take him home to his condo.

As soon as Coach was out of sight, Sebastian walked over.

"Hey," Beau said, looking up in surprise. "I thought you'd already left. Great game, by the way. Sorry I couldn't . . ." He hesitated. "It's weird to have this thing where we can't *really* talk, the way we do in private, around everyone, isn't it?"

"It is," Sebastian said. It was either going to get weirder, or it would be alright.

Unfortunately, what direction it took wasn't up to him.

Beau looked at him a little closer. "You okay? You look . . . not exhausted. But . . . worried?"

"I need to talk to you," Sebastian said. "But not here. Let's go back to my place."

"No," Beau said firmly. "I'm going home. And you can come with me, or we can talk tomorrow."

"Really? But your dad's condo . . ."

Beau rolled his eyes. "He's not even going home. I wish I could make him, but I can't."

"Oh." While this was good for him, and might allow him to finally see Beau's place, it occurred to Sebastian that this wasn't *good* either.

He looked at his watch. It was almost two, and Coach wasn't going home, but back to the office? That was sort of fucked up.

"Yeah, I'm not happy about it. But it means you can come with, if you want to," Beau said.

"Sure," Sebastian said. "I got my car, I can drive us . . ."

"Yeah, there's a spot in the garage that goes with the condo, but I don't have a car here, so I don't usually need it," Beau said. "You can park there."

They climbed into Sebastian's Audi, throwing their bags into the small trunk, and he followed Beau's directions, focusing intently because if he thought, *Beau's right here, right where you've wanted him for hours,* or *what the fuck are we gonna do?* he was liable to crash the car. Even though he was normally a solid driver.

Finally they got to the building, Beau directing him to the garage level.

He parked and then they took the elevator to Beau's floor. It was not the penthouse, but it seemed like a nice enough floor.

Beau pulled his keys out of his pocket, letting them in, and finally, *finally,* they were truly alone.

Sebastian prowled around the living room, taking it in. It was maybe even more austere than Sebastian's own place. Clearly decorated by a professional, almost no personal touches anywhere.

Beau didn't spend much time here, which Sebastian knew, because he'd been spending all his extra time—what extra time he had—with Sebastian.

"So, you gonna tell me what has you so upset?" Beau asked, flicking on a light and heading into the kitchen. He opened the fridge and pulled out two bottles of water, throwing one at Sebastian.

"Yes," Sebastian said, "but first."

He set the water down on the counter and closed the space between them in two steps, cupping Beau's face—his fucking precious, hot-as-hell face, the one that had captured Sebastian from the first glance—and kissed him.

He poured all his longing, all his uncertainty, every bit of terror of losing him, into it.

Beau squeaked in surprise, and then groaned into Sebastian's mouth, following him where he wanted to go, until they were pressed up against each other, Beau rubbing his hardening cock against Sebastian's thigh.

It took effort, but Sebastian tore his mouth from Beau's, finally, and stepped back. It wasn't a lot of space, but it was enough.

"You make me crazy," Sebastian confessed, his voice rough.

"And here I thought you were coming here to dump me." Beau's tone was light, but Sebastian didn't miss the concern in his dark blue eyes.

"No. Never." Sebastian hesitated. "Opposite of, in fact. I wanted to tell you . . . *God*, I don't know how to say this. But I think your dad knows about us."

"Oh?" Beau laughed.

Laughed.

"Do not tell me, *is that all this is*," Sebastian said, strained.

"I mean"—Beau shrugged—"it's hardly the end of the world."

"For *you*, maybe. He's not going to kick your ass. Or have you killed. Or *traded*."

"You really think he'd do that?" Beau looked surprised.

"I don't know what he'd do, he's Asa fucking Dawson. He's a wild card. He's brilliant. And whether you see it or not, he's protective of you."

"Yeah," Beau agreed. He picked up the water, picking at the label with a fingernail. "But not like that. He knows . . . we've talked about this."

"About *this?*" Sebastian felt his heartbeat accelerate. "You told him?"

"No, no, no," Beau reassured him. "No, I didn't. But yeah, we have talked about this general situation, if I ever got involved with a player. It wasn't even a stretch really, because who else do I see on a regular basis? He told me he didn't care, much, but he didn't want to see it spill onto the field. Mess up the player dynamics. It's not like I'm in the coaching hierarchy, not in a meaningful way."

"You're telling me . . . he isn't going to care." Sebastian said it carefully. Slowly. Not wanting to be misunderstood when this was so goddamn important.

Beau shrugged. "That might be a mild exaggeration," he said.

"But he's not going to kill me. Or trade me."

"You don't seem sure which is worse," Beau teased, a smile lighting up his face.

"At this point, I'm *not* sure," Sebastian grumbled. "I want to play for the Piranhas. You guys are building something special. I wanna be part of it. But I want you, too. I'm tired of hiding it. I'm tired of having to sit in different sections on the plane. I'm tired of having to avoid talking to you because it's so damn obvious we care about each other when we do."

"Then, if you want to, you could tell him," Beau said. "It's up to you, because I know what it would mean for you."

Sebastian had expected Beau to offer a lot of different advice. He hadn't expected this particular piece of advice.

"You think I should? You would be okay with that?" Sebastian asked.

"He's letting Tristan and Wade be together, isn't he?" Beau challenged.

"Tristan and Wade aren't his son," Sebastian retorted.

"Well, let me ask you this," Beau said, pulling off his glasses and taking a step closer, until he was pressed right up against Sebastian again. His voice dropped to a murmur, his face tipped up until it would be so easy to kiss him again. Sebastian wanted it. Desperately. "Are you going to break my heart?"

"What? *No*," Sebastian insisted. "Hell no. Fuck no. I'm not . . . I wouldn't."

"Then." Beau grinned. "You've got nothing to worry about."

Sebastian was struck dumb.

Struck down.

He'd known what this was, before this, because it had been rather undeniable. But he'd never given voice to the feelings before. Never before.

Because he was struck down, struck dumb; completely, irrevocably, fucking *all in* in love with Beau Dawson.

"Come on," Beau said, like Sebastian wasn't desperately trying to recalibrate his whole fucking existence to this brand-new realization, "let's go to bed. It's late."

Beau's bed was not only big, it was comfortable, and with his immediate concerns allayed, Sebastian should have found it easy to collapse into it, Beau next to him, and fall asleep.

But he didn't.

Beau's soft snores started up almost immediately but Sebastian lay there, and couldn't stop thinking.

He kept going back to one thing.

Are you going to break my heart?

If Beau said that . . . if Beau had *meant* that, that would mean that Sebastian wasn't the only one who was in love.

Beau hadn't said anything, but then it was still early. They were still feeling their way around each other.

Or else, that was what Sebastian had believed.

Now, it was becoming increasingly obvious that they'd been in deep almost from the beginning.

He'd told himself it was just sex. Only sex.

But that's not what it had ever been.

If it had been just sex, he could have fucked Beau, or let Beau fuck him, and he would've moved on, the way he'd moved on before, with every other one-night stand. But when the going got rough, or a celebration was called for, he didn't want to just touch Beau—he'd also become the one person that Sebastian craved.

He wanted to talk to him, pick his incredible brain, analyze games with him, tease him, be teased in return, he even wanted to sleep next to him, just like this, without sex as a precursor, for as many nights as Beau would allow.

And that was definitely not just sex.

He finally fell asleep, but he had dreams—dreams where he kept reaching out for Beau and not quite holding on to him.

When Beau's alarm went off, he was awake in a moment, and he knew exactly what he needed to do.

"I gotta go," he said first thing, immediately sliding out of bed. Beau blinked at him through sleepy eyes.

"And do what? It's eight in the morning."

Sebastian knew how resolute he looked. How resolute he sounded.

"I gotta take care of something."

Beau flopped back into bed. "You're going to tell my father."

"Yes." Sebastian paused. He knew exactly what he was going to say to Coach, but first, he should really say it to his guy. "But before I go..." He climbed back on the bed and pulled Beau close. "First," he murmured into Beau's neck, "I want to say that sex with you is really great."

He could feel Beau's smile, even though he couldn't see it. "Sex is really great with you, too."

"But it's not just sex with you," Sebastian said earnestly. He'd never made this speech before, though he had tried once before and he didn't think he'd handled it particularly well—but this time he was going to do it better. "It's . . . I'm in love with you, Beau. I'm here, for as long as you'll have me. And if that means that your dad kills me or trades me or gives me the cold shoulder and the worst assignments on the field, so be it. I can't do this without you. I don't even want to."

Beau pulled back, and he was so goddamned beautiful, even with his fucked-up hair, and the sleep crusties in his eyes. "I love you, too." He paused. "For longer than I've wanted to, that's for sure."

Sebastian laughed. This is why he loved this man. He would never let him just *be*, except when that was what Sebastian needed. He'd always push. Always be there, ready with a quip and a laugh and a smile.

He was, quite simply, everything that Sebastian needed.

And everything he wanted.

Chapter Sixteen

It was one thing to feel brave, tucked up in Beau's arms, the echo of his love confession still ringing in his ears.

It was entirely another to walk up to Coach Dawson's office, see him sitting inside, and gather the courage to go in there and hopefully *not* blow his career up—but the possibility, Sebastian knew, existed.

"You gonna keep lingerin' there in the doorway?"

Sebastian shouldn't have jumped when Coach's drawl wafted out of his office.

But he did.

"Uh, no," he said. Reminding himself as he walked in that he was *Sebastian Howard*, and even if the sports media had liked to say that he was washed up, that he didn't have a future in the NFL, Asa Dawson would still be stupid to throw him away like he was worthless.

He stopped right in front of Coach's huge desk. It was covered in papers, about a thousand sticky notes, all with incomprehensible scribbles, and behind it sat Coach. Looking tired, dark circles under his eyes, his skin almost gray, but he was smiling.

"Come in, sit down," Coach said magnanimously. "It's early, but you seem to be on a mission. What can I do for you?"

Sebastian sat. Then ripped the Band-Aid right off.

"It's about Beau," he said.

He's not going to kill you. He really isn't. Beau wouldn't have let you come if he thought that was even a possibility.

"Oh? What 'bout Beau?" Coach leaned forward, resting his elbows on the desk. His eyes gleamed. "He causin' any trouble for you, Howard?"

If Coach had any fucking idea how much trouble he'd caused.

If he'd been even slightly less irresistible, then maybe Sebastian wouldn't be here right now, nearly sweating through his shirt.

But no, that wasn't true, was it? Because even if Beau had been *slightly* less irresistible, Sebastian still would have fallen for him.

"Not exactly," Sebastian said. "We're . . . well, we're together."

Asa raised one single eyebrow. It was shockingly expressive, that eyebrow. He had a few strands of silver mixed in with the dark hair at his temples, but that eyebrow? Still pitch black. Beau, Sebastian realized, would age this well. He'd look this handsome and arresting in forty years. In fifty.

Sebastian wanted that. Wanted to look at the man he loved, all those years down the line.

And there was no time like the present to make that happen. He forged ahead, feeling reckless now that he'd finally admitted the truth.

"We didn't mean for it to happen," Sebastian continued, "but it did, and we're happy, and I love him. Pretty sure he loves me too. So if that's a problem for you . . ."

Coach smiled.

Not one of his slow, deadly smiles, the kind that made you realize that Coach was a hundred times smarter than you'd ever be. Instead, a happy smile. The kind of smile that seemed entirely reserved for his son, whenever he'd make a joke or silly comment or when he'd be absolutely, utterly brilliant—which, since this was Beau—happened frequently.

"If you're happy, and *Beau's* happy," he said, "then I'm happy for both of you."

"Then . . . you're not gonna kill me? Slowly? And hide the pieces under the field?"

Coach's grin widened even further. "Now, I know I've got a reputation as a tough ass, but y'all think I've actually stooped to murder?"

Sebastian wasn't sure. If anyone could, it was probably Asa Dawson. He had that killer instinct and if someone pissed him off . . . well, Sebastian knew which side he'd be taking.

"Uh," he said, hesitating.

Coach threw his head back and actually fucking cackled, clearly delighted by this.

"A man," he said when he finally stopped laughing, "doesn't even have to make his own reputation. It's made for him. The answer is no—no, I'm not gonna kill you, at least not now. You gonna keep making Beau happy?"

"Of course," Sebastian said automatically.

"Then no," Coach said, still chuckling, "I'm not gonna kill you. Not even gonna bench you, not when you're playin' so well. Better than ever."

"What about Beau making *me* happy?"

"Oh, I don't worry about *that*," Coach said, "Beau's real good at makin' people happy. He's always made me happy. Never had a day where he didn't."

"Sounds like he deserves someone to make *him* happy," Sebastian said, considering this. He'd never thought of it that way before, but Beau was the kind of guy who brought joy to everyone around him.

"If you love him for who he is, and not who you want him to be," Coach said firmly, "then you will. Beau's special. I've always known that. Glad there's someone else who does too."

"Good." Sebastian stood. Wiped his sweaty, damp palm on his jeans. Extended it. Coach stood too, and shook it, firmly. Looking Sebastian right in the eye.

"If you want to make Beau happy, then you will," he said. He paused. "And," he added, eyes twinkling again, "that'll make *me* happy, and apparently around here you wanna keep me happy."

Sebastian laughed then, a mixture of joy and relief cascading through him.

He hadn't had to sacrifice one thing he'd loved for something else.

He'd been willing.

But bless Asa Dawson, of course it hadn't come to that.

"One thing, though," Coach said, as he began to turn to leave. "I told Beau this, awhile back, back when he started workin' for me."

Sebastian waited, trying to push down the anxiety that threatened to crawl right back and take ahold of him again.

"I don't want this to interfere with what you're doin' on the field," Coach said, his tone of voice suddenly forged from steel. Sebastian was reminded of *why* everyone thought he'd totally be capable of burying an enemy underneath his football field. "If you cost us games, if you're a distraction . . ." He paused, meaningfully. "Then maybe you might wanna glance behind you at night. I've worked too hard. *Beau's* worked too hard to see this go up in smoke 'cause you can't keep your dick in your pants."

"It won't," Sebastian promised. "Actually . . . Beau's been real helpful for me, with helping me prep for my new position. I couldn't have done it without him. I wouldn't have even *considered* it without him."

The grin was suddenly back, like it had never left.

And that, Sebastian thought, was disconcerting.

Impressive, but disconcerting all the same.

"I know, Howard, I know. Beau's got good instincts."

"The best," Sebastian countered.

"And that," Coach said, walking around his desk and patting Sebastian on the shoulder, "is why I gotta make the threat, but I'm not worried. Not in the least."

Beau couldn't settle down for a nice relaxing morning after Sebastian left—his heart was still beating out of his chest from Sebastian's confession, and then his own—so instead of lazing around in bed like he'd intended, he dragged himself up and put his workout clothes on, intending to head to the facility for a workout before the weekly meetings began.

He was halfway there when his phone vibrated with a text.

It's all good, Sebastian had texted, **he's not pissed off. In fact I think he's happy for us.**

Beau rolled his eyes, but typed out a quick reply. **Glad you're not in danger of imminent death.** He hesitated and then added a second message. **'Cause it'd be really awkward if I told you I loved you and then you died.**

Sebastian's reply came through just as he was walking in, swiping his key card at the south entrance.

Not as awkward as it'd be for me, he said. **I'm meeting my agent for lunch, 'cause he's in town, so I've gone home. But I'll see you later? Dinner?**

Beau considered this, thinking about the very long day of meetings he'd be having. Usually players didn't come in the day after a game, but coaches? Beau was surprised that his dad didn't have them in a meeting the whole night right after a game.

But, he realized, there was one enormous benefit to Sebastian telling his father.

They didn't have to hide anymore.

No more sneaking around.

Lots of meetings, he texted back, **but you could always bring me one of those amazing Cubans.**

Sebastian texted back a thumbs-up.

Beau had just gotten into a good rhythm on the treadmill when his dad walked into the gym.

He pulled out one of his earbuds. "Did you sleep at all?" Beau asked. Easier, he decided, to start with the more innocuous topic of his father's god-awful lifestyle habits than Beau's boyfriend confessing about their relationship this morning.

"I did, some," Asa said, leaning against one of the weight machines, opposite Beau's treadmill. "Had a real interesting visitor this morning. Sure he's already told you I'm not gonna dismember him and bury his parts under the field."

Beau rolled his eyes. "I never thought you would. You don't give a shit who I date as long as it doesn't interfere with the team. I told him that. Maybe you could work on inspiring a little less fear."

"Ah, but that's not true," Asa said thoughtfully. "I *do* actually give a shit who you date."

Beau stopped in his tracks. Surprised. The treadmill beeped in annoyed confusion, not quite understanding why he'd stopped. Beau ignored it.

"It's not any of my business, really," his dad continued, "which is why I didn't say anything before, but Howard's a good choice. Solid. I think he really cares about you. Came into my office this morning, even though he looked fucking terrified. And I have a feeling not much scares that boy."

"Not much does," Beau agreed.

"I just thought you should know, he said good things. The right things."

Beau was pleased, even though he wasn't particularly surprised. Not after what Sebastian had said this morning, flushed with joy and more than a little terror.

"But then," Asa added, "I don't think that surprises you none. You've got a good head on your shoulders. You wouldn't have picked wrong."

"Thanks, Dad," Beau said dryly. "The accolades keep coming."

Asa shot him what Beau secretly considered his "Coach look."

"Listen, and let me pay you a compliment," he complained. "I did give him the field lecture. He agreed. Said you'd been helpin' him."

"He needed the help," Beau said, starting to jog again.

"And," his dad added slyly, "that was a great excuse to spend a lot more time with him."

Beau laughed. "Not much gets by you, does it?"

Asa shrugged. "Listen, son, life is short. You gotta take what makes you happy and hold tight to it."

"Like you did?" Beau did not roll his eyes, but it was a close thing.

"I'm married to the job, you know that. Just glad you won't be."

"Does that mean . . ."

"It means," his dad said, interrupting him with a firm voice, "that you gotta do your work, but I will absolutely kick you out of the office if you start to become anything like me."

Beau nodded, trying not to laugh. "Got it," he said.

"Now, get back to your workout. We've got the coaches' meeting in an hour, I'm sure you've got lots to prep for that," Asa said gruffly.

He turned to go, but at the last minute, Beau called out, "Hey . . . thank you. I know it's not ideal, us dating, but . . ."

Asa's smile was brilliant as he flashed it towards Beau. "But he makes you happy. And that's all I've ever wanted for you. More ideal than you'd think, actually."

"What was so important you didn't want to tell me over the phone?" Alec asked, leaning back in his chair, wiping his lips with a napkin.

"I'm . . ." Why was it harder to tell his agent and friend about Beau than it had been to tell his coach and Beau's *father?*

Maybe because Alec wasn't straight either—and he'd, as far as Sebastian knew, never really been in the closet.

It was easy enough for people to say they didn't judge.

But people, Sebastian knew, *judged.*

The way people still looked at him sometimes, that was evidence enough of that.

Even when it wasn't just any people, it was a friend.

"You're an alien," Alec teased, finishing his sentence. "You're going to head up to Mars and start a football team in space."

Sebastian shot him a glare. "I'm dating someone, actually. And no, before you ask, they're not an alien."

"Well, that would've been my first question. And my second . . . who?"

"You might not believe this but . . ."

"It's Beau Dawson," Alec finished for him, casually. "It's totally Beau Dawson, isn't it?"

"You are a terrible friend and an even worse agent," Sebastian said, even though he meant completely the opposite. "How did you know?"

"Are you kidding me? You were all worked up about him *weeks* ago. I asked you what kind of problem it was, and you *insisted*, I'll point out, that it was not an *I want to fuck him* problem. But . . ."

"In my defense," Sebastian grumbled, pushing a fry around his plate, "it was not *only* an *I want to fuck him* problem."

Alec grinned. "So, what are you going to do about Dawson the elder?"

"I told him. This morning."

"Ah."

"You don't look shocked that my face isn't busted."

"Punching you in the face for declaring you're in love with his son? Not Asa Dawson's style," Alec said, taking a sip of his soda.

"I said I was dating him, not that I was in love with him," Sebastian pointed out.

He loved Alec, he really did. But he could not imagine what dating him was like. How did Spencer do it, when Alec was already ten steps ahead of him?

But then . . . Sebastian realized that Beau was like that too, sometimes.

Okay, most of the time.

Nearly all of the time.

On Beau it was adorable and impressive. On Alec it was just annoying.

Sebastian decided that proved there was someone out there for everyone. You just had to find the *right* person. The person who fit you, like a puzzle piece.

The way that Beau fit him.

"You didn't have to say you loved him," Alec said smugly, "it was all over your face when you said his name. You're a goner, Howard, and I'll be the first to admit, it's kinda cute."

"Just kinda cute?"

"Really cute, okay? We're happy for you."

"Oh, you and Spencer are a *we're* now? How does he feel about that?"

Alec's expression was mischievous. "He loves it even more than I do, actually."

"Of course he would." Sebastian was absolutely not bitter at all about all those Defensive Player of the Year awards that Spencer had on his mantel. Or *Alec's* mantel, Sebastian supposed. Or the mantel they fucking owned together. It would be obnoxious, but kinda like Alec had just said . . . it was really cute.

"So Dawson the elder knows the truth. Who else?"

It was the moment that Sebastian had been waiting for—and dreading—since he'd asked Alec, who'd just been a few states away, to come to Miami.

"Are you asking if I'm going to come out of the closet?"

Alec's gaze remained steady. "I don't know, am I?"

"I don't want to give a big interview or make a big deal out of it, okay?" Sebastian said, feeling defensive even though he knew, *logically,* that there wasn't a reason for it.

Alec was his friend. His agent. The one person who was always going to be on his side.

Not the only one, now, Sebastian reminded himself. *Beau's there for you, too.*

"You don't have to do anything you don't want to do," Alec said crisply. "If you just want to live your life, just the way you want, that's absolutely your right."

"That's what I want. All I want."

"And we're lucky to be living in a world where you can," Alec said, his voice firm. "I'll make sure to let any reporters know that questions about your personal life continue to be off-limits. But . . ."

"But there's going to be a lot more."

Alec shrugged. "Possibly. If anyone gets wind of you dating Beau, then absolutely. He's not unknown to the media. And he's the son of your coach. That's always going to lead to questions."

"That I don't have to answer."

"No. You aren't under any obligation, but some advice?"

Sebastian already had a feeling that he wasn't going to like it, but then he'd asked Alec to meet with him for a reason. Because he hadn't wanted to just talk about this over the phone. It was too big to address so casually.

"Sure."

"At some point," Alec said gently, leaning forward, "the questions might get more annoying than addressing them would. I don't know how quickly the media is going to put two and two together and get four. It's less of a big deal now than it was. Lewis and Nicholson on your team are already together. They've become essentially a non-story for the sports media. The gossip media love them, but Tristan also . . ." Alec winced. "Also panders to that more than I'd really like. But he's young, he'll figure it out.

But you, you're older. You aren't after attention. You're not going to be posting couple selfies on Instagram or making TikTok videos about how much you love each other and how much each other's socks smell."

"Is that what Tristan and Wade are doing?"

"Oh, no, I don't know what they're doing, I very specifically *do not know,*" Alec said, laughing. "We got Tristan a social media manager, and I let him deal with that. I wasn't even fucking qualified to deal with that."

"You're totally qualified, you just didn't *want* to," Sebastian teased.

"Fine, fine, yes. But what I'm saying is maybe it would be easier to get ahead of the whole thing. Put out a little statement when the questions start to get bothersome. You don't have to say anything about you, personally—that's not their business, honestly, and there's enough queer players in the NFL now who are honest about who they are that you being not straight isn't even a story. And of course, everyone already knows Beau is gay. Just say something like *I appreciate your respect for my privacy,* and something along the lines of *my teammates and my coach support our relationship.*"

"And then?"

"And then," Alec said, "nobody has any story to write. You're together. The team knows. Coach Dawson knows. You're not breaking any rules or going behind anyone's back. It's all above board and a total non-story. Reporters only waste their time if something smells."

"Huh, okay. Well, that's . . ." Sebastian hesitated. He didn't hate the idea, at least not as much as he thought he would. "That's actually not a bad idea."

"I'll put something together, and send it over. We don't have to release it now, though we *could* if you wanted. If you really wanted to get ahead of it. You can talk to Beau and figure out a good time. Are you going to tell your teammates? Or do they know?"

"Some of them know. Friends of ours, they know," Sebastian admitted. "Tristan. Wade. Logan Banks. Paxton Kelly and Davis Abernathy."

"Of course Tristan knows." Alec rolled his eyes. "If there's any good gossip within a ten-mile radius of that facility, Tristan knows about it."

"I thought he might've told you," Sebastian said. He'd sort of expected it, because yes, he knew how Tristan was, and Alec was his agent, too. But the fact that Tristan had kept his mouth shut about something that nobody else knew about? It raised the kid a lot higher in his estimation.

"If you told him to keep his trap shut," Alec said wryly, "he's generally pretty good about that."

"Seems like he is," Sebastian acknowledged. "But I guess it's probably time for me to share with the rest of the team, yeah?"

"That would be my suggestion," Alec said. "It's going to prevent a lot of questions in the long run. Makes you look real legitimate, and not like you're just sneaking around."

"We're not," Sebastian said firmly. He paused. "You're right," he added. "I love him."

Alec's gaze softened. "I'm so pleased for you, for both of you."

"Maybe," Sebastian teased, "you should be a matchmaker, not just an agent."

"Believe me, I've been considering it." Alec's expression was wry and amused.

And because he was so smart, Sebastian thought that maybe he might actually be.

"So you saw Alec today?" Beau asked as they sat in his office, sharing one of those huge Cuban sandwiches.

Sebastian had also brought in two Mexican cokes, in the glass bottles, and he'd set another tightly closed paper bag at the edge of the desk when he'd unpacked the rest of the food. When Beau had asked what it was, Sebastian had told him it was a special delivery for Coach.

And that, Beau thought as he chewed and swallowed another delicious bite of sandwich, was one of the many reasons he'd fallen in love with Sebastian Howard. He was not only blindingly, painfully hot, he was kind and sweet, *thoughtful*. The sort of teddy bear you'd like to squeeze and then hump.

"Yeah, I wanted his advice," Sebastian said. "About . . ." He gestured between them. "I meant what I said before, I don't want to make any kind of big declarative statements. I don't want to share details of my private life with the media but . . ."

Beau followed instantly. "There's a story here. If you give a story the room to grow, it can turn into something."

Sebastian sighed. "Exactly. Alec actually suggested putting together a very simple statement, and sharing it after we tell the rest of the team. Something like, *please respect our privacy in this relationship,* and *yes, everyone knows.*"

Beau laughed. "*Yes, everyone knows.* That's a nice touch."

"That's the Sebastian Howard phrasing," Sebastian said, a tiny smile creeping over his handsome features. "I know Alec would manage to say it better."

"He could run it by Helen too," Beau suggested, referring to the Piranhas' head of public relations. "And then it would *really* be like everyone knows."

"He could do that. But I wanted to talk to you about it first. We're . . . we're in this together now. I don't want to do anything without talking it through with you." Sebastian sounded so serious, so earnest, that Beau felt like he was falling all over again.

He'd never imagined having a partner who was so conscientious of him. But after Sebastian, he knew he could never settle for less again.

Sebastian was it for him.

"I'm okay with the idea of sharing a joint statement," Beau said. "It's a good point. Alec is smart. If we dispel any questions up front, then there won't be any. Well, there will *always* be questions, but they're easy enough to ignore."

"That doesn't bother you?" Sebastian asked, still so earnest.

"That people ask questions? People have asked questions about me and my sexuality in relation to my father and football since I was seventeen," Beau said wryly.

"I mean . . ." Sebastian looked pained. "That I don't want to make a big statement."

Beau put down his sandwich, wiping his fingers on a napkin, and even though the door was open, had zero compunction about reaching for his boyfriend, pulling him into a tight hug. There were definitely some benefits to his father knowing the truth. And the rest of the team knowing it shortly.

"Listen," he murmured into Sebastian's shoulder. "I don't give a fuck what kind of statement you make. I know you care about me. I know we're in this together. That's all I care about."

Beau could feel the tension in Sebastian's shoulders slowly begin to ease. He pulled back a fraction, and could see the relief in his eyes. "You mean that," he said. "But you . . . you *did* make a big statement."

"Yeah, when I was seventeen and I thought other people's opinions of me mattered, way too much fucking much. I learned the hard way that isn't true. If you're good with you, then what you tell the rest of the world doesn't matter. If you want to scream it from the rooftops, great, if you don't ever want to share the details of your personal journey, that's great too."

Sebastian pressed a quick kiss to his cheek. "You are . . . I don't have words for how fucking amazing you are. Maybe I should get Alec to write me a statement about that, too."

"Maybe," Beau said, grinning. He returned to his chair, picked up his sandwich. "Now, you said you wanted to tell the team. How do you want to do it? When do you want to do it?"

"I don't know. That's another thing I wanted to ask you. Maybe you know the best time."

"Honestly, if I was going to guess the best time . . ." Beau hesitated. It seemed counter-intuitive, but then it had been his first inclination. And he knew enough about himself to know that usually his first inclination was the right one. "I'd say we should do it right before the next game. Like at the walk-through the night before."

"Really?" Sebastian sounded skeptical.

"Everyone's got their focus screwed on tight, and they don't have time to overreact, because they're thinking about the game," Beau said. "That was my first thought, anyway."

"I would be okay with that," Sebastian said slowly. "I do think we should check with your father, but if he's okay with it . . . then we can do that. I'll let Alec know to get the statement done, and to check in with Helen."

"Wow," Beau said, unable to stop smiling even long enough to take a bite of his sandwich, "I guess we're really doing this, aren't we?"

Sebastian's smile was at least as bright as his own. "We sure fucking are," he said.

Chapter
Seventeen

Sebastian was normally pretty keyed up before a game.

Walk-throughs were supposed to calm everyone down, double-check that everyone was on the same page with the game plan, and generally be a confidence builder that tomorrow's game was absolutely winnable.

And normally, the combination of those goals was enough to calm Sebastian down enough so he didn't feel like he'd explode out of his skin before the team took the field the next day.

But tonight, nothing was working.

He was antsy, barely able to stay in his seat, as he waited for the coaches to go through the different game plans for the next day. It was even worse because Beau wasn't there with him—he was standing up at the front with the rest of the coaches.

Alec had written the statement. Helen had signed off on it. Coach had approved of their plan to reveal their relationship at the end of the meetings, agreeing with Beau that acting like it wasn't a big deal was the best way to handle it.

Sebastian just wanted it handled and done with so he could . . . well, so he could *try* to relax.

Finally, Coach finished up and turned to Beau, standing next to him. "I know you've got one more thing you want to say," he said.

Beau nodded and that was Sebastian's cue. He got up, wiping his sweat-damp palms on his athletic shorts and ignored all the surprised looks being shot his direction as he walked up to the front.

They'd agreed to keep it short and sweet—as simple as possible. But when he got up next to Beau, he discovered that he didn't have any words at all. So he just reached out and tucked his hand into Beau's and squeezed it.

He'd let Beau deal with the words; he was better with them anyway.

"You might hear some rumors floatin' around in the next week or two," Beau said, "but Sebastian and I wanted to set the record straight. We're together, in a relationship, and it's not a secret. Coach knows. Coach's happy for us. But the last thing we want is for us to distract the team from football, so that's why we wanted to put it out there. Yes, we're together. No"—Beau paused, smiling—"it isn't really any of your business, and that's the way it's gonna stay."

For a long, tense moment there was nothing but silence.

Sebastian wanted to crawl under a chair. Not that he'd fit. But the desire was undeniably there.

It was Logan who broke the stillness.

"What?" Logan called out. "You aren't gonna be up in each other's faces all the time like Tristan and Wade?"

Everyone laughed, and Sebastian realized right then, it was all going to be okay.

Nobody cared.

They might be surprised—almost certainly because he'd never talked about his personal life and he'd definitely never divulged his sexuality, except to a few select friends—but after the shock had passed, it didn't really matter and nobody really cared.

Relief surged through him, and Sebastian glanced down at Beau, who squeezed his hand back.

"That's the plan," Sebastian said, speaking up for the first time. "No need to knock on any doors before you open them."

"Hey," Tristan said, clearly in mock offense. "We *try* to keep it at home."

"Keyword there is *try*," Beau teased.

There was even more laughter filtering through the assembled group, and Sebastian relaxed further. This was going to be okay. Nobody was going to call him names. Nobody was going to think less of him. After all, nobody thought less of Beau, right? Nobody thought Wade wasn't an absolute beast. Everyone knew Tristan ran one of the fastest 40s in the NFL.

And he was on a team that could boast of having the very first out-and-proud queer player. He wasn't on his own. He was part of a long line of guys who just wanted to play football, and love whoever they wanted to when they got home.

"We're all good, then," Coach said with a firm nod. "Like Beau said, this isn't a secret, I didn't want anyone to think they were sneakin' around behind my back. But we're focused, too, on tomorrow's game. On getting another W."

A quiet roar went through the players and Sebastian turned to Beau and grinned. "I really like the sound of that," he said, and Beau smiled right back.

"Me too," he said.

But it turned out that no matter how well they'd prepared for the Patriots, the game started out rocky.

The kickoff team fumbled the ball nearly in the Patriots' end zone, and they scored almost immediately. Then on the next drive, Pax thew an interception deep into their territory, letting them score again.

Five minutes into the game and they were already down fourteen to zero.

Sebastian jogged back to the sideline, both disgusted and frustrated with the team's play so far. They hadn't managed to stop the Patriots from scoring—but they'd been set up to fail. Expecting the defense to make a stand with only a dozen or so yards to the end zone each time was ludicrous.

And still, they might've done it, but Rose had turned a moment too late, guarding one of the Patriots' speedy receivers, and he'd gotten behind him, catching the ball and sprinting the last three yards for a score.

"Hey," Beau said, catching his arm as he passed by him. "Let's go over these plays."

Sebastian, temper simmering inside of him, wanted to tell him to fuck off. He'd have told *anyone* to fuck off right now, that's how shitty it felt.

But instead he forced himself to take a deep breath. To remember how he felt about Beau. To remind himself that it wasn't Beau's fault. That Beau deserved his respect and his ear, even when he was angry.

He breathed out once and then twice and then turned to his boy.

"Okay," he said, setting his helmet down and trying to focus on the screen in Beau's hands.

"Rose turned a second too late, again," Beau pointed out quietly. "But I'm sure you saw that."

"I did," Sebastian muttered. "Not sure it would've mattered."

"It always matters," Beau said. "You want to check in with him? Or I can?"

"I'll do it," Sebastian said, even though he didn't want to. But then, he hadn't wanted the Patriots to score two touchdowns in the first five minutes of the game, either.

It was not going to be a fun conversation, but it was going to be a necessary one.

"If you're sure," Beau said, glancing down to where Micah pacing in front of the bench, not dejected like some of the other defensive players, but actively snarling at one of the assistants who'd just brought him a cup of Gatorade. And then, *yep*, there went a helmet. He kicked it, right into the net where Dylan set up his practice kicks.

"I'm sure," Sebastian said.

It was hard, as a rookie, to deal with these kinds of situations. Sure, Micah had played ball in high school and college, but the NFL was a pressure cooker unlike any other. Some guys dealt with it by shutting down, and others dealt with it by being obnoxious asshats.

It was clear which Micah was going to be.

"Okay, well, let's go over some of these," Beau said, pointing to the tablet, "and maybe he'll calm down a bit."

Sebastian didn't think so. But this would be a good lesson for him.

Maybe, after this, Micah would stop fighting him.

It just sucked that it was going to take slogging through the trenches, down fourteen points, to make the point.

"Right here, though," Beau said, indicating one of the receivers on his tablet. "He's crossed over twice, which is not something he normally does. I think you can just pick him up in coverage. That might be one of Belichick's twists for the game. Having him go the opposite way. Hoping to fool you."

"Maybe." Sebastian watched as Beau showed him the two plays. "Or maybe he just went that way because he could."

"Keep an eye on him," Beau suggested.

"What else you got for me?"

"Couple of things," Beau said, and began to go through them in the clear, direct, utterly detailed way that had frustrated Sebastian at first, but now he couldn't help but appreciate.

After he was finished, Sebastian gave Beau a nod. "Thanks," he said. There was a part of him that wanted nothing else but to reach out and touch him. Just on the cheek. Or the shoulder. To remind himself that he was here, he was supporting him, they were supporting each other, but Sebastian knew he couldn't.

Beau had reminded him, the only way he could, by telling him everything he'd already seen and analyzed on the field, so he could be the best player he could. And Sebastian would remind him, by playing up to his potential.

Bringing home the win.

Just because the Patriots had scored twice didn't mean they'd score the rest of the game.

Armed with that attitude, Sebastian marched down to where Rose and the rest of the defense were sitting on the bench, watching as Pax and the offense rallied, slowly but surely making their way down the field.

Old Pax might've let that interception shake his confidence, but he was standing tall in the pocket still, making risky throws, secure in the knowledge that his receivers were going to play as lights out as he was.

"Guys," Sebastian said, approaching the bench. "Let's get our shit together, okay? They've scored twice. Fine. No reason they have to score again. I'm gonna shut them down over the middle. Nobody gets in. Nobody gets out. Let's hold the edges, and, Rose . . ."

Micah glared at him.

"Rose, let's go over that last play."

Micah's jaw jutted out. "You my coach now, Howard? Seems like you aren't playing corner anymore 'cause you *can't* play corner, so maybe you should shut the hell up."

"You said you wanted me to help you, this is me helping you. You're turnin' around a second too late. Your timing's still off. Fix it."

Sebastian waited for a beat, and then another one, expecting that Rose would respond, but he didn't. Just kept glaring at the same poor piece of turf in front of him.

"Fine," Sebastian said in clipped tones. "Do what you want. But you better fucking cover Abrams better. 'Cause he's runnin' all over you."

Micah still said nothing, and so Sebastian flopped down on the opposite end of the bench, and let his temper flare and then cool as he watched the offense drive down the field and at the end of a gorgeously long drive, eating up tons of clock, score a touchdown.

Pax threw the ball to Wade, on a beautiful little out route, and he dove into the end zone, putting his whole body into making sure the ball crossed the plane.

Sebastian fist-pumped with the rest of the bench, excited and stoked that they'd cut the lead, and then it was time for him to go back out onto the field and do his part.

The Patriots had one of the best coaches in the NFL. Love him or hate him, Belichick never came less than fully prepared, with lots of little wrinkles and tricks, always ready to trip up the opposing team.

And Sebastian intended not to be tripped up.

Still, that meant that even though the defense was playing its hardest, the Patriots *were* able to move the ball.

For every time Sebastian either tackled the running back for no gain or the ball dropped to the turf, at the feet of one of the receivers, they made a tough third down, pulling plays out of their asses and moving the ball *just* enough to keep on the field.

It was frustrating, and infuriating, and Sebastian had known it would be, had known exactly what to expect, but it still got to him.

It was third down again, and Sebastian was puffing inside his helmet, the darkened shield beginning to fog up despite all the anti-fog technology that had been applied to the plexiglass. He aligned himself with the running back, because it was third and four, and he wouldn't put it past Belichick to run the ball just because he was contrary like that and *could*.

But then right as the quarterback was calling the count, as Sebastian's body braced for the moment when the center snapped the ball, he saw a flash out of the corner of his eye.

That receiver that Beau had pointed out earlier, and he was aligning himself differently than he had been—he was going to cross over, just as Beau had predicted.

Sebastian shifted his weight, and not taking his eyes off the running back for a second, because he didn't want anyone to know he'd seen through the play, watched as the ball landed in the quarterback's hands.

Sebastian sprang into action, pushing his body right up against its limits, watching and waiting until the receiver was just about to receive the ball, because any earlier would be a penalty. Then, the moment he was safe, he reached out with all the technique that Coach Brett had drilled into him, tackled the receiver to the turf, the ball falling just a split second later.

Exultation roared through him in a rush of joy. He'd done it. He'd stopped them and the Patriots would be punting now, giving the offense another crack at scoring. At tying the game.

First things first, he helped the receiver up, who glowered at him, but then he made a savage fist pump into the air, roaring. It had felt like this, back in the day, when he'd first started playing corner, like the world was his oyster, and he couldn't make a wrong move.

When every player on the field had both feared him and worshipped him.

And it was going to happen again.

Beau had been right. He wasn't washed up. He wasn't a failure. Success wasn't any less of a success just because it looked different.

He jogged back to the bench, feeling everyone slap him on the shoulders and back and rear, congratulating him on a great play.

Yes, it had definitely felt like this. And it was going to feel like this again.

Beau was standing right next to the bench. He was fucking beaming. "You caught him out," he crowed in delight. "You listened."

"Of course I fucking listened," Sebastian answered. "You're the smartest guy I know, Beau."

Beau grinned. "Thanks," he said.

He didn't have to say it, but it was there in his eyes all the same. *I love you*, and *you've made me so proud.*

"Now," Sebastian said, "let's win this fucking game."

At halftime, the score was nowhere near what Beau had expected.

But then he'd not expected the complete breakdown of special teams *and* the offense on the first few plays of the game either.

Five minutes in, they'd been down by fourteen points, and now they were up seven.

It wasn't where he'd been expecting they'd be standing at halftime, but considering how wild the game had been, Beau would absolutely fucking take it.

His dad's hair was equally as wild, like he'd been running his hands through it during every moment of the first half. And his own, Beau realized as he caught a glimpse in one of the glass panels as they jogged through the hall towards the locker room, wasn't much better.

"Circle up," his dad called out as soon as the bulk of the team had made it to the locker room. "We might've been down, but you just fucking proved you're never out of a game. That's the fight I want to see. The fight I give a shit about."

Beau watched as the players around him nodded. Sebastian was over on the far end, jersey off, adjusting one of his pads. He glanced around, looking for Rose, because he knew Sebastian had tried to talk to him and he hadn't gotten through to him. The next person to try would be him. And if that didn't work, they'd enlist his father, who could put the fear of God into anybody.

Between his dad and Coach Brett, Beau challenged anybody to keep their shitty attitude alive and kicking.

But Rose wasn't there. Finally, Beau saw him, jogging in at the tail end of the line, behind a few of the support staff members. The last fucking player to make it to the locker room.

This, Beau decided, was ending now.

Was it frustrating to give up a touchdown in the first few minutes of a game? Absolutely. Was it even worse to give up two? No question. But nobody else had quit or gotten belligerent. Just Rose.

And that was bullshit.

"Hey," he said, cornering Rose by the end of the locker room. "We gotta chat."

Micah shot him a belligerent look. "What about?"

Micah Rose was not even close to the first asshole that Beau had ever dealt with. And he wouldn't be the last. When he'd first started working with his dad, nobody had wanted to listen to him at all. But he'd gotten through to them, because he was stubborn as hell and also refused to let petty insults get to him, and eventually, players had learned that what he had to say was valuable and they should listen.

Rose would eventually get there, too. But if he was under the impression that a little scowling would get to Beau—he was sorely mistaken.

"Your timing is off. Just like Sebastian keeps saying. If you'd turned just a fraction of a second sooner on that second touchdown drive, he wouldn't have caught the ball. And then it happened again, on that last drive. You still turned late, but luckily the throw wasn't quite on the money and you were able to tip it away at the last moment. But you keep being behind, playing reactive, you're gonna give up a lot more touchdowns."

Micah opened his mouth. Clearly to argue. But Beau held up a hand.

"No," he said. "I know Sebastian is working with you. I know he's giving you tips on when you should be turning. I've even *seen* you do it right. Fucking listen to him, okay?"

"You're just a pussy assistant who couldn't play a down of football if your life fucking depended on it," Rose sneered.

It was not the worst thing Beau had ever been called. He supposed he should be glad Rose hadn't pulled out the worst insult in the book. "Don't care," Beau said in a clipped voice. "Fucking listen, okay?"

"You think letting Howard fuck you makes you important? It *doesn't.*"

It was Micah Rose's worst luck that at that exact moment, his father had finished his speech, and the players were breaking into their positional groups, and the locker room was quieter than it had been.

Which meant that *everyone* heard the bullshit that Rose was spouting.

It wasn't just the worst luck for Rose though; Beau wasn't happy about it either. He'd pulled Rose aside, sure that he'd be getting a variation of this speech, because he hadn't wanted anyone else to hear.

But now Sebastian was standing, and the look on his face was murderous as he stalked over to where the two of them stood.

Shit.

And Sebastian wasn't the only one watching. Logan had stood up too, and on the other side of the room, he could see Tristan and Wade looking, and worst of all, fucking absolutely the worst of all, his father's gaze was glued to the two of them.

Double shit.

"You think spouting that crap makes you a *man?*" Sebastian sneered, his voice carrying through the locker room, which had gone dead silent. "Makes you a good football player? It sure fucking doesn't."

"Listen," Beau said, turning to Sebastian and putting a hand on his chest, pushing him back just a little, "I'm handling this. Let me handle it."

Sebastian shot him a look full of disbelief. "He just insulted you."

"Yes, I know," Beau said. "I'm very smart. I can usually tell when someone insults me. *Let me handle it.*"

Sebastian doled out one more single look that promised pain—utter, unbelievable pain—to Rose if he didn't listen. Or if he was stupid enough to insult Beau again.

Beau wanted to tell him it wasn't worth the effort. Rose was going to do whatever he was going to do. He was young and hungry and didn't know how to deal with the emotions that came with playing professional football. Everyone thought they could handle it.

A lot of guys couldn't. Not at first.

"Okay," Sebastian finally said. "Okay." And to Beau's pleasant surprise, he stepped away. But before he did, he dropped his voice, so low that only Beau could hear. "But only because I know you can deal with this shithole on your own."

"Yes, I can," Beau said firmly.

He turned back to Rose, who was still sneering, like he'd enjoyed that exchange. Like he thought he'd understood what that exchange meant.

But he couldn't possibly.

Rose thought it meant that Sebastian was weak and small, conceding to someone he saw as even weaker and smaller than Sebastian was. But what Rose didn't see—what he was incapable of understanding—was that Sebastian hadn't conceded to Beau's request because he was weak and small. He'd done it because he knew just how strong Beau was.

How entirely capable Beau was of taking him apart, all while never laying a single finger on him.

It wasn't Sebastian making himself small.

It was proving how big he thought Beau was.

How much faith he had in Beau.

How much he loved him.

And Beau realized he'd never loved Sebastian as much as he did in that moment.

"We're not in our locker room in Miami," Beau said to Rose, "we're in Foxboro. But it doesn't matter if the words aren't written there." He gestured to where *Equality - Perseverance - Loyalty* was written on the wall in the Piranhas' locker room. "They still matter. They're the fucking foundation of this team. And you *will* embody them, even if you don't respect them. Even if you don't respect me. I don't care if you hate me, I don't care what you think of me. As long as you turn at the right fucking time."

Rose didn't say a word.

Beau took that as agreement, and turned, heart still beating a shade too fast, to talk to his father.

But before he could, Rose muttered something, the word that Beau had really hoped he wouldn't pull out.

Not in a locker room full of at least half a dozen queer athletes who were all looking for a reason to demolish the asshole's face.

But nobody had ever claimed that Rose was smart.

He said it, and Beau froze in his tracks. Mind working in overdrive.

Sebastian was at least five steps away. But he could close that gap like it didn't exist. But he wouldn't run Beau over to get to him.

Beau stepped in between, but it turned out that Sebastian wasn't who he needed to worry about.

Logan charged right past Beau and pushed Rose against the wall, trapping him with his much bigger body, skewering him with his fist in his stomach and his flat, furious gaze.

"Shit," Beau heard his father say and staff and coaches swarmed around them, surely with the intent of pulling Logan off Rose, but nobody actually did. Which, Beau realized, said it all.

"I've had just about enough of your bullshit," Logan said. "You say another fucking word, and I'm gonna feed you your own balls."

For a long, interminable moment, nobody moved.

Beau took that to mean that if Logan *did*, nobody would much disagree with his handling of the situation.

"Banks," Coach barked out, walking closer, staff and other players moving out of the way until he was right next to them. Logan hadn't let Rose move a muscle.

Beau had known the center was strong, but he hadn't realized he was *this* strong.

It was an impressive display.

And if he pushed it any further, he was going to get kicked out of the game, and if they had any hope of keeping their lead and improving on it, they would absolutely need him helping Pax to lead the offense.

"Sir," Logan replied. Still not moving.

He hadn't punched Rose once. Only held him.

It wasn't even technically a fight, because Rose hadn't been able to get loose enough to fight back.

It was just Logan proving, with an amazing display of tenacity and strength, that he could take him apart if he chose.

"Let him go," his father said. His voice sounded so calm that anyone else might think that he wasn't bothered.

But Beau knew better. This was a step past an Asa Dawson that screamed and yelled. This was a truly dangerous Asa Dawson.

Logan let him go and Micah stared at him. Then switched his glare to Coach.

"Rose," Coach said, still deadly calm, "we're a team. We respect each other. Even when we don't like each other. You know what that means?"

Rose shook his head. Mutely.

If only, Beau thought, he'd been smart enough to stay this quiet earlier.

"It means that we listen. It means that we take advice and we let ourselves be coached. It means that we're *bigger* than just ourselves. Today, you're just a player, spouting nasty insults that none of us need to hear. So you can stay on the bench the rest of the game, and consider what that means for your future. You can join us, or you can stay there. What happens next, it's up to you."

"But . . ." Rose protested and his father held up a hand. Resolute.

"Howard," he said next, "you ready to play corner again?"

Sebastian glanced over at Beau, and then back at his father.

Beau was usually very good at predicting what people would say and do. He'd known that Rose had some small-minded crap he was working through, but then he hadn't entirely expected him to act out in this way.

But Sebastian? He never could have predicted what he'd do next, and he believed he knew Sebastian better than just about anyone.

He knew him, and he loved him.

"Sir, with all due respect . . ." Sebastian glanced over at Rose. "I'm not a corner. Not anymore."

His father raised an eyebrow. "You're not?"

"Sir, I'm a safety. A really fucking good safety. You put me at corner, I can play corner, but . . ." And Beau knew how much this next admission cost him. Or maybe, Beau thought as Sebastian actually began to smile, maybe it didn't cost him anything at all. "But I'm gonna be better for you out there as a safety. Every single play, I'm gonna be better there. We wanna win, you put Rose out there on the field."

His father looked just as surprised as Beau felt.

"You don't want me to bench him?"

"I know the worst punishment in the world for a corner. It's not sitting on the bench. It's playing and having receivers scorin' on you. Which is gonna happen if he doesn't learn how to listen to advice."

"Means we could lose, if he keeps givin' up touchdowns," his father said, and to Beau's shock, it sounded like he was actually considering Sebastian's idea.

"Yeah, but he won't ever do it again after that, not if he wants a job in the NFL," Sebastian said with a wild grin. A grin Beau wanted to kiss right off his face.

"Thought all you ever wanted was to play corner again," Coach pointed out.

"Yeah, I did too," Sebastian said, but then he shrugged. "One constant in life is change, isn't it? A really smart guy told me I'd be a great safety. And guess what, he was right."

His father nodded. "Okay. Rose." He glanced over at Micah. Still sullenly leaning against the wall. "You're in. But you better fucking shape up, okay? I'm not here for any of this bullshit. And

. . ." He paused. "If you ever insult my son again that way, they'll be lucky to find pieces of you under the field."

He clapped his hands, and the knot of people slowly began to diminish as the team got prepped to head back onto the field for the second half.

Beau realized as he watched his father jog back out of the locker room, that while he'd never *needed* his father to defend him, because it meant he'd learned how to defend himself, it sure didn't feel terrible either.

After the wildest, craziest halftime that he could remember experiencing, Sebastian wasn't sure what the vibe would be when the team took the field for the second half.

If they'd come out flat, he'd not have been surprised.

If they'd come out fighting and pushing hard to win, he wouldn't have been shocked, either.

But luckily for the team, it was more the latter than the former.

It was like Rose's words had galvanized them, and brought them together as a team. And enough of them were queer—or queer-friendly—that no doubt Rose had pissed them off.

But instead of that anger making them want to give up, it had pushed them harder to win.

It was late in the fourth quarter now, only two minutes left in the game, and they were up four points. All they had to do, Sebastian thought as he jogged onto the field for the Patriots' final possession, was not give up a touchdown.

And that might've been easy enough but there was still Rose out there, holding down the corner spot. He'd been better, this half, but not perfect.

Between every drive, he and Beau had gone over to where he sat, at the very end of the bench, anger practically emanating off of him, and had talked to him.

Not with him—because that would have meant he needed to actually converse back—but at him. And maybe he wasn't responding verbally when they'd given him advice, but he was listening.

And that, Sebastian had decided, was a good enough first step.

The guy was an asshole, but then so many of them had been assholes as rookies.

It wasn't that unusual, and there was always the chance he could grow out of it, given the right coaching and the right opportunities.

But he and Rose were still never going to be friends, even if he turned out to be not an asshole, because he was still probably going to be a homophobe, and *fuck that noise.*

Sebastian set up in the middle, not for the first time realizing how much he enjoyed really letting his mind work alongside his body, analyzing what the quarterback was doing, analyzing how the play might unfold, and what position he could put himself in to make the best possible move on the ball.

Then the ref blew the whistle and Sebastian tensed, moving to the side, and then the other side, waiting that long, interminable second, as the quarterback dropped back, and then he sprinted across the field, because he knew it was going into the deep middle.

Right where Rose was.

Rose was on the receiver, shadowing him closely, and then right as Sebastian *would've* turned, if he'd been on him, Rose did, reaching up at just the last second and batting the ball away, letting it fall to the turf.

One down, Sebastian thought as he returned to the huddle, three to go.

They might have kicked a field goal on fourth down, but these were the Patriots—they'd be going for the win. Which meant they'd have to play lights-out defense for all four downs.

Second down.

The Patriots did something they were famous for—they broke out the running back, sending him sprinting down the sideline, and Sebastian, always aware that could happen, was in exactly the right spot, and tackled him to the ground.

He came up with a yell, feeling the blood rush through him leaving him feeling no pain, no soreness, no stiffness. He was ready to go. He could play for another hour if they needed him to.

Two down, two to go.

Third down, and Sebastian could feel the defense getting excited—and the offense getting antsy. They were going to make a big move. He could feel it. Gesturing to Rose in the huddle, he pointed to the Patriots' fastest receiver, making it clear that he thought they were going deep.

Rose nodded. Appearing, at least in this situation, to lose his animosity.

Sebastian was right. The moment the quarterback dropped back, the line holding back the defensive ends with a resolution they hadn't had all game til now, he knew they were going for the win right here.

There was only forty-five seconds left. They clearly thought this was the shot, and they were taking it.

The receiver that Sebastian had pointed out streaked down the field, Rose in hot pursuit, and Sebastian abandoned the middle and fell back, joining him.

With Sebastian joining Rose, the receiver was double covered, but that didn't seem to daunt the quarterback. He pump-faked and then threw, putting all his strength on the ball.

Sebastian tracked it through the air with his eyes, and decided, at the very last second, that if Rose was going to cover the receiver, he was going to make a play on the ball.

It had always been risky for him to switch his attention from the receiver to the ball when he'd played corner. He knew too many corners who got burned way too frequently, because they were trying to be a hero and catch interceptions. A corner's job, Sebastian believed, was to make sure the receiver wasn't in a position to catch the ball.

Not to catch it for him.

But Rose was there, and Sebastian decided he was going to trust him. Maybe he wasn't trustworthy, but they were teammates and that was the foundation of a team. Trusting each other.

So he angled his body, and stretching out, he felt his fingertips just brush the ball and making one last valiant effort, he pushed and reeled it in, falling to the ground with it tucked securely under his armpit.

Dimly, he heard the ref's whistle, knowing the play was over. Knowing he'd caught the ball.

All they'd have to do was send Pax out to take a knee, and the game was over.

They'd won.

Sebastian looked up, and there was a hand, outstretched, ready to help him up.

To his complete shock, it belonged to Rose.

He took it and let Rose help him to his feet, and to his *continued* shock, Rose gave him a quick embrace and said, "You're a fucking beast, man. I can't believe you caught that ball."

Sebastian couldn't either.

And when he finally jogged back to the sideline, inundated with players grabbing him and congratulating him, Beau was waiting at the bench, a smile on his face.

"That," Beau said, tipping his head towards him, "was absolutely fucking amazing."

Sebastian had only two words go through his head before he dropped the football, forgotten, and pulled Beau into a big, sweaty hug.

Fuck it.

Well, technically two followed by three.

Because *I love you* followed really close after.

Epilogue

"So you're the boy who convinced my Bastian to come out, huh?"

Chloe gave Beau a look across the table that made Sebastian sweat a little harder. There'd been part of him that had been very excited for this. And another part entirely that had been dreading it. What if his mom didn't like Beau? What if she decided that he was too much like his fucking asshole father and dismissed him before she could get to know him and realize that he wasn't?

You like Beau. You love Beau.

But the shadow of his long-departed dickwad of a father loomed large, even still.

It wasn't like Chloe believed every white man was like his father, but Sebastian could feel her hesitation as she'd sat down. She'd want the very best for him, because she always had, and she'd make sure of it, too. That was just like his momma.

Even if he already knew that there was nobody better for him than Beau.

"Momma, Beau isn't a *boy*, he's a man," Sebastian reminded her, but Beau's expression—his *smile*—never wavered.

"Oh," Beau said, "I didn't convince him of anything. He did all of that on his own."

"Really." She looked unconvinced, shooting the look over the top of her menu as she perused it.

"I told you, I didn't want to talk about it necessarily, but I didn't want to hide either. Not anymore. And not here."

"You're glad you came to Miami, then," she said.

Sebastian nodded. And then realized this was as good a chance as any to convince her that Beau was worth every bit of trouble he'd caused him. And more. So much fucking more.

"Not just 'cause it's more queer-friendly," Sebastian admitted. "Though that's really nice, too. Not gonna lie about that. But . . ." He glanced over at Beau. "I found someone who gave a shit about me, who believed in me, who wanted me to play my best football still, and who loves me too."

"There was a time," Chloe said, sipping on her iced tea, "that you'd have died before playing anything but corner."

"Times change," Sebastian said firmly. Ten weeks into the season he was not just glad he'd switched, he was *loving* the switch. Beau had been right about everything that mattered. Once he'd stopped fighting, once he'd stopped pushing to keep his speed, and he'd let his body play the game it could still play, he'd seemingly gotten even better.

With every down he played at safety, he felt more and more at home.

And the record of the Piranhas seemed to reflect that.

"I know he wasn't the biggest fan of the idea at first," Beau said, "but I just knew it was the perfect fit for him. Nobody, and I mean *nobody*, wants your son to succeed more than I do."

Chloe raised an eyebrow. It was nearly as expressive as Coach's. "Even when he fights you on it?"

"You raised a fighter," Beau said, leaning forward, eyes gleaming, "and yeah, he's gonna fight things, especially when he doesn't understand them. But he's also crazy smart, and he knows when it's right to give up the fight and take it in a new direction."

She nodded thoughtfully. "I didn't know what to think when Bastian told me about you," she said. "But now I realize what he sees in you. You're young, and you're hungry. You probably remind him of him, ten years ago."

"Momma," Sebastian said, trying not to panic.

"I'll take that as a compliment," Beau said, his smile so wide he nearly had dimples, "but I'm older than I look."

"Oh?"

"Listen, I know what you're unhappy about isn't my age. Maybe our skin color isn't the same, and maybe we come from two really different backgrounds," Beau said. "I'm aware of it. But we both love the same thing, and even more, we love each other."

"I suppose," Chloe said, cracking a smile for the first time, "Bastian told you I'd be a tough nut to crack."

"That might've been something we discussed."

"But not much flusters you."

Maybe not much flustered Beau, but Sebastian would fully admit that he was sweating through his shirt now, even with the restaurant's AC blowing strong and cold. But Beau? He was cool as a cucumber. It would've been annoying, if it wasn't so damn admirable.

"Nope, Ms. Coleman," he said solemnly. "I wasn't raised to blink."

"You should call me Chloe," she said, her voice warming up. "And no, I bet you weren't. Your daddy have any problems with this?"

Beau shook his head. "Sebastian told him. Came clean. Said we didn't want to sneak around. And that's what he mainly doesn't like. The sneaking around."

"Hardest thing I've ever done," Sebastian offered. "Tellin' Coach."

"But you did it," his momma said, admiration in her gaze as she looked at him, "even though it was hard. You turned out real good, and I can't even take all the credit."

"Oh," Beau said with a smile, "but you really should."

"I can't," she said, with a firm voice. "I might've raised him, taught him right from wrong, encouraged him to play hard and work hard, but he's a man now, with you. I didn't do that. I couldn't do that. You made him want to do that, just by being you. So if you want to be together, that's fine by me."

"That means a lot to me," Beau said. "I hope you'll stay for a few days. Meet my father."

Chloe grinned. "I'd like that a whole lot. I do love college football and he's a legend. Maybe y'all should come down to the Keys, after the season's over. Get some fishing in. Relax on the beach. It's great down there. Nice easy life, not so much like here, in Miami. Everyone always pushing."

"We'd like that," Beau said, nodding. "Knoxville was different too. Not bad different, just different. Miami's a whole different kettle of fish."

The waiter arrived then, to take their orders, and Sebastian tried to relax, order another beer, as his mother and Beau shifted into small talk about places they'd lived, where *his* mother lived.

"She moved all the way to New York?" she asked after the waiter had taken their orders.

"She says she loves it there. Personally, the city makes me tense," Beau admitted. "Too much going on. Too much noise. So many people. But she loves the community of artists she's found there."

"Oh, she's an artist?" Sebastian could hear the interest buried under his momma's casual question.

Beau nodded. "She likes working in different mediums, but a lot of oils and mixed media. Likes going dumpster diving, and in New York, that's an experience."

"I prefer my clay, but you could say that some people think that gettin' your hands dirty is gettin' your hands dirty," Chloe said sagely. "I'd like to see some of her work."

"Momma is an incredible artist, too," Sebastian added. "She throws the most beautiful clay pots. So many bright colors."

"I brought some for that horrid white and beige tomb of yours," she teased. "Brighten it up a bit. Though I see you hung some nice pieces on the wall."

"It wasn't a home before, but . . ." Sebastian glanced over at Beau. They hadn't decided completely, but Beau was already spending seven nights a week at his penthouse anyway. It seemed pointless to keep two places if they were living together at one. "But it's becoming one now."

"And that," Chloe said with finality and approval evident in her eyes, as Sebastian gazed over at Beau, "is all I ever wanted for you."

"I've got it now," Sebastian said. Reached over and took Beau's hand, squeezing it. "And I'm never gonna let it go."

Ready for more football action? How about friends-to-roommates-to-lovers and a fake relationship?
-Check out *Playing the Player*, the next Miami Piranhas book, out now!

Can't get enough of Sebastian and Beau? Check out the bonus scene, *AKA Yes, Coach Dawson knows his son is hooking up with Sebastian Howard*, here.

INTERESTED IN READING MORE OF
BETH'S BOOKS?

CHECK OUT A FULL LIST OF TILES
BY SCANNING THE QR CODE
OR VISITING HER WEBSITE

WWW.BETHBOLDEN.COM/BOOKLIST

WANT TO FOLLOW BETH?

MAKE SURE YOU NEVER
MISS A RELEASE?

SCAN THE QR CODE BELOW
OR VISIT HER WEBSITE
FOR A SOCIAL MEDIA LIST,
NEWSLETTER SIGNUP,
AND SO MUCH MORE!

WWW.BETHBOLDEN.COM/ABOUT

www.ingramcontent.com/pod-product-compliance
Lightning Source LLC
Chambersburg PA
CBHW060429310726
48977CB00001B/110